STOKE MY DESIRES ROGER & LEONIE PART II

STEELE INTERNATIONAL, INC. A BILLIONAIRES ROMANCE SERIES BOOK 4

CHARMAINE LOUISE SHELTON

CONTENTS

FREE BOOK

Get the start of the STEELE International, Inc. A Billionaires Romance Series with *Discover My Desires Sebastian & Lola Prequel* **FREE!**

Click Cover Below or visit **bit.ly/CLBooksNewsletter** to subscribe to my newsletter for latest news and launches, books from my author friends, and sizzling reads in book promotions. Plus, start reading the steamy billionaire romance *Series Prequel* of Sebastian Steele and Lola Lewis.

Their stories. Their discovery of unknown desires…

ALSO BY CHARMAINE LOUISE SHELTON

STEELE INTERNATIONAL, INC.
A BILLIONAIRES ROMANCE SERIES

Discover My Desires Sebastian & Lola Prequel
(Available Exclusively to Subscribers)

Fulfill My Desires Sebastian & Lola Part I

Heighten My Desires Sebastian & Lola Part II

Ignite My Desires Roger & Leonie Part I

Stoke My Desires Roger & Leonie Part II

Justify My Desires Roger & Leonie Part III

Deepen My Desires Sebastian & Lola Part III

Capture My Desires Malcolm & Starr Part I

Embrace My Desires Malcolm & Starr Part II

Cherish My Desires Malcolm & Starr Part III

A Trilogy of Desires Sebastian & Lola Parts I-III

ABOUT STEELE INTERNATIONAL, INC. A BILLIONAIRES ROMANCE SERIES

Welcome to the titillating world of the multibillion-dollar global company and the love affairs of the family that controls it.

STEELE International, Inc. is a series of interconnecting Billionaire romance. Follow the Steele family as they fly around the world chasing the women they love and their happily ever afters. Get ready for glitz, glamour, and steamy romance books. What's better than that? The Jet-set Lifestyle has never been hotter...

The Desires Series is not for the tea set; it's for the top-shelf vodka straight up in a pretty crystal glass coterie!

Don't miss any of the sizzling romance books in the STEELE International, Inc. A Billionaires Romance Series:

Discover My Desires Sebastian & Lola Prequel
(Available Exclusively to Subscribers)

Fulfill My Desires Sebastian & Lola Part I

Heighten My Desires Sebastian & Lola Part II

Ignite My Desires Roger & Leonie Part I

Stoke My Desires Roger & Leonie Part II

Justify My Desires Roger & Leonie Part III

Deepen My Desires Sebastian & Lola Part III

Capture My Desires Malcolm & Starr Part I

Embrace My Desires Malcolm & Starr Part II

Cherish My Desires Malcolm & Starr Part III

A Trilogy of Desires Sebastian & Lola Parts I-III

A Trilogy of Desires Roger & Leonie Parts I-III

A Trilogy of Desires Malcolm & Starr Parts I-III

Series Extras

Series Playlist

ABOUT STOKE MY DESIRES ROGER & LEONIE PART II

The tempestuous, fiery love affair of Roger The Responsible and Supermodel-cum-Interior designer Leonie The Lion continues to spark in part two of their billionaire romance story.

With his Pretty Kitty back in his life finally, Roger expects days of peace and nights of passion. But life holds many surprises, including unwelcome interest by another. Leonie draws on the strength of her feline namesake to save their reignited romance time and again.

Love tested, legal troubles, hospital emergencies... Who said watching paint dry is boring?

Join this white-hot pair as their turbulent romance takes them to villas set in the hillsides of Beverly Hills and Capri, above the azure waters of the Mediterranean in Cannes, opulent Parisian manoirs, and high-in-the-clouds Manhattan penthouses in this electrifying romantic suspense Sexy Fantasy.

Their love story is a standalone second chance romance trilogy in the series. Get a glimpse of their dynamism in other books.

Anthem: "Secret" Madonna
https://www.youtube.com/watch?v=EPHUZenprKc

Playlist:
https://www.youtube.com/playlist?list=
PLXwYvn0e218Bx18MlEj1svXS-8-NachjU

Visit CharmaineLouiseBooks.com

"*I* am so very proud of you, Leonie. You've accomplished your dream, babe. You did it and everyone will celebrate with you tomorrow. I love you so much."

"*Merci, Mon Cœur, je t'aime aussi.*"

Roger's words from earlier this evening linger in my mind as I lie here wrapped in his powerful arms. The heat of his body still consumes me after we made soul-stirring love for hours. I bask in the glow of our lovemaking and in his praise. Both mean the world to me.

I snuggle deeper into his embrace and smile to myself as even in his sleep Roger tightens his grip to hold me possessively, never wanting to let me go. He murmurs my name and rubs his cheek against my hair with a sigh of contentment.

My mind turns back to how far we have come from almost two years ago.

. . .

THE MEETING my best friend Lola Lewis had to expand her lingerie company Lola's Coterie with STEELE International, Inc. set off a chain reaction for her and for me. She met the love of her life, Sebastian Steele. I met his younger brother, Roger.

I giggle to myself as I think back to his initial reaction when he walked into the wrong conference room and came upon my half-naked voluptuous body. To prepare for the fashion show portion of Lola's presentation, the models, glam squad, and I were using the room. Roger caught more than an eyeful as I stood before him in a thin, silky thong that covered my bare mons and nothing else.

His mouth gaped and his gray eyes popped out of his head comically. An impressive bulge grew to punch against the zipper of his bespoke trousers.

"They're only breasts, *chéri!*" I teased him as I cupped them in my hands for emphasis. "No need to look so stunned!"

Transfixed in a daze, he licked his lips. Then beat a hasty retreat when someone cleared their throat.

During the fashion show, Roger sat in the correct conference room with an unblinking intense stare. His expression never changed as scantily clad models strutted past him—me, *The Lion* included. His gorgeous eyes tracked our moves. But he didn't show interest or displeasure. He was a hard read.

Boy, was I wrong...

Who knew my being the spokesmodel and sashaying my way through the fashion show would result in an unexpected two-month-long relationship?

Our insta-attraction sparked further when Roger blocked other suitors from me at LEVELS New York. Lola surprised me with her purchase of seven-day All Access membership passes for us to experience the flagship of the three luxury BDSM and dance club—Paris and London have locations, too. Global and Local All Access Membership or Dine & Dance Membership options for the über-wealthy and high-profile people who prefer discretion.

On a night I ventured alone, Roger absconded me. We moved from the Peepshow banquette to one of the private suites. Our tryst turned into an evening of sharing our lives and goals. A release of our souls to the other. I'd never felt so connected to a man as I did with Roger.

We ended my week in New York City bound for Paris on his Gulfstream 650 and bound at the hip.

While in the city—where funnily enough we're both based—our relationship continued to flourish. Roger guest lectured one of my classes at Paris American Academy. It was a natural fit as he's the President of STEELE's Residential Properties Division, and I was completing my interior design bachelor's degree. Of course Dalia Shaw, another student, flirted shamelessly with Roger. Later that night, he and I role-played naughty schoolgirl punished by her professor at LEVELS Paris.

Despite the good times, Roger's control-freak ways drove a wedge between us as he constantly nitpicked my coursework ethic as too lax. When he publicly harangued me, then had a fight with my seat mate Antonio Vasquez at our end-of-the-semester reception, marked the beginning of the end.

Roger apologized to me. He paid for Antonio's medical costs and gave him a sum of money in recompense. In addition, Roger had STEELE Paris' Human Resources team set up an annual paid internship program for two students awarded in perpetuity.

Happy to move on, our relationship progressed until we had the horrible blowup. The last argument that led to the end of our short-lived relationship. Sadly, the immediate electricity of what I thought was our *coup de foudre* fizzled.

A shudder runs through me as I recall how the numbness of despair hooked its tentacles into my heart. Then ripped it out when Roger so callously told me he wanted "a serious-minded partner and not a wayward woman who cannot stay focused for over five minutes."

As I made my way from the pleasure we had just shared in the surf at Palmilla Beach to the luxury villa beside STEELE Cabo San Lucas, I could barely keep the tears from falling. It made my pain even worse when Roger refused to relent as he pinned me with his stoic stare. That damnable intense expression he gets when he's being pigheaded. So, I left.

Three weeks later, my tender heart cut anew when at the Grand Prix after party in Monte Carlo I saw Roger cozy up with Verónica Casal. The Spanish supermodel had her claws in him, and he didn't appear to mind at all.

Despite me being with Giovanni Mattei, the anguish was genuine. After the Cabo fiasco, I couldn't help but return to the arms of my on-again-off-again paramour. I needed some way to soothe the pain in my heart.

Gio and I fell back into our agreed upon relationship: to the public we were the hot, passionate couple; in private, our amorous encounters never reached intimate penetration. So once again, I put up with his seeking full release with others as long as I was not a witness to his rendezvous.

Yet, it was not enough.

Eight months later, Roger insisted upon speaking to me. Until then, I ignored his phone calls and text messages. Finally he reached me while I was visiting Lola at Sebastian's penthouse duplex in The STEELE Tower. The clan occupies the top floors of the mixed-used property where their company's headquarters are on Fifty-seventh Street and Fifth Avenue—Billionaires' Row. I was in New York to help Lola with her wedding plans.

Roger was adamant to make amends.

"Please Leonie. For the sake of Lola and Sebastian, let's set our situation aside. Put their minds at ease about how we'll behave at their wedding. I promise I will not bother you. Okay?"

I agreed. The mind-blowing kiss he gave me to seal our agreement reignited my desire for my love.

Ever the fighter—Roger trains as a boxer—he and Gio

came to blows at Lola's Coterie Dubai's opening night party just two months later. And a week before the wedding…

After which, Roger left a heart-wrenching voicemail asking me to forgive him and to tell him what to do to make things right with us. I couldn't resist him.

I can never resist him.

FORTUNATELY, that was then, and this is now.

Roger and I realize we need each other and respect each of our ways: Roger exacting and me more carefree. We truly are *un coup de foudre*—a second chance version. So we've learned to adapt to one another. But also to take on some of the other's qualities. Roger loosened up and doesn't have to stick to a regimented way. I focus more on the tasks at hand and not flit around. We make our relationship work.

And it does.

Over the last six months we've been back together, Roger and I have grown and our relationship has matured. We get it and each other. At last.

"ROGER! WHERE'S MY MAKEUP CASE?!"

I yell as I storm in from the bathroom wearing a Lola's Coterie sheer silk, flesh-toned bra and thong set.

It's hours later and I'm trying to get dressed for my

graduation ceremony. Nothing is going right so far: I forgot to set the alarm; my toe decided to jam itself against the cabinet when I kicked it closed; cramps battling my insides. Now my makeup is missing…

Merde!

Roger of course is all cool and collected, fully dressed as he sits on the sofa in his primary bedroom. Meanwhile, I'm running around like a madwoman.

He has the absolute audacity to eye me from my toes up my legs over my belly to my hips. Then he tilts his head as he stares at my breasts, transfixed again. This fool is eye fucking me!

I let him have it.

"Ow, fuck!"

He exclaims as he rubs the side of his head.

"Stop ogling me! I asked you a question, Roger!" I bellow as I raise my comb to take aim at his stupid head since my hairbrush wasn't enough to knock some sense into him.

Can't he see how stressed I am??

I nearly blow a gasket when he asks if it was necessary to ding him upside the head. I refuse to answer. Instead, I pivot on my heels and storm into the bathroom as I mutter obscenities in French

No sign of my makeup case, I head to the dressing room. At least my strapless white jumpsuit and skin-tone strappy sandals go on without a hitch. I let my mahogany hair loose from the topknot to cascade down my back in silky waves to my ass.

D'accord!

"Leonie, I don't care if you get pissed. But I will not let you be late to your graduation, babe," Roger says.

I turn around to find him standing in the doorway to the dressing room. Damn is he sexy... all six feet, three inches of him.

Roger Steele could be a male supermodel. His sultry gray eyes and ebony hair slightly long, cut to skim his ears and neck along with the angular cheekbones and cleft chin of his clean-shaven face. The olive skin tone doesn't completely hide the shadow of hair beneath the surface.

But at this moment, he makes the mistake of running his hand over his burgeoning bulge. Does he think of anything besides sex?!

I growl at him as I lift the corner of my lip to flash my incisor. *The Lion* is not pleased with her mate.

He chuckles, not at all bothered by my histrionics.

"Besides, you're glowing, Kitten. You don't need any makeup. Let's go," he commands.

I glance up and study him. I decide he's not fucking with me. So I nod and not argue with him. My golden caramel-colored skin is flawless thanks to genetics, clean eating, and regular exercise. My mother is Tunisian and my father Parisian. They taught me at an early age to treat my body well.

"Fine, let's go," I respond as I sweep past him.

Roger shakes his head and chuckles some more.

"I heard that!" I snarl as I stalk out of the bedroom door with my cap and gown in my hand.

We take the family's private elevator at The STEELE Tower Paris to the garage. Similar to the New York City Tower, it's mixed-use with commercial and residential space plus the largest mall in Paris. Being in the *quinzième* with spectacular views of the Seine and of the Eiffel Tower adds to its appeal. Location. Location. Location.

Roger's driver Eric Vogler has the Black Badge Rolls-Royce Cullinan ready. We'll pick up my parents Guy and Josy Beaulieu from my family's ancestral home *Le Beaulieu Manoir* in the wealthiest neighborhood of the *seizième*. Eric offers me congratulations and I thank him with a hug.

Once settled in the plushy SUV, I relax. Then smile at Roger and take his hand as he sits beside me.

"Thank you too, *Mon Cœur*," I say. "I didn't mean to bite your head off."

He leans in to whisper in my ear, "Later, you'll have my other head down your throat. So don't fret."

I snort and slap him on the chest, "You Steele men are cretins without a doubt!"

He brings my hand to his lips and kisses my palm. Then slides them to my inner wrist where he kisses it softly.

I whimper and stroke his face with my fingertips.

"I love you, Roger, so much," I whisper. "You've supported me and believed in me. Even when I argued with you. The completion of my degree would have been a lot harder and taken more time without you. You pushed me and made me realize I could do better if I just focused more. *Merci, Mon Cœur*."

Roger takes a moment to collect himself from the

effects of my words. I truly love this man more than he can ever imagine.

He kisses me with such passion that we don't realize we've arrived at my parents' home until they get into the SUV. Now it's my turn to feel overwhelmed as they praise me. I can only whisper my thanks. Roger gives his handkerchief to me to dab the tears from my eyes. My heart bursts with joy surrounded by my loved ones.

We arrive at Paris American Academy. I rush to join the other graduates, slipping into my gown and placing my cap on my head. My nerves have my stomach in knots. I feel queasy, but ignore it.

The excitement is palpable as I make my way to the side of the stage. I peek out to spot my crew. I'm so excited everyone came to celebrate with me.

Lola and Sebastian along with Roger's parents Morgan and Shelley, his second oldest brother Malcolm, Harris and Haley fraternal twins and the youngest flew in from New York City. Plus Blair Thomas and Billie Chandler Lola's personal assistants-cum-close friends, Starr Knight who became another close friend after we attended her fitness retreats came on Patrick Rockett's private jet—Billie's Scottish billionaire beau. The Paris locals include Luc Montaigne Lola and my billionaire mentor and Blair's not-admitted *Le Renard Argenté*, Lucien Jackson, Roger's cousin, and Joel Bailey and Hettie Fuchs, Roger's close friends.

Boy, will this surprise them, especially Roger...

"For the first time in the history of Paris American Academy, the student with the highest grade point average and the student voted upon by their peers is the same individual."

The Academy's president pauses as a hush falls over the crowd. He glances out at the students, then continues.

"Please join me in congratulating this year's valedictorian... Mademoiselle... Leonie Beaulieu!"

The crowd erupts in applause.

As I sashay onto the stage, I wave and smile at the audience thrilled they're delighted for me. It took more time than usual since I maintained my modeling career full-time. And I didn't focus as I much as I could have...

The president and I hug, then he raises our hands in victory. Yes, this is a tremendous success for me. I deliver my valedictory of anecdotes and inspiring stories. It's well received. I end in thanks to my parents, Lola and Luc, and Roger.

"Also, I thank the love of my life. His support and belief in me was unceasing. Even when faced with my fierce lioness."

The audience laughs, and I smile as I continue.

"Without him, my completion of my degree would have been a lot harder and taken more time. He pushed me and made me realize I could do better if I just focused more. You are so dear to me, Roger. *Merci, Mon Cœur. Merci pour toujours.*"

I'm ecstatic when Roger rises and responds, *"Je t'aimerai pour toujours,* Leonie Beaulieu."

My happiness reaches its peak as I blow a kiss to him and he catches it.

Once the ceremony ends, the graduates and faculty go to the reception area to await the guests. I take a spot by the door to get an unobstructed view of my family and friends. Roger hurries over and sweeps me off my feet. I cradle his face between her hands and kiss him fervently.

Wolf whistles draw us apart, to which I throw my head back and laugh.

Roger puts me down reluctantly when Lola wants to hug me. It's a glorious moment as everyone shares their congratulations and well wishes.

I glance around for Roger and see him standing to the side, watching me intently. My amber eyes meet his gray orbs, and I wink. He chuckles as he returns one to me.

The reception is lovely. But we're ready to go to the restaurant at STEELE Place Vendôme. Lucien—*The Sexy Chef*—runs the restaurant along with several other businesses that Jackson Corporation partners with STEELE. As a surprise, he prepared all of my favorite dishes and desserts. While we enjoy after-dinner drinks in the private room, I call for everyone's attention. They turn expectantly towards me as I stand at the table.

"Thank you, everyone for celebrating my big day with me. It marks a new page in my life. So, I want you to be the first to know my plans."

I pause and smile at everyone gathered before I continue.

"As of now, I plan to work full time at STEELE Paris as a newly promoted project designer. I will model only for Lola's Coterie and for the global cosmetics company."

They offer more congratulations as they toast me, and I beam.

A sharp pain zings my belly. It's enough to make me cringe. But I ignore it, not wanting to ruin the moment.

Roger distracts me when he stands and takes me by the hand to lead me to the center of the room.

I smile at him as he brings my hand to his lips and kisses it.

My vision blurs just as Roger drops to one knee. The pain is excruciating. Bile rises in my throat as a warm sensation seeps from my core.

"Leonie!" Lola screams.

Roger swings his head towards Lola, who's pointing at me. Then he turns to me.

Confused, I glance down as my eyes follow their stares. A red stain blooms on the white of my jumpsuit. My eyes widen in fright when I notice the blood—the source of the warmth and pain.

"What the fuck?!" Roger yells.

I drag my eyes to his as I touch my belly, stricken with another zing and reach for him, feeling faint.

"Roger—"

My vision goes black as I fall into his arms.

ROGER

"*M*onsieur et Madame Beaulieu…"

Those words from two days ago continue to haunt me along with visions of Leonie pale and soaked with blood and of her lying limp in my arms.

I choke back a sob as I hold her small hand in my larger one, stroking the back of it with my thumb gently.

"Baby, please… Please don't leave me… I love you so much…"

My sentence trails off when a knock on the door to her private suite cuts me off. I shift in my chair beside Leonie's hospital bed to glance towards the sharp rap. Then call for the person to enter. Doctor Pierre Berger walks in briskly, exuding the confidence of being the best in his field.

And the best is what he is as Luc pulled rank as the major benefactor of the hospital.

After we learned the cause of Leonie's affliction, he demanded the top OB-GYN attend to her. Not just of the hospital, but of all the country. As the multibillion-aire CEO and Chairman of the Board of his family's multigenerational, global banking empire Banque Montaigne, he used his considerable influence to procure Dr. Berger. Since this is the top hospital in Paris, Dr. Berger has his affiliation with it and serves as their OB-GYN department director and a practicing doctor.

Yeah... OB-GYN...

Leonie's affliction is actually a pregnancy. Dr. Berger estimates she's eight weeks pregnant... With my child.

When the emergency room doctor entered the waiting room, Guy and Josy responded eagerly to know the status of their beloved *Trésor*. He introduced himself as Leonie's attending physician and ushered them from the room for privacy. But they held back and told him I could take part in the conversation as her fiancé. I was thankful for their recognition and hurried behind them.

Lola's soft cries intensified in alarm as I left. My heart beat in my chest wildly.

The ER doctor led us to a separate room where he gestured for us to sit.

"Mademoiselle Beaulieu is in stable condition now," he pauses to gaze at each of us before he continues. "We put her under heavy sedation to help her body to heal itself more efficiently."

Josy's mournful wail made the hairs on the back of my

neck rise. Guy pulled her into his arms as he rubbed her back. But kept his obsidian eyes riveted on the doctor.

Despair caused an anguished cry to escape my lips. But I also watched him, hoping for some words to reassure us.

He sensed our need for more, the doctor continued.

"Are you aware of her medical situation?" He asked with his gaze on me.

Taken aback, I stammered no.

Guy's eyes raked over me for any sign of guile.

My face reddened, torn between anger he would think negatively of me and in embarrassment I didn't know something was wrong with my woman.

The doctor nodded.

"I see. Mademoiselle Beaulieu may not have known either, as it is in the early stages. It's quite—"

"Early stages of what, man?? Get it out already!"

I exploded, not able to take another second as my mind went into overdrive on "early stages" of the worse diseases imaginable.

The doctor had the decency to appear chastened and rushed on in his explanation.

"She is pregnant. Congratu—"

"What the hell??"

"*Que voulez-vous dire?!*"

"*Quoi?! Mon Dieu!*"

Leonie's parents and I shouted in unison. Then peppered the doctor with questions of how. He turned to me and gestured as if to say ask him, not me.

Guy and Josy turned to me.

My mind blanked. I stood and paced. Then stopped and ran my hands through my hair.

A smile spread across my face. This was just what I wished for as Leonie and I strolled through the grounds at *Le Beaulieu Manoir*. I envisioned her playing with our children on her family's ancestral lands. My heart soared then, but plummeted when I took in the anxious expressions on Josy's and Guy's faces.

Right... Blood... Fainting... Under heavy sedation...

Fuck me!

I dropped back into my chair and shook my head. I recalled Guy's words to me during dinner the first night I met Josy and him.

"Leonie is a special gift of her mother and mine. Madame Beaulieu and I tried for many years to conceive. Many painful miscarriages and the resulting agony finally gave fruit to our magnifique petite fille. After she was born, we could not have any more children. She means everything to us."

Yeah... Fuck me.

"You are the father, *oui?*"

The withering look I gave the doctor made him sit back in his chair as though I physically punched him in the chest.

If my mobile hadn't rung, I would have done it. I kept him pinned with my stormy gray glare as I barked, "Steele."

"Rog... Roger... Pl... Please tell me Leonie is okaaay..."

Lola's distressed plea pulled me back from the brink. I had to get my shit together and take control of this situation. I gave my head a firm shake to clear the disorder.

"Yes, don't worry, Lola. We'll be in shortly."

Her sigh of relief filled me with determination to get back on track. I sat forward and asked the doctor about the well-being of my woman and my child.

He confirmed they were both stable and would require follow-up with an OB-GYN. I asked the cause of the bleeding. The doctor told us bleeding was common in the early stages of pregnancies, and it appears as though sexual activity led to repeated impact with her cervix.

My stomach dropped as I recalled the hours of love-making we made the night before. Being well-endowed with ten inches and wide girth, Leonie often told me I reached the end of her channel. The sensation of pain morphed into pleasure for her as I stretched her tight pussy to accommodate my cock.

This was my fault. Damn.

Guilt seared my soul. Leonie and our child were in danger because of me. Fuck.

Josy reached over and squeezed my hand, drawing my attention to her.

"It is not your fault, Roger. Do not take the blame. Leonie is young and strong—"

Josy choked back a sob, more than likely at the memory of her suffering. Guy soothed her, then looked at me.

"Roger, Josy is correct. You are not at fault," he starts. Then says as much to Josy as to me, "Decades have passed since our experience. Medicine and technology have improved. The best medical team will care for our *Trésor*. I promise we will get through this with a positive outcome."

Since only one or two people could see her at a time in the ICU, we decided Josy and Guy would go first. I returned to the waiting room to fill the others in on the details.

No sooner had I opened the door than everyone spoke at once asking about Leonie. My heart swelled at their love and concern. Guy was right, we'd make it together.

* * *

"Bonjour Monsieur Steele," Dr. Berger says as he crosses the room to shake my hand.

I rise to greet him, but continue to hold Leonie's hand. I'm not letting her go for even a moment. My mother could barely persuade me to shower and change.

"Doctor Berger, good morning," I respond, noticing the rest of his team as they file in behind him. I nod in greeting. Then return to my seat, scanning Leonie's face for a reaction.

I realize she's still under heavy sedation, but I know she can hear. I squeeze her hand to let her know I'm not going anywhere.

"We have good news."

My head jerks up when I hear Dr. Berger's statement.

"From what the tests show, Mademoiselle Beaulieu and your baby are progressing positively. We will wake her from under sedation now."

"Thank you, Doctor Berger! I'm sure her parent will want to be present. They just stepped outside for some fresh air. I'll call them now," I respond as I pull my mobile from my jeans pocket excitedly.

The doctor speaks with his team while we wait for Josy and Guy to arrive. Shortly, they burst through the door, their elation palpable. Josy hurries to my side and takes my hand, smiling up at me. Guy stands beside her and greets the doctor.

The anesthesiologist steps forward and administers the drug through the IV. Guy and I watch him intently—no mistakes allowed.

Josy joins us as we expel a collective sigh of relief when Leonie's eyelids flutter and she licks her lips. I say a silent prayer of thanks.

The doctor and a nurse tend to her while we stand to the side. I hate the lack of control I have over the situation. I feel responsible and useless. Only able to wait for others to take care of my responsibilities. My eyes drift to Leonie's still flat belly beneath the covers.

Wow. My baby is inside of her, growing stronger every day. I'm in awe of Leonie. She and our child will want for nothing. I will use every ounce of my power to protect and to provide for them. Mine!

My mobile vibrates. A quick glance at the screen shows it's my mother. While still keeping my eyes trained on Leonie's face, I back from the bed slightly to answer.

"Roger! Honey! We're in the waiting room. Sebastian saw the doctor and his team walk by! What's happening?"

No one returned to the US. Instead, we commandeered the waiting room, turning it into our base. Once again, Luc used his sway to arrange cots and comfortable chairs, tables and power strips, and a catered food area. They gave us access to the staff locker room facilities—although I use the bathroom in Leonie's suite. The locker room is too far for me, even if it is only one floor below us.

"Leonie and our baby are fine, Mom," I respond. "The anesthesiologist is waking her up now."

The joyous scream from Lola is deafening. My mother has the call on speaker so all in the waiting room could hear. The sound carried over my phone despite not being on speaker. The doctor and everyone in the suite peer at me, and I shrug. Then disconnect the call after I promise to call them when she awakens.

"Rrr... Rog... Roger?"

ROGER

"*P*regnant? I'm pregnant? Are you sure? This makes little sense... You must be mistaken..."

Leonie's voice trails off as she tries to make sense of what Dr. Berger tells her.

She's been awake for an hour and started asking what happened as soon as she realized she was in the hospital. But the doctor thought it best to allow Leonie time to adjust from the sedation reversal before answering her questions. Her parents and I agreed.

Instead, the doctor monitored her vitals, and the nurses helped her to use the bathroom and to shower. I had to hold back a possessive growl when Leonie's gown dipped dangerously low, almost revealing her full breast. It was bad enough the outlines of her plump nipples poked against the thin material.

Even half out of it, Leonie glanced at me and with a shake of her head reached to adjust the negligible garment.

I preferred to care for her, particularly the bathing part. But I let it go for now. I don't want to jar her or cause any discomfort. However, I sent a text message to Lola to request some more suitable loungewear delivered from her lingerie boutique pronto.

Dr. Berger gave the all clear for Leonie to eat. So, Lucien called her favorite restaurant of his and ordered a variety of dishes for her. The tantalizing aroma of lobster bisque, consommé, steak frites, and roast chicken with boiled vegetables filled the room. I haven't had a decent meal in two days, so whatever she doesn't eat, I'll finish!

Now, both of us—rather all three of us sated—Dr. Berger smiles at Leonie.

"*Oui*, Mademoiselle Beaulieu. You are most definitely pregnant. I estimate eight weeks, in fact."

Leonie's gorgeous amber eyes widen, and she peeks at me from beneath her long eyelashes.

"But I'm on birth control. I... I didn't do this on purpose. I'm sorry," she whispers as tears glisten in her eyes.

I reel from her words. My mind tries to find answers.

On purpose? Why the hell would I think she got pregnant on purpose? I may be a multibillionaire. But Leonie comes from a wealthy Parisian family that dates back to the eighteenth century and the royal court. Plus, she's a multimillionaire on her own from her modeling career.

Could it be she doesn't want a baby? Or she doesn't want a baby with me??

Fuck!

I draw on my ability to control, to reign in my emotions.

"Sorry?? What are you sorry about, Leonie?"

"Please allow me to address your birth control," Dr. Berger intercedes. "Birth control is not infallible. Medications like antibiotics or not taking the birth control at the same time consistently or other factors can impede its effectiveness."

Leonie nods, still stricken.

"When did your last menses occur?" He asks.

She thinks for a moment as she leans back against the pillows.

"It ended before Roger and I went to the South of France two months ago," Leonie responds.

"Well, that aligns with the tests. Now, I must inform you of your options. Should you wish to not move forward with your preg—"

"*Mais bien sûr!*" Leonie roars like a lioness protective of her cub as she places her hand on her belly.

"Leonie please!" I growl, unable to contain my caveman instincts to protect what's mine.

We shout at the same time and stare at each other. I take a second to realize she wants to have my baby. Thank fuck!

"Oh Roger, you do want to have a baby with me!" She cries, relieved.

* * *

I BUNDLE her onto my lap and bury my face in her silky hair. I take a deep inhale of her scent, the classic sultry perfume Dior's Pure Poison's blend of florals with amber and musk fills my nostrils. Mine!

Quietly, the door of the suite clicks closed. Dr. Berger left us for privacy.

Leonie's tears dampen the front of my long-sleeved t-shirt. I rock her in my arms and croon words of love and forever. They rumble from my chest to hers; the calming vibration eases the tension as Leonie melts against me.

"Of course I want to have a baby with you, my precious love. We are having our baby and any others. You are mine, Leonie Beaulieu, as are your children. All mine to love, cherish, and protect forever. You have nothing to be sorry for, sweetheart."

She nods, but my wet shirt muffles her response since she pressed her mouth against it.

I ease back and cradle her face in one of my hands as the other continues to hold her in my firm embrace.

"I love you so much, Roger. But I'm scared... The bleed-ing, that's not normal... My... My mother's—"

I cover her lips with my fingertips and shake my head.

"We will not speak of the past, only of our future. Your father and I promise we will provide the best medical and technology available. Luc found Dr. Berger, and he is the absolute top in the field of OB-GYN in all of France. This hospital scores the highest rating; Luc is the major benefactor. All you need to do is relax and enjoy your pregnancy. You maintain the support of our families and friends."

I pull back to stare at her intensely, "Do you understand?"

Leonie acknowledges my Alpha male in control and responds yes. As she peers up at me, Leonie's amber eyes glow with the fire inside of her stoked once again. My *Lion* is back.

*　*　*

"Oh, Lola, don't cry, *Chérie*! We're fine."

Leonie smiles and pats her belly lovingly to reassure her best friend as they sit on our bed under a cashmere throw.

"Don't worry, *mon amie*!"

Dr. Berger discharged Leonie earlier this morning with orders for a month of activity restriction, no stress, and to monitor for cramps or excessive bleeding after sexual activity.

I could barely look the doctor in the eye when he mentioned the sex part. Fuck me if my big dick didn't hurt my baby, or rather babies... We may just have to pause on the lovemaking...

The news of my cock hitting her cervix caused the bleeding surprised Leonie—not the best when a woman is in the early stages of pregnancy. She peeked at me to gauge my reaction.

Since I already knew, I maintained a neutral face. No

need for me to freak her out, even if I was still recovering from the news.

I stared at the doctor to avoid her questioning gaze. So, she returned her attention to Dr. Berger's commentary. Inwardly, I sighed with relief. The plan is to avoid that conversation as much as possible.

Now, we're home in our penthouse. As soon as my head was on straight, I had all of Leonie's pertinent belongings moved here. A closet company reconfigured two of the guest rooms to accommodate her vast wardrobe.

How many handbags, shoes, and little black dresses can one woman own?? Sure she's a model who's given tons of clothes and stuff, but damn.

Most of Leonie's toiletries and such were already in our bathroom. When she's up to it, we can go to her duplex to get her personal items. For the time being, I had her photo albums put in the family room. Then set up another room as her studio for painting and sketching. Since she needs to cut back on activities, I arranged for the start date of her full-time position as a project designer delayed until further notice. So I made an office for her from another room.

The floor-through penthouse below the one my siblings use just became available. My parents agreed to move into that unit so I could expand mine into a triplex with their current floor. My hope is the project will preoccupy Leonie, and she won't be pissed I delayed her job at STEELE. Besides, we need room for our growing family.

The thought makes me smile. But even though I told

Leonie not to think of the past, I can't help visions of her mother's experience from lurking in the back of my mind. I pray we don't go through the same hellish struggle.

"I know, but you scared the absolute shit out of me, Leonie!"

Lola's exclamation brings me back to the bedroom.

"The blood stood so bright against the stark white…" Lola trails off as she shudders and hugs herself, tears shimmering in her hazel eyes.

"Babe, Leonie and the baby are fine. Don't stress her out," Sebastian says as he stands beside Lola and rubs her back to soothe his wife.

The platinum wedding band glints on his ring finger.

Which reminds me, I didn't have the chance to complete my proposal to Leonie. She hasn't mentioned me being on one knee at the restaurant. So I wonder if she remembers. Nor did she respond one way or the other when the hospital staff referred to me as her fiancé.

Regardless, tonight I plan to rectify the situation. Tomorrow will not dawn without Leonie wearing my ring. My woman, my baby, my ring—mine.

"Sebastian is right, Lola! Only happy thoughts," my mother adds from the sofa by the window as she wraps her arm around Josy's shoulders.

Josy nods and says, "*Oui, chérie!* This is a time of joy and celebration!"

Our fathers agree and decree only the best care for Leonie and their grandchild.

"*Absolument!*" Luc concurs.

Almost everyone surrounds Leonie. She sits like a queen holding court as though in her private chambers in Versailles. Our bedroom may not be as ornate. But we added a sofa and some chairs to the existing loveseat and bench to accommodate her visitors. The spacious room provides ample footage.

Vases filled with flagrant flowers sit on almost every surface here and throughout our penthouse from Malcolm, Harris, Haley, Lucien, Blair, Joel, and Hettie. Before they flew back to the US, Starr, Billie, and Patrick dropped by with more bouquets and well wishes.

We kept the media from finding out since we were in a private room at the restaurant. Other patrons could not see who the medics rushed from the establishment. The restaurant and hospital staffs, bound by solid nondisclosure agreements, cannot disclose anything.

Our lives are private and will remain so. The less fodder given to the media, the better. As with most old money families, the Steeles and Beaulieus like media coverage to further our business gains, but prefer intimate aspects to remain private.

"Yes, we will celebrate our blessing and ensure the best care for mommy and baby."

I declare as I place my hand on top of Leonie's resting on her belly and smile affectionately.

"*Oui, Mon Cœur,*" Leonie purrs as she cups my face.

"But first..."

I lower to one knee beside the bed as I remove the little navy blue velvet box out of my jeans pocket. Then open it as I take a deep breath and pray nothing interrupts me this time.

With Leonie's left hand held in my grasp, I say the words that have burned on my tongue for months.

"Leonie Beaulieu, I love you with all of my heart, body, and soul. You mean more to me than anything in this world. I want us to spend the rest of eternity together. Marry me, my love."

Leonie sits stunned. Then tears pop out of the corners of her gorgeous amber eyes as she chokes back a sob.

The twenty-five carat Asscher cut diamond ring set in platinum is a sight to behold. So I expect her shock. The exquisite beauty has as much fire in it as our spark-filled relationship.

The ring is a family heirloom given to one of my paternal great-great-grandmothers as a gift to commemo-rate the birth of an heir. I chose it from the family's collec-tion for that very reason and explain its provenance to Leonie as I place the impressive ring on her finger.

"*Oh, Mon Chéri, c'est exquis, merci...*" She murmurs in awe.

"Oh, don't you just love the Steele men and how they just expect you'll say yes without waiting to put their ring on it!"

Lola's remark makes everyone laugh as she hugs her best friend.

"There can be no other answer, babe!" Sebastian chuck-les, not embarrassed by his alpha tendencies.

"Definitely not!" I add before I kiss Leonie silly.

"Let her get some air already!" Haley exclaims as she pushes me out of the way to hug Leonie. "Congratulations, sister! Now I have two to balance the four beasts... Um, I mean brothers!"

"Whatever, baby girl," Malcolm jabs as he leans in to hug Leonie, too. "Now, we have two more busybodies to watch after!"

"Yeah, youngin, respect your elders!" Harris adds despite being only a few minutes older than his fraternal twin. "Welcome to the family officially, Leonie!"

"Yes, welcome, sister!" Sebastian adds as he moves our siblings out of the way to hug Leonie. "And welcome to you, our Little One!"

Leonie laughs as he pats her belly.

"Thank you so much!" She says smiling as she glances around the room at our loved ones.

When her gaze returns to mine, I grin with my eyes full of love.

LEONIE

"**W**hoop, whoop! Don't hate! We've got the best rings ever!"

Roger has been insistent I rest and relax. So for almost two weeks, he has only allowed me to move about the penthouse. No lifting, no carrying, no sudden moves, no sex...

He sensed I was about to lose it and booked my favorite spa to cater to my every need. To make sure no one disturbed me, he reserved the spa exclusively for Lola, Blair, Hettie, and me.

Lola's gleeful outburst bounces off the walls, overpowering the peaceful music playing in the tranquility room of the spa. I can't help but laugh as she bounces and shimmies in the plush suede chair. She waves her left hand causing not only her engagement ring to sparkle, but her hand harness, too. Both have ginormous diamonds that glitter in the light.

I gaze adoringly at my gigantic ring and smile like the Cheshire Cat. Not one to boast, but... Gotdamn!

I recall Elizabeth Taylor's response when Princess Margaret proclaimed the actress' Krupp Diamond ring, she dubbed My Baby, as "very vulgar;" "Yes, ain't it great?"

Well, my ring is like it, only eight carats smaller than the famous one Princess Margaret hated on.

I tell Lola the story, and we titter as we do our happy dance. The Elizabeth who was famous for her astounding jewelry collection is her icon and inspired her to create Lola's Coterie. So it overjoyed her when Sebastian gave her an engagement ring, a tad bit smaller and in the same emerald cut as her idol's Ice Skating Rink ring. Another Steele heirloom piece.

"Your rings are beyond stunning," Blair sighs as she holds my hand in hers to gaze upon the sparkler. "What woman wouldn't want a flawless rock on her finger? I mean, you're both will zillionaires. Who would expect any less?"

Hettie laughs and quips, "Right! Give me vulgar any day of the week, month, year, princess! Now go sip some haterade from a golden, jewel-encrusted chalice, honey!"

Our laughter turns into snorts and guffaws until tears roll down our reddened cheeks.

After I catch my breath, I turn to Hettie.

"You and Joel have been dating for a few years now and living together. Do you want to get married?"

Joel met Roger at a business function some years ago. Outside of his family, Joel is Roger's closest friend. In the time they've known each other, Joel began a relationship with Hettie. They too met because of business. He's an investor in real estate, and she's an attorney who specializes in commercial property law. They share a half-through flat in The STEELE Tower Paris a few floors below Roger and me.

Hettie stares at the bubbling, layered-stone fountain in the center of the room. The hypnotic sound of the splashing water captivates her while she ponders my question.

For a moment, I sense I struck upon a sensitive topic and wish I hadn't asked. Hettie and I have been friends for only a few months after Roger introduced us at dinner with Joel. Since then, Hettie and I have gone shopping and had lunch a few times. Perhaps it's too soon for personal probing. But I'm so used to sharing relationship details with my other girlfriends, that I didn't think twice about asking Hettie.

"We have. He claims we 'have a good thing going… As it is. No signs of marriage on our horizon. I'm way too young to commit for the rest of my life.'"

She sighs and glances at the rest of us. Then continues.

"I, on the other hand, would like to get married and start a family before I turn thirty-three in two years. Hell, Joel acts like he's in his twenties. He'll be thirty-six in a few months!"

We nod encouragingly and offer her words of support.

"If Sebastian *Alpha Playboy* Steele can settle down, Joel can too! Just give him some time," Lola says.

I smile and add, "Billie's adage 'why pay for the cow if you can get the milk for free?' Might give you a hint of what to do to encourage Joel to put a ring on it... Move out or at least not be as readily available to him. Give him reason to miss you, if you know what I mean."

Blair claps and bobs her head repeatedly.

"Exactly! I found the more attention I paid to Luc and the more I made myself accessible, the less he responded to me. It's a man's nature to chase and conquer, you know..."

Although not as forthcoming with their relationship, Lola and I surmise Luc and Blair are a steady if not committed couple. Luc being the refined *duc* never discusses his intimate relationships with us. Blair has taken on his trait and keeps mum, too.

We also know Luc's concern with their age difference. He's seventeen years older than Blair. Despite being in his early fifties, the super sexy *Renard Argenté* continues to turn heads. His deep blue eyes glitter like sapphires. Black hair with some gray sprinkled in it adds to his distinguished appearance. His body remains fit with regular workouts and healthy eating. The nickname Lola and I gave to Luc goes beyond appropriate for the attractive, fifty-one-year-old man.

It's only heightened Blair interest in Luc. She's not at all put off by his age. Obviously, she learned her lesson and cut back on the shameless flirting she did before they dated.

Hettie ponders our words, then sits up straight, throwing her shoulders back.

"You're right! Joel was a lot more attentive before I moved in with him. He always popped around my flat with pastries for breakfast or a bottle of wine and popcorn for a night of Netflix. Funny enough, my sub-tenant just finished their lease and moved out last week. I haven't had a chance to let it. It's a sign!"

She throws her head back and laughs.

"Just as I believe in *un coupe de foudre*, I believe in signs and all point to you getting your ring sooner than you thought!" I giggle.

"Go, girl!" Lola whoops.

"Yay you!" Blair adds, giving Hettie a high five.

We chat some more while we finish a light lunch of salads and citrus-infused water the staff brought us after our last treatment.

"Pardon me, mesdames, but are you ready for your next sessions?"

The general manager's question cuts into our conversation.

We've had body polishes, waxing, aromatherapy, reflexology, and massages. Now it's time for manicures and pedicures. Dutifully, we troop behind our aestheticians to yet another room.

I peek at My Baby engagement ring as I place my hand on My Baby belly and smile. I'm thankful for a man who loves me and who's not afraid to commit to me and to our child. My smile widens when my "vulgar" ring blings as the wall sconces catch it in their light.

. . .

"I SWEAR, Leonie, you're glowing and I don't think it's from the facial. Hot Momma Alert!"

Hettie laughs as she wets her finger and sizzles it against her hip.

"*Merci!* I do feel a whole lot better now," I respond, my tinkling laughter joining hers.

"Yeah, you gave us a major scare. But we'll only talk about positive things! 'Positive vibes,' as Starr says!" Lola chimes in.

Blair turns to Lola, "And what about you, missy? When are you popping out a mini Sebastian?"

Lola amber eyes widen and she puts her hands up to ward off Blair's questions and shakes her raven-haired head vehemently.

"Bite your tongue, Blair! I hadn't planned on a relationship and look what happened! I'm thankful, yes. But Sebastian and I are nowhere near being ready for kids. For now, Lola's Coterie is my baby and STEELE is his!"

We laugh at her dramatic reaction.

"So, bestie, you don't want to be pregnant at the same time as me? How much fun—"

"Don't you dare put the whammy on me, Leonie Beaulieu! I mean it! Stop laughing at me!" Lola screeches.

The rest of us laugh so hard, we nearly fall out of our chairs as we wait for our nails to dry. Lola glares at each of us before she cracks up at her hysteria.

My mobile vibrates in my robe pocket, interrupting our taunts. Roger insisted I keep it near so he could easily reach me. I know he's putting on a brave face for me. But he's just as concerned as I about my mother's experience. Neither of us wants to face such pain. So I didn't argue about his request.

"Ciao, *Mon Chéri!*" I answer in a chirpy voice. No need to add to his worry.

He breathes a sigh of relief before he responds, "Ciao, my love. How are you doing? Are the sessions okay? The general manager assured me the treatments are safe for pregnant women. According to the schedule she sent to me, you should almost be done. Are your nails dry? Should I have Eric bring the car around to pick you up now? He's just—"

"*Mon Cœur,* take a breath! We're fine! Don't worry," I say to stop his drilling. "Yes, we're drying our nails. But I'm not ready to leave just yet. I'll call you ten minutes before. Okay, *Mon Chéri?*"

Roger sits in silence for a second, then agrees.

"Aw, he's so concerned. How sweet!" Lola says as I put the mobile back in my pocket. "Roger *The Responsible!*"

"*Oui,* so responsible, he delayed my start date at STEELE for the 'unforeseeable future' without asking me..." I grumble with a frown. "Then tells me he has a project to keep me busy once I feel up to it... Morgan and Shelley are moving into the penthouse below the one you and Sebastian are in. We're going to take over their old one. I get to manage the combination of the two penthouses into a triplex..."

Lola fidgets and avoids my eyes.

"What? Spit it out, Lola Steele!" I demand, sensing my best friend knows something she isn't sharing with me.

She defers her answer in favor of adjusting her topknot to get it just so...

"Spill it now, Lola..." I repeat, pinning her with my most fierce glare.

She snaps to attention and mumbles under her breath.

"What? You know we can't hear you, Lola!" I exclaim as I lose patience with her stall tactics.

"Okay... Okay already! Baz mentioned Roger being adamant to push back your start date when you were under sedation. I agreed it was a good idea."

She raises her hand to stop me as I interrupt.

"You do not understand how frazzled Roger was... He wouldn't let anyone take you out of his arms... He tried to bogart a nurse to get into the emergency room... He was inconsolable... Morgan and Shelley were so concerned. But Roger regained control as soon as the ER doctor explained you were pregnant and the bleeding was normal."

Lola lets me absorb her words. Then she continues.

"Remember, he's the one out of all the siblings who's the most in control—the most straight and narrow. He had zero control over your and your baby's wellbeing. He got his shit together pronto, though. So cut him some slack, sweetie."

Tears well in my eyes. I had no idea. Roger has said

nothing, and I'm sure he told everyone not to mention it. He keeps saying he only wants me to be happy and to have a healthy stress-free pregnancy. I cannot ask for anything more.

However, I can do something for him...

ROGER

"Why hello there, Monsieur Steele."

Leonie's seductive purr draws my attention away from the paperwork I have in front of me. My eyes nearly fall out of my head when I gaze up to find her leaning against the doorframe of my home office. Her voluptuous body on display for my hungry eyes.

Barely there red stretch-tulle embroidered with flowers and satin trim for a bra and matching panties set peeks out from beneath a red satin floor-length robe. The plump nipples of her fuller breasts poke against the lace like succulent dark berries, begging for my mouth to engulf them.

Leonie's belly may still be flat. But her hips flare, and my hands itch to clutch them as I pound into her tight, wet pussy.

Her long, shapely legs ending in fuck-me mules are the perfect length to wrap around my neck...

Fuck!

My cock grows along my thigh as it hardens inside of my gray sweatpants. Thankfully, the soft material allows for stretch. However, the crewneck collar of my black t-shirt feels like it's choking me. The temperature in the room increases, and my skin heats.

I shake my head to clear the instant lust that shoots through every fiber in my being for my mate.

No, calm down, boy. I can't harm her and our baby again.

She saunters into the room, exaggerating the sway of her hips, then stands before my desk akimbo. I have to grip the edge until my knuckles turn white. It's the only thing I can do to keep from jumping up and throwing her over my shoulder to carry her off to our bedroom and ravish her.

Damn! Two weeks and no Leonie, and I'm at my breaking point.

Get it together Steele… Your woman and your child first, caveman.

"*Amoureux*, I want to thank you for treating my girls and me to a wonderful spa day. They pampered me and drained all tension. Except for one," she purrs as she trails her long red fingernail over her shimmery caramel-colored skin. My ring on her finger sets sparks off in the light.

I gulp when she pinches her right nipple between her fingertips and mewls. Her amber eyes narrow to slits as she whimpers from the pain in the pleasure. My dick jumps.

Breathlessly she says, "I know you're busy catching up

with work. But I wanted to let you know just how thankful I am for your thoughtfulness, *Amoureux…*"

Leonie's voice trails off as she sashays around my desk and squeezes between it and my chair. Then slides the paperwork off to the side before she plops her lush ass on top. My eyes trail up her thighs, riveted to the wet patch on her panties. The scent of her arousal wafts up to fill my nostrils and stokes my inner caveman desires.

Fuck. Me.

"You don't mind, do you, *Amoureux?*" She asks with hooded eyes as she uses the tip of her nail to lift my chin.

My stormy gray orbs meet her golden amber gaze. I'm fucking captured by her spell. Captured.

"*Oui ou non?*"

She whispers in my ear as her long nail scrapes along the cleft in my chin. Her warm breath combined with the rasping sound as her nail goes across my five o'clock shadow is the last straw. I shudder from the effort to keep my hands gripping the armrests of my chair and not her ass. I ache to scoop her up and ram my fat, long cock inside of her wet, tight pussy.

Again, I shake my head.

That's what caused her to bleed, jerk! No!

"No, Leonie. I mean yes… I do mind," I say as I stand.

Before I can stride away, she wraps her legs around my waist and pulls me back in place.

"Roger, you do not understand how my hormones are raging… I need you. I need you inside of me, *Amoureux… S'il vous pla"t.*"

Trapped, I cannot resist her siren's call. But I must try...

"Leonie, my love, are you sure? I'm afraid to harm you and our ba—"

She cuts off my words as she covers my mouth with hers. The intensity of the passion in her kiss blows my mind. It obliterates all fear. I give in. But I will not lose control.

To temper my rampant desire, I take the reins. I cup her face in my hands as I tilt it to just the right angle and tangle my tongue with hers. She tastes like the iced lemon ginger tea she's started drinking instead of her Réserve Jean de Lillet Blanc.

Her soft purrs as I dominate her lioness make pre-cum bead on the tip of my dick.

As though Leonie is telepathic, her small hand slides over my rock-hard, six-pack abs to slip under my waistband and encircle my throbbing cock. The girth won't allow her fingers to touch. But the long, pressured strokes she applies more than make up for any shortcomings.

I groan into her mouth when she pinches the leaking slit. My entire body poised for release. Not yet.

My hands travel over her full mounds to heft their extra weight. More than a handful, and my hands are sizable. Perfectly mouthwateringly plump.

When I tweak her nipples at the same time, she growls and arches her back. Yes, her buds have become sensitive because of her pregnancy. I roll the distended tips between my fingers. Leonie moans as she scoots forward to the edge of the desk, tugging my cock free of my sweatpants.

It bounces against my abs just below my navel. Losing her warm hand amplified by the cool air.

Leonie stops our entwining tongues and peers at me from beneath her long eyelashes.

"*Amoureux*, I ache for you," she pleads with hooded amber orbs.

I tease her pussy seam through the soaked stretch-tulle as I watch her face to witness her in the throes of ecstasy. Her eyes close.

"Open your eyes, Pretty Kitty. I want to see your pleasure mount," I command.

She complies and leans back on her hands as she widens her thighs to give me better access.

I slip two thick digits beneath her slick panties and coat them with her essence for a natural lubricant. Once they're fully covered and Leonie writhes on the desk begging for more, I slide them inside of her pussy. The gentle strokes brush against her G-spot, and she cries out in bliss.

"Oooh, Roger... So good... So good," she pants.

"I know, Kitten. I'm going to make it so good for you, I promise," I croon.

My fingers move inside of her wet warmth. Then I scissor them to prepare her pussy for my cock. She rocks against the base of my palm, soaking it with her juices as an orgasm steamrolls towards her. I speed up my pace, alternating the rhythm, then admonish Leonie when her eyelids shutter. She jerks her head, and her gaze return to mine.

"Good girl, Kitten," I praise her as I pinch her engorged clit. "Cum for me."

Leonie breaks beautifully for me. Her body quivers as a sheen of sweat glistens on her skin, and she keens in untamed pleasure.

My wild cat purrs as I continue to stroke her pussy, bringing her down from her climax gently. Her soft cries drive me to the edge again.

I rein it in and kiss her passionately.

She wraps her hand around my dick and scoots almost off of the desk to line her pussy up with my bulbous head slippery with pre-cum.

When the tip enters her wet, warm channel, we both groan. Thirteen days, seventeen hours, thirty-eight minutes, and we're finally as one again.

The sensation as I stretch her with my girth makes me hiss. Then growl when she contracts the muscles of her inner walls. Her greedy pussy pulls me in deeper, almost to my base.

Fuuuck!

I gather the strength to withdraw before I hit her cervix. I remain ever mindful—Roger *The Responsible* Steele...

"Mmm mmm... *Non*," Leonie whines, saddened by the unexpected loss of contact.

I ease back in as I pluck her breasts out of the bra to rest atop the soft cups. Her fully aroused nipples beckon to me. I lick one of the tips. Then suckle it into my mouth, surrounding it with heat as her pussy gushes around my dick.

"Ooooo... Oh!" Leonie coos, then cries out as I nip her

sweet bud.

My hips flex to drive short and long strokes of my cock at a leisurely pace. The pace ensures she feels the velvety steel texture and every inch of my pulsating dick as it grazes her inner walls. I shift the angle to dive deeper. But avoid the delicate entrance to her womb.

We lose ourselves in the sensuous dance of the ages. A sexual thrall overtakes us as we reach an unchartered level of cloud nine simultaneously.

A spine-tingling sensation shoots through my body and jets out my dick as I spew more of my seed inside of Leonie. The amount so copious I could impregnate her all over again if it were a possibility.

"Rogeerrr! *Mon Dieu!*" She screams, my name falling from her lips repeatedly as I take us over the edge.

"Take it... Take all of me... Fuuuckkk!" I bellow as I throw my head back and roar my release, my body shuddering from the force.

I collapse back into my chair with Leonie straddling my hips, still bound together.

The sound of our heavy pants and the smell of our carnal sex permeate the room. I close my eyes to revel in our blissful connection as I stroke Leonie's back. She nuzzles her face into my neck and sighs. Neither of us is inclined to move. So we rest.

"I KNOW when you made me pregnant."

My hand pauses with the fork of jerk chicken and

steamed vegetables halfway to mouth. I glance at Leonie across the table in the dining room.

After we soaked in the bathtub, we heated up two Anita Green's delicious and healthy prepared meals. Leonie's no cook, and I don't have the inclination to waste time in the kitchen. So we either go out to eat, order in, or eat the meals.

Anita is Norman Green's—my boxing trainer and STEELE business partner—wife. Along with being a highly followed yoga instructor with a flourishing practice, Anita recently finished culinary school at Le Cordon Bleu. Then started a meal plan delivery service.

Norman is a former world heavyweight champion for nine years straight. When I met him at STEELE Las Vegas after his last bout in the ring, I offered him the opportunity to open chains of branded gyms through our Entertainment Properties Division. One for underprivileged youth and another as exclusive elite training facilities for the über-wealthy and star athletes. He accepted and took me on as his first private client.

Norman added Anita's customized plans to the paid offerings of the elite facilities and complimentary healthy snacks to the youth. She also took over the food services in both chains. They rank as the most popular couple in the fitness world.

I have to put the tasty morsel back on my plate and sit back to stare at Leonie.

"How do you know?" I ask.

A beatific smile spreads across her glowing face—Anita

designed a meal plan specifically for the nourishment of a mother and growing child as Leonie's meals.

"It was during the night we spent in Cannes," she says triumphantly as she rubs her belly.

I cock my head and think back on that unforgettable night of passion.

"Oh, baby... You feel so fucking good... So hot and wet..." I grunt with pleasure.

Leonie writhes beneath me with her wrists bound to the headboard above her. She pulls against the silk restraints fruitlessly as her fists clench and unclench. I can tell she needs more.

I move one hand from her hip to place my thumb in her slack mouth. Without hesitation, she suckles it eagerly. Once it's sopping wet, I pull it from her mouth with a pop and sit back on my haunches. Still connected, I lift Leonie up to settle her on top of my muscular thighs.

In this position, I have better access to her luscious body. My lips trail down the length of her elegant neck to wrap around one of her pebbled nipples. At the same time, I pull her round ass cheek aside to expose her puckered hole. Then press the pad of my wet thumb against her back entrance. The painful pleasure makes her tighten the muscles in her pussy and ass. I grunt from the force on my throbbing cock.

I plunder her bottom hole with my well lubricated thumb and use my powerful thighs to pump my dick up into her greedy little pussy.

"Aaahhh!" Leonie screams.

Her back bows, and she keens as each thrust hits the end of her channel. I can feel her pussy walls flutter as an orgasm peaks. She rides me fervently to reach her impending climax.

"Fuuuck... Leoonnieee!" I roar as her release triggers mine with a blinding jolt down my spine to my balls and out the tip of my dick.

Inside of her, my shaft swells impossibly larger, bumping into her cervix before hot ropes of my seed bathe her womb. Another wave crests over us as we continue to pound our bodies driven by the innate need to mate. Our frenzy desire to sate our carnal needs.

When the last drop of my life-giving essence flows from my body to Leonie's, we fall to the bed. No longer having the strength to maintain our position. Fully drained, we lie on the bed in a state of bliss.

"I love you, Leonie Beaulieu," I murmur in a voice thick with emotion as I brush my lips against her temple.

She lifts her head from my sweat-soaked chest where my heart beats in sync with hers to gaze into my eyes. I nuzzle my cheek into her palm as she strokes my face and rubs her thumb across my lower lip.

"I love you, Roger Steele." She says in a voice hoarse from her screams of mind-blowing pleasure.

I kiss her fingertip and cradle her head back against my heart before we fall asleep.

"Huh, you think? Well, it was most definitely intense. Damn," I respond as I shift in my chair to reposition my enlarging cock. "I guess you can say my most caveman-like moment."

I tease as I squat beside Leonie and cover her belly with my large hand.

"Mine!" I state possessively as I kiss first her lips, then my baby. "How are you, Lil Cub?"

Leonie giggles and runs her fingers through my collar-length ebony hair. She massages my scalp and sighs.

I glance up at her. Then straighten when I see her amber eyes glisten with tears.

"What, baby? What's the matter? Does something hurt?" I ask, holding back the panic.

Leonie shakes her head, her waist-length mahogany hair falls over her face like a wavy curtain. I brush it back and cup her chin to force her gaze to mine.

"Tell me," I command.

She takes a deep shuddering breath, closes her eyes, then reopens them to respond.

"I… I want everything to be okay…. And not worry you or anyone else…"

My heart aches. I pull Leonie from her chair and cradle her on my lap as I re-take my seat.

"Hush, baby. It's all right. You and our baby are fine. You're not worrying anyone and especially not me," I murmur.

She tilts her tear-soaked face to gaze into my eyes, studying me.

"If anything should happen, Roger, promise me you will take care of our baby."

What the everlasting fuck?!

No way am I going to allow that to pass.

"Leonie, understand me clearly. If for any reason I have to choose between you and this baby or any other, I choose you always. You mean everything to me. We can try for another baby, or we can adopt a baby in need of a wonderful home. But you... You are irreplaceable, my love. Call me selfish. But I will not live without you, Leonie."

She speaks. But I cut her off with a firm shake of my head. I don't give a damn how harsh it may sound. But it's the damn truth.

"No! This is nonnegotiable. And we will not speak of such things ever again. Do you understand?"

Leonie nods, still sad.

"Words, Leonie. I will have your words," I demand.

She takes some time to consider.

I feel her body stiffen, and she sits up tall. The surrounding energy vibrates anew. Then Leonie stares me straight in the eye with a fiercely determined expression.

"*Oui*, Roger. You are right, *Mon Cœur*. We will move forward from this moment on with only positive thoughts and words of love. You are the most responsible person I know"—she smiles brightly as she strokes my cheek—"But we will share the responsibility of our blessing together. I don't want you to think you have to be strong for both of us. I will not neglect your needs either."

Tears blur my vision as my heart soars with so much love for this woman of mine. She gets me like no one else. I couldn't have asked for a better woman. I chide myself when I recall the awful words I said to her when we had the horrible argument in Cabo San Lucas. The one that pushed her past her limits and drove her out of my arms.

"Leonie, you were 'clear' with me on the jet. Now let me be clear with you. I want a serious-minded partner and not a wayward woman who cannot stay focused for over five minutes. You consistently flit around and avoid your studies. Coming up with excuse after lame excuse. You want people to respect you. But you cannot respect yourself."

I give a silent prayer of thanks she forgave me and we understand one another better. I shake my head to banish the offensive words—'only positive thoughts!' Now here we are engaged to be married with a growing family.

"Well, since you decided to delay my start at STEELE… I may as well start the penthouse makeover project and not remain idle any longer," Leonie says, drawing me from my musings.

I kiss her arched eyebrow, and she giggles as she swats me away.

"Seriously, Roger! You caveman! From now on, we discuss things as a couple before we make decisions," she admonishes me. "But, *Mon Chéri*, you are correct again. I'm not quite up to a hectic schedule."

Leonie pauses and stares at me with skittish eyes.

"Not that I'm flitting around or making any excuses! *Non!* I want the position!" She cries with her hand over her heart as a vow.

I throw my head back and laugh uproariously. Yeah, Leonie and I are on the same wavelength!

How can it get any better?!

LEONIE

*J*keep telling myself I told Roger not to worry, and we'd only have positive thoughts going forward. But I'm still nervous to hear what Dr. Berger will say after he examines me this morning. It's been just over a month since my graduation celebratory dinner.

My stomach still knots whenever I think about what happened. I can't help it.

Just like now as I stand in the all white, Carrara marble and glass walk-in shower. The temperate water sluices all over my body from the multiple jets. Even though it's big enough to hold four and the calming scent of lavender wafts around me, I feel claustrophobic.

I lean my forehead against one of the glass walls and close my eyes. My lips move in a silent prayer: the safety of our baby like a mantra. I finish with deep breaths like Starr taught me during our last Skype yoga session.

She designed a prenatal program with guidance from

Dr. Berger and told him she would act as my doula during delivery. We meet six days a week for an hour. The sessions include asanas, pranayama, meditation, and yoga *nidra*. The yogic breathing I've done in other classes. But I never tried yogic sleep.

Starr insisted it would relieve stress by placing me in a sleep state during which she would guide me in mediation. The first time we tried yoga *nidra*, I didn't only "reach a deep level of relaxation." But fell asleep, then woke myself with my loud snoring!

I smile as I think of my health and wellbeing focused friend. The worry lifts—just a little…

"What's so funny, Kitten?"

A shiver runs through me despite the warm water as Roger's huge hands slide along my flanks and hips to cover my belly. My belly that's no longer flat as a washboard. Our baby has made itself known by pushing my tummy out to make room.

I place my smaller hands over his and melt into his loving embrace. His strength seeps into every cell of my body to center me better than all the eight limbs of yoga combined.

"I'm thinking of Starr and how I snored during my yoga *nidra* session," I respond with a giggle.

Roger chuckles as his lips drag along the side of my neck, leaving a trail of open-mouthed kisses. At the sensitive juncture of my neck and shoulder, he sucks the skin into his mouth. The pulls intensify, guaranteeing a mark.

My mate never lets a day go by without claiming me. I

moan and press my ass against his thick shaft, eliciting a grunt from him.

"Naughty, Pretty Kitty," he rumbles in my ear. "You want your little pussy stretched before the doctor examines you?"

I mewl and rub against him some more. That's exactly what my body craves.

His deep chuckle reverberates through me. In response, my core pulsates as my juices flow in anticipation of Roger's massive dick filling it.

He shifts to the side. The sound of wet skin on skin smacking echoes in the shower.

I gasp from the shock of Roger spanking my ass.

"Oh no, Pretty Kitty. You will not have my cock interfering with your examination. But you will have a spanking for your untimely desires," he croons with his lips pressed against the shell of my ear.

I dance on the tile. But Roger's firm grip around my waist prevents me from slipping. He may punish me. But he would not endanger our baby or me.

My pussy swells and my clit becomes engorged from the arousal building within me. My juices slip from my core to coat my inner thighs.

Merde! I. Want. My. Mate. Now.

As though sensing the peak of my arousal, Roger drops to his knees behind me and grips my hips. He tilts my pelvis to angle my dripping pussy lips to his mouth. A long swipe of his tongue along my seam drives me to my toes as I slap my palms against the steam-slicked glass wall.

Roger's eager feasting of my sweet pussy exemplifies his hunger to the point of greed. The slurping sounds blend with his guttural growls and groans of satisfaction to reverberate around us. His fingers tighten on my hips to lock me in place when my body quivers with the start of an explosive orgasm.

When his tongue wraps around my clit and his thumb breaches my puckered hole, I lose all control. My head falls back and I yowl. The sound slices through the air.

"Oh. Oh. Oh. Aaaaaahhh!!"

The intensity of the onslaught of many waves cresting one after the other dragged on by Roger's continued banquet brings me to my knees.

Roger, not sated fully, guides me to all fours with my ass high to the shower floor, never moving his mouth from my wrung-out pussy.

Another climax takes me and I drop my forehead to the cool marble as a strangled cry falls from my slack mouth. My pants come quickly and I close my eyes, unable to take anymore.

"Roger, please…"

In response, his passionate growl vibrates through my pussy.

"Aaahhh…"

Not until Roger licks the last drop from my thighs does he pull me onto his lap. He cradles my heavy head against his powerful chest. The hypnotic beat of his heart along with his soft murmurs of love fill my ears as I drift into a blissful state of orgasm overload.

. . .

"Bonjour, Mademoiselle Beaulieu and Monsieur Steele. Please have a seat in the east parlor and a nurse will be with you shortly."

I thank Dr. Berger's cordial receptionist as I return her welcoming smile.

His office inhabits the ground floor of his grand personal townhouse with a separate entrance for patients. The receptionist sits at an ornate desk in the foyer. One of the front salons serves as the waiting room. While the other salon has two secretaries seated at desks with guest chairs in front of them. Wooden file cabinets line the wall behind them.

Roger and I admire the fine architectural details and rich decor befitting of the impressive mansion as we make our way to the salon.

Another couple sits on one loveseat and glances our way as we enter the room. Recognition fills their eyes when they see me.

Roger and I haven't released a statement regarding our engagement yet. We decided to wait until I met with the doctor again. Roger didn't want the media, bloggers, and gossips going crazy like they did when Sebastian and Lola announced their engagement. The media already dubbed Sebastian, Malcolm, Roger, and Harris as the STEELE Quaternity—the most sought-after of the world's eligible billionaires.

Toss in my popularity as an internationally known

supermodel, and it would increase tenfold. All it takes is one person to see us and wham! Broadcast news! I agreed I wasn't ready for the added stress.

Now, Roger nods in greeting, and I smile. Might as well get used to people's reactions, I muse. My pregnancy will show soon enough, and my engagement ring isn't exactly subtle. Besides, I want the entire world to know Roger is mine! He's not the only possessive one in our relationship.

With his hand on the small of my back, Roger guides me towards a seating area furthest away from the couple. As we pass them, the man gawks at me openly. Undoubtedly envisioning my sexy *Sports Illustrated Swimsuit Issue* covers and my seductive Lola's Coterie billboards. Roger glares at him, and the man shifts his gaze immediately.

Inwardly, I shake my head and roll my eyes. Staring at me while seated next to his woman...

"Fucker! He keeps it up, and I'll rip his eyeballs out," Roger growls as we sit.

I cover my mouth when a snort of laughter pops out. Roger side eyes me, and I turn away to stifle more snorts.

"You like that fucker staring at you, or are you laughing at me, Pretty Kitty?"

Instantly, I cease all laughter at Roger's Alpha tone. I curse when my pussy clenches with need.

"*Plus jamais, Mon Cœur,*" I purr.

Roger grunts. Then sits back with his legs spread. He holds my hand on his muscular thigh. The caveman dominates the space and claims his mate in full view of an interloper.

I flip through a pregnancy magazine on my lap with one hand. To distract Roger from glaring at the man, I show him some articles as we wait for the nurse.

When she arrives, we follow her to an examination room that could pass for a bedroom except for the table with stirrups attached in the middle of the floor. Once she leaves with instructions for me to put the gown on with the opening in the front and no underwear, I slip out of my silk wrap dress, lingerie, and strappy sandals.

Roger shifts in his seat, and I glance at him over my shoulder as I shake my ass to give him a show.

"Leonie…" He warns.

I giggle and sit on the edge of the table. As I look around the room, I notice the medical equipment artfully hidden in plain sight. My nerves come back, and I take a deep inhale. A knock on the door precedes my exhale.

Roger glances at me, and I nod.

"Come in," he calls.

Dr. Berger and the nurse smile as they walk in.

"Bonjour, Mademoiselle Beaulieu and Monsieur Steele. How are you doing?" He asks.

All eyes turn to me, and silently I repeat my mantra for the safety of our baby before I respond.

"Much better, Dr. Berger. We've followed your precepts, and the low-level prenatal yoga sessions have helped to lessen my stress."

He nods, then continues, "Any cramping or bleeding?"

Roger squirms.

"*Non*, none at all, doctor," I answer confidently and smile at Roger.

He returns my smile and sits up, reassured.

"*Très bon!* Let's do your examination first. Then your ultrasound," Dr. Berger states.

The checkup proves all is indeed much better.

Relief fills me. Next, the scan. I'm excited to see our Lil Cub!

The cool gel on my belly makes me shiver, and Roger who now stands beside me squeezes my hand in his to support me. Without glancing away from the screen, I smile in acknowledgment.

The images before me make no sense at all. So I wait for Dr. Berger to say something in explanation.

He leans forward to peer at the monitor more closely. Then sits back with a frown as he shakes his head. He reaches out to turn a knob for the volume.

The sound of an irregular heartbeat fills the quiet room.

My world collapses. Every negative thought races through my mind. The awful experiences my parents faced come to the forefront. All positivity vanishes in a puff of smoke. Pouf...

Merde!

Unconsciously, my grip tightens on Roger's hand to the point of pain as I hasten to sit up. The wand slips off my belly and my gown falls open. I don't give a damn.

"What? What's wrong? Why does its heart sound funny? *Mon Dieu!*"

I cry in French, unable to think in English.

My eyes fill with tears, and I feel as though the walls are closing in on me. Panicked, I swing my gaze from Dr. Berger to the nurse to Roger and back to the doctor.

"Tell me!" I demand.

"What the fuck?! Answer her!" Roger bellows.

Dr. Berger raises his hands, palms out in compliance as he shakes his head.

"*Non, non!* You misunderstand! Nothing is wrong! You're fine! Your babies are fine!" He exclaims as his words tumble from his mouth.

The room falls silent again as we stare at the doctor. Then Roger and I yell at the same time.

"*Qu'est-ce que tu viens de me dire?!*"

"Babies?!"

ROGER

"*O*h, *Mon Trésor!* You're glowing! How beautiful you look!"

Leonie's mother exclaims as she hugs her treasured daughter to her bosom tightly. Tears glisten in her eyes. But Josy doesn't allow them to fall. Her soft amber eyes so like Leonie's shut as she squeezes her even more. Her lips move as though in silent prayer.

Guy beams at his wife and only child as he stands next to them in the foyer at *Le Beaulieu Manoir*.

His brawny six-foot-four-inch frame towers over the mother and daughter pair. He's a foot taller than petite Josy. Even with Leonie in sky-high heels, he has two inches on her.

"Oui, *Mon Trésor*, absolutely spectacular!" He agrees, grinning broadly.

Guy's voice booms around the grand entryway of their

palatial French Rococo mansion. Set on twenty acres on the outskirts of Paris in Neuilly-Auteuil-Passy, their ancestral home is one of the finest in the wealthy neighborhood. And Guy is the epitome of the Alpha male of the estate, with his finely tailored clothes that underscore his fit physique and statuesque frame.

Leonie gets her height and wavy, mahogany hair from her father and the lush curves and eyes from her mother. Personality wise, she's a combination of Guy's bold confidence and Josy's elegance and warmth.

I wonder who our twins will favor. The Beaulieu leonine amber eyes and aristocratic demeanor. Or the Steele signature gray eyes and dominant tendencies. They'll definitely match the height on both sides, even if Josy is the smallest of us all. However, as long as our babies are healthy, it doesn't matter.

"And you, Roger. Good to see you, son!"

Guy claps me on the back and draws my attention to the room.

Since Leonie and I became engaged, he's taken to calling me son. He explained he's thrilled with his daughter, but a son is a welcome addition to their small family.

I'm thankful he's accepted me. Not one to fear anything or anyone, Guy's frank warning when we first met makes him one to acknowledge as better to have as a friend than as a foe:

He leans forward. His obsidian eyes bore into mine.

"Do not fuck my daughter over or you will pay the price."

I train as a boxer and can hold my own. However, Guy is a force to take into consideration. He may be in his early sixties, but he's studied jujutsu for decades. He's just as comfortable in the French salons as in the back alleys. It's best for all parties involved, we're on solid footing.

"Good to see you, too, Guy! You look well," I respond heartily.

He nods and gestures toward the all-glass solarium that overlooks the rear rose garden. Our regular spot for the Sunday brunches we've enjoyed over the last several months. We pass the now familiar salons on our way. I spot new items Josy must have added from Beaulieu Enterprises, SAS's ever-changing stock of high-quality antiques, antiquities, and fabrics.

Over the centuries, the Beaulieu's continued to grow their merchant business. Now, Guy as the *président* has expanded it into a multibillion-dollar enterprise.

While Sebastian was in Paris after his honeymoon, we met with Guy and his team to discuss partnership opportunities. They impressed Sebastian. He made the alliance between STEELE International, Inc. and Beaulieu Enterprises, SAS his first big deal since being named the new CEO by our father. Morgan, who took part int the meetings via video conference, gave his approval.

Their company is privately owned and Leonie is the heir apparent. After our engagement, Guy expressed his wish for me to take on the helm with Leonie when he retires. Leonie made it clear she is not interested in running the day-to-day responsibilities as she wants to focus on her interior design career.

We agreed we would incorporate Beaulieu within the STEELE organization. But Leonie will maintain majority control with our children, taking on the company at the appropriate time. The Beaulieu company will continue to pass on to the next generation as it has for centuries.

The future addition pleases Sebastian and my father. Morgan and Guy admire one another as equals. It's the perfect solution for both companies and families.

Leonie and I arrived early to spend some time with Guy and Josy before my clan joins us for brunch. They're ideal in-laws—no hovering, no forcing themselves into our lives, no judgment. Even with their concern for Leonie and the babies, neither Guy nor Josy force their way in our relationship. Although I wouldn't mind at all.

"Tell us about Dr. Berger's assessment of your wellbeing, *Mon Trésor*," Guy says as we settle on sofas near the wall of glass.

The view of the manicured park-like grounds with the stables, tennis court, and swimming pool with cabana is peaceful. A pleasant respite from the bustling city. No wonder Leonie raves about her happy childhood. Who wouldn't with such a lovely place to grow up?

"Oh, *Papa*! All is good!" Leonie exclaims clapping her hands as her amber eyes glow and her cheeks blush. "But we want to wait until we gather everyone before sharing any details."

She turns to smile at me and takes my hand in hers.

I nod at her lovingly and respond, "Yes, Leonie is doing very well! Dr. Berger is pleased with her progress."

"*Bien, bien!!*" Guy slaps his muscular thighs with both hands. Then wraps an arm around Josy to hug her close.

She closes her eyes with a contented sigh and leans into his massive chest.

My smile widens as I take in their joy.

Leonie kisses my cheek, and I place my hand on her belly as its outline presses against her buttery soft, black leather shirt dress.

We spend half an hour chatting about everything from Josy's latest recipes and philanthropic endeavors to Leonie's yoga escapades with Starr.

"And Roger joined one of my sessions... You know, since Sebastian takes classes with Starr. You should have seen how Roger tried to analyze each asana. Starr was very patient with him. While I threatened to ban him from future sessions!" Leonie tells them.

"Now, don't tease Roger, Leonie! That's not nice," Josy admonishes, then continues. "You know how very serious he is!"

Her laughter tinkles around us—light and high. Only in her early fifties, she keeps a youthful quality. Another trait I'm sure Leonie will inherit from her.

"Roger, practicing yoga will help with your boxing. The focus and breathing will enhance your technique," Guy adds.

"Yes, I can see those benefits. Despite what Leonie says, I will join one or two of her sessions"—I put my fingertip to her lips when she protests—"But I won't interfere. Starr is an acclaimed teacher who I trust implicitly."

"Fine!" Leonie huffs.

The chime of the doorbell pauses our conversation.

Since they give the staff the weekend off, Guy goes to the entry and returns with my parents, Sebastian, Lola, Malcolm, Harris, Haley, Luc, and Blair. Our cousin and Lucien's older brother Lachlan, the President of Liquor at Jackson Corporation, is in town from his home base in Aberdeen, Scotland. He has business at their Paris offices this week. He follows Haley into the solarium.

"Leonie, honey! You look marvelous!" My mother Shelley gushes as she pulls Leonie into an embrace.

"Indeed! Nice and healthy, young lady!" Morgan adds with a warm smile sparking his platinum eyes.

The rest of the clan offers more hugs and words of well wishes.

"Leonie, it's so good to see you well," Lachlan says as he double kisses her cheeks.

This sly fucker. Lachlan always uses his Cary Grant movie-star looks to woo women. I growl low in my throat, and he laughs, draping his arm around Leonie's shoulders.

"Calm down, Papa Caveman! I'm off the market!" Lachlan winks.

A stricken sound behind him makes us turn.

Haley stands staring at Lachlan. Her gray eyes widen behind her glasses. Scarlet flushes her cheeks as she turns away quickly.

Lachlan's usual Alpha Dom bravado falters as he

watches her stalk towards the sideboard. She takes a flute filled with a Mimosa and gulps half of it.

I clear my throat, then cock my head at Lachlan when he faces me again.

He averts his gaze and gives Leonie's shoulders a last squeeze before he steps away.

I glance up and my eyes meet Sebastian's as he stands stoically.

"*Mon Cœur?* Are you ready?"

Leonie stares up at me with her hand on my chest.

Whatever the fuck is up with Lach and Haley, if anything, will have to wait until after Leonie and I share our glorious news.

"Yes, my love. You want to tell them?" I ask.

Leonie shakes her head and pats my chest, "*Non*, you."

I wrap my arm around her waist and kiss the top of her head. Then linger as I inhale her scent mixed with the blend of florals with amber and musk of her perfume. Divine.

"Everyone, please take a flute to toast our fantastic news," I say, glancing at each face around us.

Lola claps and whoops as she heads to the sideboard. The others follow. I pick up two glasses of Leonie's new favorite drink, iced lemon ginger tea, and hand one to her.

A hush falls over the room as everyone gazes at us raptly.

I loop my arm back around Leonie's waist and raise my glass in the air.

"Leonie and I are expecting…"

I pause for effect while Leonie giggles.

"Bro, if you don't spill it, I'll hack into the doctor's medical records right here, right now!" Harris threatens as he whips out his latest innovative gadget.

Haley pulls her mobile from her handbag and poises her fingers over the screen as she glares at me.

I don't doubt one of our two tech wizzes will do just that if I don't finish fast enough.

"All right! All right!" I laugh.

I lift my glass high and shout, "Identical twins!!"

An uproar of boisterous cries of surprise and glee mixed with claps, feet stomping, and sharp whistles fill the solarium. Everyone speaks at once as they go wild with glee.

They sweep Leonie from my arms by either Josy and Shelley or Lola, Haley, and Blair. Her joyful laughter makes my heart leap. They surround her as they rub her belly and kiss her face.

"Damn, bro! Twins??"

"Congrats, man! Hot damn!"

"Well done, son, well done!"

"*Félicitations, fils!*"

"Holy cow! The caveman made his claim without a doubt!"

"Excellent, Roger! *Bon travail!*"

"Tag! You're next, Baz!!"

The most incredible sensations flow through me, igniting every fiber of my being with an electric charge. I chuckle when I think of how Leonie calls our love affair *un coupe de foudre*. How apropos!

"Well, Roger, honey, you and Leonie certainly have your work cut out for you! Wedding plans, penthouse makeover, delivery! Josy and I volunteer to assist with all!"

I throw my head back and laugh uproariously.

"Of course, Mom! I've heard through the grapevine about your military strategies and tactics..."

Now it's Shelley's turn to laugh loudly. She wipes the corners of her eyes before she responds.

"I have no doubt! I take full responsibility!"

"*Oui!* So much to get done! But first, we eat!" Josy adds.

Leonie nods enthusiastically as she pats her belly and points to her mouth.

"Time to feed the babies!" She exclaims.

Everyone laughs and heads to the delicious dishes arranged on the buffet. The tantalizing aroma of savory and sweet foods fills the air. Josy blends traditional Tunisian and French fare of meats, vegetables, and baked goods. Our mouths water in anticipation.

Lucien, who's joined us at some brunches, claims he's going to use her recipes for his restaurants and eateries.

Josy quipped how he might as well since Leonie refuses to learn them as is the family's way to pass the recipes down through the generations.

Today's lively conversation is a perfect match to the festive atmosphere. Everyone is excited Leonie and I decided to find out the babies' sex at the eighteen-week scan.

"We have enough to get done without worrying about what colors to use," Leonie laughs.

"We need more girls!" Haley declares. "We have more than enough testosterone and overinflated egos to last a lifetime!"

Neither Sebastian nor I miss the wince Lachlan makes at her declaration. Once again my eldest brother and I share a a glance. Lachlan is his best friend. So I'm sure Baz will get the truth out of him.

Haley will prove to be harder to crack since she insists we stay out of her love life. I must admit it has to be hard to have four older brothers who intimidate any guy she dates. Not to mention no one is good enough for our father's princess. Only our mother sympathizes with Haley.

Oh, well... Too bad, Baby Sis.

"How much time do we have to prep for this wedding?" Lola snickers.

Sebastian gave her little time. He refused to wait. I don't blame him one bit.

"You are lucky I allowed you any time, Lola," Sebastian says in his Alpha Dom voice with his eyebrow cocked.

I chuckle to myself when Lola lowers her gaze as her face flushes with heat, and she squirms in her seat.

Every man at this table is an Alpha male. Some have the extra Dom characteristic. So no one bats an eye at Sebastian and Lola's D/s exchange. Hell, my brothers and I peg our parents as having a D/s marriage!

The women we love are all independent, smart, feisty, and bring something to the table other than their good looks. Some may be subs, some not. A need drives each male to provide the utmost pleasure to their mate. However, all play is consensual between adults who respect one another and their limits.

Leonie is not a sub and I'm not a Dom. But I dominate her in the bedroom. And she loves it!

A small hand glides along my inner thigh beneath the linen-covered table. Fingertips dance across my crotch. Then give a squeeze to the burgeoning bulge.

I have to take a sip of my iced tea to hide my unexpected groan.

Meanwhile, Leonie captivates all with her tales of yoga, my "zealous attentiveness," and her changing eating habits, including a desire for salty things. At which point, she tweaks my cock in emphasis.

Fuck. Me.

Yeah, this morning, she made an almighty meal of my dick. Just thinking about her decadent feast makes me swell. I have to adjust my lengthening cock surreptitiously to lessen the pinch of the zipper teeth on my trousers.

"*Oui, oui!* Roger has mastered my needs. He expects them before they even form in my mind!" Leonie says, laughing at her private pun.

"So when is the wedding date?!" Shelley demands.

"Well... Honestly, I'm ready to marry Roger right now. But I've always dreamed of a fairy-tale wedding. I want time to create it and to cherish every moment from idea to honeymoon." Leonie whispers.

I cup her chin in my hand and turn her head to bring our eyes on a level. Then I kiss her lips gently.

"Whatever you want, my love, it is yours. Just leave the honeymoon to me. For all intents and purposes, you are mine. My ring, my babies, my woman. Mine." I respond.

Tears well in her eyes. A reminder of how her "hormones rage inside" of her as she reminds me daily.

"However, I have my limits. I will not wait more than a few months," I add.

She leans her forehead against mine and inhales deeply as we share breaths for a moment.

"Fine. Four months... I need four months from today. Enough time to plan our wedding extravaganza, redo the penthouse into a triplex, and prepare a gorgeous nursery for our bundles of joy."

Leonie sits back to stare me in the eye directly. Her amber eyes ablaze.

"D'accord?"

"Oui, Mon Amour, d'accord! I promise you will have your fairy-tale wedding no matter what."

"Well, thank goodness! I can do four months! Josy?" Shelley says, clapping her hands.

"Oui! Oui! Four months is fantastic! Mon Trésor will have the wedding of her dreams!" Josy responds jubilantly.

"Well then, a toast to four months!" Guy stands at the head of the table and raises his crystal flute.

"To four months!"

The chorus rings around the solarium.

Leonie smiles at me with such a profound expression of love on her face.

My heart bangs against my chest. I will do all I can to ensure the love of my life always has that look permanently etched on her gorgeous face.

My lips find hers and my hand rests on her belly bump.

All. Mine!

ROGER

"*T*ell me how Leonie is doing?"

My Vibram Fivefingers-clad feet pound the roof-top track of Norman Green's Elite Training Facility. The Champ and I run around the course as part of my cardio for this morning's training session.

It's a clear sunny day. So they withdrew the retractable glass roof into its casing. The sounds of the city drift up the six stories and remind us we're still in the heart of Paris' bustling business district. The location proves the ideal spot to attract high-powered titans of finance, real estate, media, and other industries. The waiting list for membership stands at four months long.

I lift my face to the sky, enjoying the sun on my olive-toned skin. Sweat glistens on my face and neck even as the wind whips around us. The moisture-wicking fabric of my shirt and training pants keeps my body dry. Which is a good thing since Norman has me doing a balls-busting workout. And the run is the warm-up...

Now he's asking questions. Sure he cares about Leonie's wellbeing. But it's also a test of my endurance. Can I talk comfortably while running laps? Or does the effort cost me my breath? I give Norman the side eye.

"Look, Steele, I want to know how she's doing, seriously! You had Anita and me worried! Talk to me, man," he says sincerely, holding his hands up as he runs beside me.

That's one reason members clamor to train with him. He gets in it with you. A man who doesn't just talk the talk. He works out right along with you. All in.

"Thanks, man. I appreciate your concern. Leonie is doing really well. In fact"—I pivot to jog backwards—"Call me Big Poppa... We're having identical twins!"

Norman's firm jaw drops, and he stops short in surprise.

I jog in a circle, throwing my hands in the air. I'm a true player. Take dat. Take dat!

Identical twins!

Every time I think about them, a big goofy grin spreads across my face. Leonie just laughs and shakes her head whenever she catches me spacing out, smiling to myself. She's dubbed me Big Poppa after her favorite rapper, The Notorious B.I.G.

"Shut up, Steele! You got it like that, man? Damn!" Norman chuckles as he shakes his head.

He and Anita have a little girl named Antonia—a combination of their names. He's the only one of my friends who has children. So, he's become my source for firsthand experience.

"As I said, call me Big Poppa!" I toss over my shoulder as I return to our run.

Norman catches up to me with ease.

"Congratulations, Big Poppa! They say twins run in the family. But man, I tell you... Double the after-midnight feedings, diapers, crying. But oh so worth it," he says as he slaps me on the back.

We settle into our run for another lap. Then head inside for some footwork training followed by the heavy and speed bags. I notice an improvement on my focus in my speed bag work from my new yoga practice.

Even though I told Leonie I would join her sessions, I only come in during the mediation or yoga *nidra* portions. Instead, Starr teaches me separately based on my needs assessment. She found I would benefit from Ashtanga, as it requires strength and stamina with the added memorization of the sequence element. It appeals to my intense nature.

"Anita had your and Leonie's meals for the week delivered to your penthouse. She wants you to know she added more of the jerk chicken Leonie enjoyed," Norman tells me as we walk to the locker room after our session ends.

"Great. Leonie will be ecstatic. Give Anita my thanks," I respond. "Too bad you can't join the guys and me tonight at the lounge. Lachlan has a new blend we're testing."

"Yeah, I know. It sounds like a good time. But Anita and

I have plans for date night, dinner and the ballet, I can't break."

I nod, understanding I wouldn't change my plans with Leonie either.

"Next time," I say as we shake, and I clap him on the shoulder before we head into the locker room.

"Count on it. Ballet or bros?" Norman says.

"Bros!" We reply in unison.

Our deep chuckles bounce off the travertine-tile walls as we stride to the showers.

"NOW THIS IS my latest creation. No one but the craft team has tasted it. You, my brothers, will be the first beyond the walls of Jackson Corporation to experience this exquisite blend of—"

"Give us a damn snifter already!" Joel interrupts Lachlan's razzle-dazzle speech.

"Here, here!" Lucien adds as he picks a Baccarat crystal snifter off of the tasting table.

We're in one of the glass-enclosed tasting rooms at Jackson Smoke&Scotch the new lounge Lucien opened five months ago. In the Place Vendôme/St. Honoré area on Rue Saint-Honoré, it quickly became the spot to see and be seen for old society, fashionistas, and celebrities. *The Sexy Chef* has a way with food and drink as much as with women.

Tonight is no exception. He's invited a few ladies to what was supposed to be our Guys' Night Out. Sure, the three women are beautiful and dressed provocatively. But none can compare to my Pretty Kitty. Who I left at home lying on our bed in a silk negligee writing in the baby journal I gave to her.

Leonie's fuller breasts overflow the lace cups as her succulent nipples poked through. She left her mahogany hair hanging down to her the curve of her ass, partially covering one eye. My very own Jessica Rabbit.

Without even trying, Leonie is irresistibly sensual. Not like the brunette who just touched my chest. Uh, no...

"Pardon me," I say as I step away to pick up a snifter.

Just as I pass her, she grips my forearm to stop me.

"Aren't you Roger Steele? As in the STEELE Quaternity of billionaire brothers?" She asks, her little pink tongue flicking over her overly inflated lower lip.

I stare at her hand on my arm, then back at her with my eyebrow cocked.

She titters and squeezes.

Where did Lucien find this one? Damn.

The press release went out two days ago announcing the engagement, wedding date, and congratulations on the expected birth. The news spread like wildfire. The Internet blew up. Bloggers sent into writing frenzies. Trending social media hashtags #TheLionCaught, #SteeleScoopedII dominate feeds.

Guests who attended Sebastian and Lola's wedding call my mother for invites. My office and Leonie's modeling agency flooded with calls for interviews. Two Steele bachelors off of the market in eight months prove fodder for the media and society alike.

However, this woman missed the memo...

"Yes, I am Roger Steele"—she preens and bites her lip—"And no, I am not interested, as my gorgeous fiancée is at our home waiting for me. So again, pardon me."

I extricate my limb from her grip and stride to the tasting table without a glance back. That should answer her question and prevent any further advances. One can hope I muse as I take a hefty gulp of Lachlan's self-proclaimed best damn Scotch ever...

"That hottie was all over you, bro," Joel says as he appears at my elbow.

I glance at him as I cradle my snifter of what actually is an excellent blend. Lachlan wasn't being a blowhard after all. The taste of chocolate and dried fruit mix well together. The trademark bite drags along the back or the throat before settling with a warmth in the stomach. Tasty.

"No thanks. I've got an all-natural hottie at home. In fact, I'm not staying much longer. I planned on a Guys' Night Out. Not a meat market where I'm on the hook," I reply as I glance at my Vacheron Constantin Patrimony Traditionnele.

Joel chuckles as he takes a sip of his Scotch, eyeing the red head across from us.

I pin him with my intense stare.

"What the fuck, man?" I demand.

Joel doesn't look away from the woman as he responds absently, "What?"

"Well, let's think about it, shall we... Hettie Fuchs... Your girlfriend. Sounds familiar?" I deadpan.

Now his attention drifts away from the redhead. Joel's arctic blue eyes flash as he glares at the wall. He snorts and finishes his Scotch in one long swallow.

Oh, boy. This can't be good, I muse.

"Oh, you mean Miss I'm Moving Back Into My Apartment Out Of The Blue??" He growls scowling into the empty snifter.

Nope. Not good at all.

"What the hell did you do, Joel?" I ask, positive he had to do something to make Hettie leave after they've lived together for so long.

"How do you suppose it's my fault, Roger?" He says snidely.

I sigh and glance at my watch again. Enough of this shit. I belong home snuggled up with my woman, not being harassed by a stranger and arguing with a friend. Give me a damned break already.

"Well first, Hettie committed herself to you. So she wouldn't just up and leave. Second, did it occur to you she may want more than what you're offering, Mr. I'm Way Too Young To Commit?"

I throw his words back at him from the first time we were in this very lounge talking about our relationships. I also realize I'm thinking from a female's perspective. Leonie is rubbing off on me...

Joel looks uncomfortable as he loosens the Prince Albert knot of his silk necktie. He stiffens, and I glance up to see the redhead sidling over to us with a seductive smirk on her face.

"Hi, would you like some help with that?" She purrs, batting her long eyelashes at Joel as she reaches for the tail end of his tie.

He jerks backwards as though burned and shakes his head vigorously.

"No!" He collects himself and softens his response. "No, thank you. Actually, I have a girlfriend."

"Well, I don't see her here," she presses on. "And you seem tense, sweetie."

Her hand slips up his tie as she flicks her long fingernail on his exposed throat.

Joel catches her wrist and removes her hand. Then he cocks his eyebrow and responds, "No. Thank. You."

Damn, is it the Scotch or what? These women are super aggressive tonight. I turn my back to refill our snifters as I shake my head in disbelief.

Fortunately, the red head takes the hint and moves on to where Lucien and Lachlan stand chatting with the other two women.

I watch Lachlan and wonder if Sebastian got any details from him about Haley. Lachlan senses my intense stare and glances in my direction. I give him the I-see-you chin bob and sip my Scotch.

Slowly, he returns my nod. Undoubtedly knowing what I'm thinking.

Not blood cousins. Rather, our mothers have been best friends since they met in New York as young women before either married their billionaire husbands. As a result, the Steeles and Jacksons grew into a tight family unit, and the children consider themselves cousins.

Close or no; blood or no. I'll kick Lachlan's ass if he fucks with my baby sister. I'm sure Sebastian made that clear to him before he returned to New York City.

"You're right, bro. I fucked up with Hettie."

Joel's confession brings my focus back to him.

"What happened?" I ask, concerned for both of my friends.

He sighs and tells me how she asked him flat out if he planned to have the cow for free. He had to explain that one to me. It made sense and reminded me of Leonie's hesitancy to move in with me and Lola's back and forth with Sebastian. Somehow, I realize they're behind this one. I keep that theory to myself and let Joel continue.

"I miss her. I mean badly. But I can't just go crawling back. You know what I mean?" Joel asks, looking like a lost puppy.

I clap my hand on his shoulder and squeeze it.

"Man, take my advice. Go get your woman and put a ring on it already!"

I gesture towards Lachlan and Lucien. Then to the two of us.

"What would you rather... Women who only want you for your name and wealth? Wasting time on those who don't give a fuck about you the man? Or a woman who's been with you for years and loves you for you? And all she wants is your commitment to her as she's given hers to you. Doing things your way all this time... Come on, man, it gets old. Trust me!"

Joel takes a moment to consider my speech. Then nods his head.

"You're right. This last month showed me I had a good thing with Hettie, but it could be great. Well... I guess they'll be hashtags about us next."

He laughs and touches his snifter to mine in a toast.

I join in his laughter and finish my Scotch.

"And on that note, I have a sexy as fuck fiancée curled up in my bed. Gotta fly!"

Joel chuckles and places his snifter next to mine on the tasting table.

"Right with you! I have to send a text message to my shopper to ask the manager of Harry Winston to open real quick for me. Then I'm dragging Hettie back to my cave where she belongs. This time with my ring on her finger!"

Our boisterous laughter fills the room. The others turn to gawk at us, and we salute them.

Then waltz out the door whistling *Going to the Chapel of Love* between chuckles.

I CAPTURE the image of Leonie curled under the covers on my side of the bed with her head resting on my pillow when I return to our penthouse. Her wavy hair fans across the silk pillowcase. The contrast of the mahogany and the cream frames her beautiful face. One boob popped out of her negligee, enticing me with its pebbled tip. But I let her rest as she appears so peaceful.

Instead, I stride into my dressing room and swap my bespoke three-piece suit and custom shirt for a pair of navy silk pajama bottoms. After I brush my teeth and wash my face, I return to stand at our bedside.

Leonie is so gorgeous. A natural, effortless beauty who takes my breath away. I glance down at the profile of her baby bump and my smile widens. MILF Alert! I'm a lucky so and so.

I open the little navy velvet box and set it on the night-stand. The two large pear-shaped diamonds and the pavé diamonds in the platinum band of the *toi et moi* ring sparkle in the lamp's glow. Leonie left one on for me. The identical, flawless stones will act as a reminder of our twins every time she sees it, I think as I place it on her right ring finger.

Leonie sighs and murmurs my name in her sleep as she unconsciously closes her fist on her new ring.

How symbolic, I think as I kiss her forehead softly. Then slip under the covers behind her. I spoon my body around hers with one hand on her belly and the other on her breast. Happily, I join her in a peaceful slumber.

LEONIE

"*H*ow are Blair and you doing, Luc? Long distance can put a strain on a relationship."

I mask my burst of laughter with a cough at Roger's out-of-the-blue question. Ever since he played counselor for Joel and Hettie, he's offering advice like the Love Doctor!

In reality, Roger did well with our friends.

Joel proposed to Hettie a week ago, and she's in seventh heaven. She was more blown away by his unexpected popping of the question when he showed up at her flat late at night, than she was with the flawless twenty-carat, cushion-cut diamond!

Hettie did a FaceTime call with me the next morning from the bathroom while Joel was still asleep in bed. She couldn't contain her excitement any longer. She had to tell me and show her stunning Harry Winston ring right away.

Later at lunch, Hettie shared more details about his

proposal from the doorman announcing she had a visitor to Joel dropping to one knee when she opened the door to them not making it to her bedroom.

I covered my ears and responded TMI—too much information!

They chose a date six months from now. Like me, Hettie desires the wedding of her dreams and Joel is more than willing to do what she wants. He's just happy she's decided to spend more time at his flat. Hettie told him she was only moving a few of her items back in. She plans to stay the majority of the time in her flat.

"I told Joel, 'you only have the cow part-time!' He groused about it. But I stood firm."

Now, Roger, Luc, and I are on board Roger's Gulfstream G650 headed to LAX. Since Dr. Berger cleared me for work, Lola and I decided I would get in some photo shoots before The Twins took over my body. The photographer can PhotoShop my babies bump without taking away the integrity of the images.

My role as her exclusive spokesmodel will continue throughout my pregnancy. As previously planned, I'll do appearances at Lola's Coterie boutiques and at the high-end retailers that carry her collections. Interviews—print, television, radio, online—will run according to the media schedule.

Once The Twins grow larger, I won't model the lingerie and loungewear anymore. The evening wear collection won't fit my new frame either. So over the next few weeks, I'll pose for the camera. In the words of my modeling godmother, Rupaul: I better work! Shantay, shantay, shantay!

Roger insists I'm a MILF and still every man's sexy fantasy.

I don't disagree. A pregnant woman is a beautiful reminder of the power of nature and the strength of a woman.

Besides, I don't have any issues with my body. I embrace my curves—full C-cup breasts, slim waist, grip-worthy hips, round ass, and all. My healthy eating and exercise habits won't change. So, the only weight will come from The Twins as Dr. Berger recommends.

I intend to rock my fitted dresses, skin-tight leather pants, and bikinis. Plus, strut in my stilettos. Just add my name to the list of Hot Mamas: Hilaria Baldwin, Blake Lively, Ciara, Jennifer Lopez, and more!

Lola says she has a surprise for me. She refused to give one hint even though she knows the anticipation drives me crazy. Never mind, I'll know soon enough. Well, in another eight hours…

But the expression on Luc's handsome face proves the entertainment on this flight increased tenfold!

Luc is of the upper echelons of society. A man with a genteel upbringing and impeccable manners who does not discuss his private affairs. Period. Lola and I tease him mercilessly. But Luc remains mum.

Roger sprang the question on him just as he took a sip of his Chateau Lafite Rothschild. Luc sputters dribbling the pricey potable down his clean-shaven cleft chin. The crimson shade of his face matches the wine's hue. Luc's denim blue eyes widen, aghast at such an intimate question.

Even though he's known Roger for almost two years, he's known Lola and me far longer and doesn't share with us. So his shock is real.

And laughable. Cue the popcorn!

We started eating dinner a moment ago with casual conversation. Now, I sit back to enjoy the show.

"Hey, are you okay?" Roger asks as he passes a linen napkin to Luc over the formally set dining table.

Despite being thousands of feet in the air, we dine on fine porcelain dishes with sterling silver flatware and crystal stemware. The delicious six-course meal prepared by one of Lucien's restaurants, then delivered to the private jet for the flight attendants to serve.

Luc dabs his full lips as his eyes flick between Roger and me.

My amber eyes dance with mirth as Luc struggles to regain control of his emotions. Poor Luc, I've never seen him so flustered. He must be serious about Blair.

"Roger, while I appreciate your concern for my... personal affairs, I prefer to keep them private," Luc responds finally as he pins Roger with an intense stare.

Not chastened, Roger continues.

"I understand and respect your preference. I merely ask because a friend of mine inquired as to Blair's romantic availability..."

Luc's jaw drops, and he blinks rapidly as he absorbs Roger's newest remarks.

Merde...

I wonder if he's serious until I feel a nudge to my thigh beneath the table. I stop myself from reacting and reach for my iced lemon green tea.

"Well, that is not for me to say. Now is it?" Luc rejoins.

Roger nods agreeably as he removes his mobile from the breast pocket of his suit jacket. His fingers fly across the screen.

"What are you doing?" Luc asks sharply as he leans across the table, eyeing the device like a snake.

Roger doesn't bother to glance up, just continues to type.

"Oh. Sending Blair's number to my friend so he can ask her on a date while we're in Beverly Hills. You see, he met her at one of Lola's Coterie's openings. He's in town at the same time as us. But based in New York... like Blair. No need to worry about long-distance romance. Huh?"

Luc loses all of his aristocratic cool as he snatches Roger's mobile from his hands.

"Now wait a minute! You cannot just give out Blair's number to some random man!" He huffs.

Roger feints aggrievement as he sits back in his chair openmouthed. He says not a word as Luc rages on about his boorish behavior. Then he pauses and narrows his eyes at Roger.

To his credit, he doesn't alter his facial features under Luc's arctic glare.

"You're fucking with me, Steele..."

Roger throws his head back and howls with laughter. Then smirks at me as he waggles his fingers in a vee.

"Two for two!"

* * *

THE EXHILARATING sensation that rushes through my veins when the flashes flicker, the photographer calls for angles, and the music blares reminds me why I love to model. The glitz and glamour of it all thrills me!

"Darling, tilt your face towards the light for me!"

The opulent Beverly Hills Mediterranean-inspired estate that was the backdrop for the iconic movie *The Godfather* serves as my plush playground. I'm lying on a chaise beside the sparkling swimming pool, surrounded by three arched pavilions.

The latest set for Lola's Coterie Beverly Hills is in a vibrant fuchsia hue that complements my caramel-colored skin. The lustrous stretch-silk satin trimmed with coral lace is the buttery soft material for the bra, briefs, and suspender belt. The matching robe flows from my shoulders to puddle on the grass beneath the chaise.

My hair cascades down my back in shiny waves with a fuchsia bow tied like a headband. The makeup artist kept the look fresh and dewy.

I'm channeling Old Hollywood Glam—portraying the wife of a movie studio mogul. Instead of a male model playing the role, Lola insists Roger do it. At first he was hesitant. But Sebastian and Luc goad him on. While the marketing team explains how a campaign featuring us would drive sales, being we're the trending couple.

The camera loves his devastatingly handsome visage. After a bit of direction, he picks up the poses and cues from the photographer easily.

Roger grins at me as I tilt my face to the light. The direction of which aligns my mouth with his crotch as he stands over me.

The photographer wants sizzling... Well, he's getting it in an abundance. And I'm not complaining... Yum!

I lick my lips and wink at him seductively. I swear his cock twitches in his white swimming briefs. The outline of his length and the curve of his tip apparent in the tight material.

"Great, Roger, flex those rock-hard abs and thick thighs of yours!" Calls the photographer.

Roger bites his lip to keep from chuckling. But he does as requested.

When he mouths MILF, I can't help but crack up. Doubling over the chaise, snorting in a very non-MILF way. I cackle so much, my breath catches. So, I hold my belly, falling back onto the chaise.

The makeup and hair teams rush over to fix my face from the tears and bow I dislodged.

Roger swats them away as he checks on me. When he deems I'm fine, he motions for them to proceed. He stands on guard behind them with his arms crossed over his powerful chest; the biceps flexing. He's a sexy Roman gladiator.

"Leonie! What's gotten into you?" Lola admonishes.

"Him!" I snort as I point to Roger, then to my babies bump.

Everyone on the set joins in my laughter.

Roger smirks like right, I made them babies.

After the pool scene and more shots in different lingerie, we move to the stone terrace for the evening wear collection. These dresses are Lola's most recent addition—a take on the lingerie as gowns befitting Hollywood award shows' and premiers' red carpets.

The sparkly peach sequin-covered georgette gown is drama overload. Wispy feather-embellished sleeves tickle midway down my arms. Designed in an elegant wrap silhouette with ties to adjust the fit. Then falls to a floor-sweeping train that trails behind me as I sashay towards the fountain. My long, toned legs, lengthened by the cream-colored strappy sandals, show with each stride. The gown reminiscent of a silver screen siren's luxurious dressing gown.

I smile at Roger as I near him, standing in a custom tuxedo beside the fountain. His eyes shimmer liquid silver in the sun as his lips curve into an alluring smile.

Roman gladiator turned James Bond heartthrob.

I slip my hand into his outstretched palm.

"Why hello there, Monsieur Steele."

Roger smirks and leans down to murmur in my ear, "Hello there, Pretty Kitty. I have something for you."

He reaches behind him to the fountain's rim for a large, flat velvet box. Then holds it aloft.

I press the crystal closure and gasp when I see a suite of rich, pure yellow and white diamonds glowing against the black suede. My eyes fly to Roger's.

He smirks as he pulls the necklace out and drapes it around my neck. Next he closes the bracelets around my wrists and slips the ring on my right index finger—I never take off my toi et moi ring. He holds his hand out with the dangling drop earrings for me to put them in place. Then he slides the comb in my hair. With a satisfied nod, he steps back to admire his gifts.

"Merci, Mon Cœur," I purr as I rub my lips across his, wrapping my arms around his neck.

Roger's hands rest on the curve of my ass as he pulls me close. His thick cock presses into my belly.

"Hold it! Don't move!"

The photographer shouts as his camera clicks in rapid succession. Capturing our classic embrace.

"HONEY, you are lit up like the Christmas tree at Rockefeller Center!"

Billie teases me since I refused to take off my new baubles.

"Ho, ho, ho! Well call me Santa!" Roger chuckles as he kisses my radiant hand.

"Thank you, Santa Baby," I purr.

"See... That's what got you preggie in the first place!" Lola exclaims.

"Oh, don't tease them. They're so cute!" Starr chimes in, her dimples flashing as she smiles.

We're gathered at the steak restaurant in STEELE Rodeo Drive for dinner on our last night. Billie flew in from Las Vegas for the week and Starr joined us. Blair sits leaning into Luc, who's been super attentive the whole trip.

"They're my rockstar yoga couple!" Starr adds.

We met with her every morning for in-person sessions at her Starr Light Fitness & Wellness Beverly Hills. I miss her live energy and hands-on adjustments. What a treat!

She's promised to fly over next month and stay for a week. She knows Anita from the yoga world. They have plans to catch up while Starr is in Paris. She's going to ask Anita to partner with her on my sessions. Since my pregnancy is progressing, Starr wants a teacher in the room with me. Roger and I think it's a great idea.

"Okay. Besides, it'll help with the authenticity of the new maternity lingerie collection... Surprise!"

Lola's announcement catches me off guard, just as she hoped.

"What do you mean?" I ask, excitement bubbling up at the thought I'll still be able to model and not just talk.

Lola claps her hands and shimmies in her seat. Her hazel eyes shine.

"I want you to collaborate with me on a sexy maternity lingerie and loungewear collection! We can design the pieces together as you go through the stages. Plus shoot campaigns with you and Roger all along!"

She pauses and gazes at me steadily. Suddenly serious.

"As long as Dr. Berger gives his approval. We will not overtax you," Lola adds.

It's my turn to clap and shimmy in my seat.

"How exciting! I already have some ideas! Like a bra with removable cups to allow The Twins to feed—"

"Hey! That's enough!" Roger cuts me off, growling at the mention of my breasts in front of other men.

"Cue the scene—Caveman Roger drags Leonie by the ponytail back to his den..." Lola jokes.

"And you are next, Lola," Dom Sebastian interjects.

Luc turns to Blair and asks, "Do you have anything to add, Blair?"

She blushes bright red from her hairline to her ample bosom.

"No, Sir!"

Billie chokes on her glass of Marcassin Estate Chardonnay. Then stares gobsmacked at Blair.

Lola's shocked eyes snap to mine, and we burst out laughing.

Le Renard Argenté is Dom Luc! Who would have thought? I guess their relationship is definitely doing well after all. Long distance be damned...

LEONIE

"The bright lights of Las Vegas always give me a thrill! I love the partying, dining, and the cheers when people hit it big… The baccarat table is calling my name, baby!"

Starr exclaims leaning closer to the window, her excitement palpable.

"It never gets old for me. Even after years of living here. I love Vegas!" Billie adds as she peers out of her window. Her Savannah, Georgia accent still prevalent. Forever a Southern Belle.

We finished the last business in Beverly Hills and now jet to Sin City for Lola's Coterie Las Vegas. The campaign for the latest collection exclusive to the boutique needs to get done earlier than expected. Thanks to The Twins!

Billie and Starr flew with Roger and me aboard his G650 private jet. Luc opted to fly with Blair on Sebastian's plane. As much as Luc wants to spend time with Blair, I'm sure he's equally happy to avoid any further intimate questions from Roger…

I glance out of my window to take in the view of the world-famous Las Vegas Strip. Starr is right. The neon lights stand in stark relief to the darkness of the night desert beyond. As the jet flies into McCarran International Airport, the lights are like beacons luring travelers to the revelry of the "What Happens in Vegas, Stays in Vegas" city.

Only since the boutique opened, have I spent as much time here. Monte Carlo and Macau are my choices for gambling. Yet, just as others, I'm drawn to Vegas.

"We'll definitely hit the tables after dinner," Roger says as he squeezes my hand resting on his lap.

I turn away from the sparkling vision and smile at him as I scan his handsome face.

He hasn't shaved. So the five o'clock shadow adds to his sex appeal. The photographer for the Vegas shoot wants Roger to have an edgier appearance. This time the scene is the Alpha playboy meets the seductive showgirl.

"Your refusal to add points to our Mile High Club earns you no orgasms for the rest of tonight, Pretty Kitty…" he murmurs in my ear huskily.

I shiver from his warm breath tickling my skin and the subsequent jolt of electricity that zings my pussy. But no way was I going to have sex while Starr and Billie were on board. Even if the bedroom is at the back of the jet with plenty of space between us. Uh, no.

Soon we're headed to STEELE Las Vegas in Roger's Black Badge Rolls-Royce Cullinan, driven by Eric, who accompanied us on the trip. Starr and Billie ride in one driven by a STEELE chauffeur. The two five-diamond resort and casino properties in the middle of the action on the Strip are magnificent. Each soaring tower features the signature STEELE gray glass. They shimmer from the neon lights' reflection on their surfaces.

The valet opens the doors on the passenger side while Eric opens the other for us. Roger takes my hand just as Starr and Billie hop out of their SUV. We stride through the ornate, but tasteful main lobby towards the private reception foyer for the twelve Bridge Penthouses.

They're designed to attract high rollers and the über-wealthy clientele. The penthouses act as a bridge to connect the two properties with the mall between them from the ground level to the third floor. Roger and I will stay in his penthouse that's on one of the top six floors. While Billie and Starr share another; Sebastian and Lola in theirs, and Luc and Blair in a fourth.

As we pass through the lobby, various staff members greet Roger by name. A few of the woman watch the girls and me.

I smirk and run the fingers of my left hand through my hair. Their eyes bulge out of their sockets when they spy My Baby. Yeah, sweeties… He's very much mine.

Cameras flash to our left, and we turn to the source. What appears to be a soon-to-be-bride and her gaggle of girlfriends recognize us. No doubt the images will show up on Instagram shortly.

Used to the commotion my presence causes, I smile and

wink. Roger keeps his typical intense stare straight ahead, even increasing his speed.

"No respect," he huffs.

I giggle and rest my hand on his forearm to soothe him.

We reach the etched-glass, double doors for the doorman to allow us entry to the separate foyer of the Bridge Penthouses. Beyond are three reception and two concierge desks, four sitting areas, and a bank of three private elevators, each accesses two of the Bridge Penthouses in this tower.

"Hey, we just arrived. I can't wait to hit the casino floor!" Lola says as she shimmies, her hazel eyes lighting up like the Strip.

"Where are Luc and Blair?" I ask, glancing around the expansive room.

"Their penthouse is in the other tower. Billie and Starr are in one here," Sebastian responds.

Hmmmmm, *Le Renard Argenté* prefers privacy so much so, he and Blair are not in sight of the rest of our party...

Lola must think the same, because she titters as she shakes her head.

The receptionist brings card keys to Billie and Starr. Roger and Sebastian's penthouses have entry plates coded to their palm prints. So we have no need for keys.

The porters take our bags via the service elevator as we ride up in the guest ones for each of our penthouses. We agree to meet in the foyer in an hour.

"Finally, alone! You think you can avoid me much longer, Pretty Kitty?"

Roger's deep baritone wraps around me as much as his arms as he pulls my back to his front. He bends his knees so his thick length nestles against my ass.

"*Non, Amoureux, jamais,*" I purr as I grind against him.

Roger slips his hand under the hem of my bohemian, red floral and geometric motif silk-crepon mini dress. The dainty, flouncy ruffles of the tiered skirt pose no barrier to his wandering fingers. His other hand slips the bow out of the slim ties at the neckline to cup one of my heavy breasts. The slightly fitted bodice shirred along the bosom provides room for him to explore.

"Aaahhh, *Amoureux...*" I moan as he flicks my sensitive nipple with his fingertip.

When two of his thick digits breach my pussy folds, I groan and increase my grinding on his dick with my ass.

Roger's arousal mimics mine for some forbidden pleasure.

The last time we were in the throes of ecstasy on an elevator, Lola and Sebastian caught us. My leg wound around Roger's hip and his hand cupping my pussy. Our mouths connected with our tongues dueling for control.

Merde...

"So tight... So wet... So sweet..." Roger says as he withdraws his fingers to suck them clean in his mouth.

The sound of his slurps intensifies my desire for him to finish what he started.

"Roger," I whine, arching my back.

He tweaks my nipple as my breast fills his hand even

more. Then returns to his fingers fucking my dripping core.

The juices slide down my inner thighs, and I ache for release. The pressure builds as I ride his fingers, humping my mons against his palm to reach my climax.

WHAP... WHAP... WHAP

"Aaarghhh!" I snarl as Roger spanks my swollen pussy lips. The last strike hits my engorged clit, and I jerk, half ready to cum and half ready to run. "Owww!"

"What did I tell you only an hour ago, Pretty Kitty?" He growls.

"No... orgasms... for... the... rest... of... tonight, Pretty Kitty," he repeats in my ear huskily.

Each word marked by a swat to emphasize his horrid statement.

Fuuuck!

The doors ping as they open onto the foyer of the penthouse. Unsatisfied and aroused achingly, I sag against Roger as he leads us through the doors.

"No fair!" I cry. "You can't possibly expect us to make love on a plane with other people on board, Roger! Now I have to suffer?!"

He chuckles darkly and strides to one wall of windows. I trail behind him like a petulant child, causing him to tug me along by the hand to keep up.

Once again, he stands behind me and holds me in his powerful embrace. I sigh at the feel of being in my man's arms and at the sight of the Strip shining brightly all around us.

We stand in silence for a moment, absorbed in our separate thoughts. Roger kisses the top of my head and reminds me it's time to get ready for dinner and fun at the casino.

"Well, Mr. Steele, if I cannot cum, neither can you!"

I quip as I sashay ahead of him to the bedroom. Then squeal when he swats my ass.

"We shall see, Little Kitty. We shall see," he chuckles again.

* * *

THE FOUR DAYS in Las Vegas lead to our New York City leg of the whirlwind Pre-The Twins Modeling and Marketing Push for Lola's Coterie. No pun!

We'll spend the next five days in the city. Then go out to the Steele Southampton Village waterfront family compound for the remaining four.

Billie stayed in Vegas while we flew a red-eye flight plan to arrive this morning. Today, Roger and Starr insist I rest. I don't disagree. A break is very much needed as I notice my stamina decreasing because of the activity.

At fifteen weeks, my body adjusts to the horny hormones, needing naps, and growth spurt of my belly. I feel as though it was just a minor bump only yesterday. A woman's ability to adapt is amazing!

"Remember to breathe with intention, Leonie. Inhale to reach; exhale to return. Your breath will guide you through the postures."

Starr's melodic voice guides me through our session.

Roger surprised me with a custom yoga studio in our penthouse. Starr helped him to fill it with every yoga-related item imaginable. Mats thick enough to protect my knees; straps to extend my reach as my belly grows; wool blankets to keep me warm during Savasana. Not to mention the candles, meditation pillows, and a *Puja* space.

I love it!

We finish the opening sequence and move on to the standing asanas. As we flow through each pose, I allow my mind to focus on the movement and my breathing. Starr is right. The breath sets the way.

"Hi, ready for me?" Roger asks as he joins us for yoga *nidra*.

Starr smiles and nods to the mat, bolsters, and blanket she set up for him next to my space.

"*Bien* sûr, *Mon Cœur*," I reply, holding my hand out to him.

Roger smiles at us and takes my hand as he lowers himself to a cross-legged position with ease. Once seated, he kisses my cheek. Then turns to Starr expectantly.

"Namaste, Enlightened One," he says, placing his palms together at his heart center and bowing his head to her.

"Namaste, Sassy Student," she says as she returns the gesture.

We laugh good-naturedly.

Starr helps us to get into comfortable positions as we lie supine on the mats. She places the bolsters under our knees and necks. Then, like babies, she swaddles us in the blankets, ensuring we're covered fully. Before she steps away, she places lavender-scented pillows over our eyes. Starr dims the lights and allows the candles to glow around the studio.

Her soothing voice guides us through the session from consciousness to a state of semi-consciousness. The mental countdowns and memories she asks us to invoke keep us from falling into a slumber. Not like my first few sessions where my snores woke me!

The forty-five minutes pass blissfully. The sound of chimes brings us back to full awareness. We recall how far we could count and the recollections from the past. It's amazing how my practice has improved.

Fully rested with the equivalent of three hours' sleep, I feel rejuvenated. Roger and I head to our bedroom while Starr goes to her guest suite on the other side of the penthouse. We insisted she stay with us since we have more than enough space since it's a floor-through property.

Situated high above the Manhattan streets, it's on the fifty-second floor of The Steele Tower skyscraper. Through the gray-tinted, floor-to-ceiling windows, the city stretches out with unobstructed views. The prime location at the southwest corner of Fifty-seventh Street and Fifth Avenue is in the heart of Billionaires' Row.

Central Park to the north, the Hudson River to the west, the East River opposite, and the rest of Manhattan to the south from Midtown to Battery Park. On a beautiful, cloudless day like this morning, the vista draws you to gaze out of the windows for hours.

But not this morning. Roger and I have plans to shop the baby boutiques and lunch at La Goulue It's my favorite restaurant in New York. I'm ordering the *Moules sauce Poulette* or *le Pavé de saumon aux lentils.* I'm so excited to have time to go while we're here. Mmm mmm mmm!

Roger and I decided to pick up unique items for The Twins in each city. While in Beverly Hills, we found some cute clothes and toys including two giant cuddly bears Roger had to get. They took up more space than the humans on the jet!

After a quick shower, I change into a fiery tonal-orange and white patterned mini dress cut in a classic shift silhouette. The button-fastening tabs at the sides and sleeves adjust the fit and coverage. Perfect for my growing babies bump.

I pair it with beige with black tip Chanel ballet flats, a woven Bottega Veneta Cabat handbag, and classic Versace shades. In New York, so I have to rep The Notorious B.I.G. with the vintage black and with gold accents sunglasses. My hair has grown so much, I pile it atop my head in a messy bun.

Roger opts for a navy v-neck cashmere sweater, dark denim jeans that stress his firm ass and luscious bulge perfectly, and black Gucci loafers. He shaved his stubble showing his cleft chin and left his tousled hair to air dry. His dove gray eyes covered by the silver metal and pale blue lenses of his Tom Ford aviators.

Sexy Big Poppa! Rawr!

"The contractors sent an update for the renovations.

Did you have time to read their email?" He asks as Eric drives us to the first boutique.

"*Oui*, I saw it. But haven't answered since I'm waiting for my latest AutoCAD files to come back from the graphics team. What did you think of their estimated time-line for completion?" I respond, flipping through my emails for their message.

"Okay, but not good enough. We need them to cut off three weeks," Roger starts. "Two need to be for the deco-rating to complete and a week for us to settle back in. We will not wait until seven days before your due date. We need to be ready early."

I smile to myself. As he mentioned, it's not unusual for twins to arrive at thirty-six weeks. Roger's been reading books on twins and babies in general. He's gotten into the habit of spouting off facts and details. He's read more than me!

"What's so funny?" He asks, cocking his eyebrow at me.

"You've become quite the expert... Roger *The Respon-sible* Steele!" I tease.

He smirks and shakes his head.

Eric stops the car on Madison Avenue and we hop out of the Rolls-Royce Corniche. A friend who owns a textile company recommended the boutique. She supplies the fabrics for their clothes and nursery items.

"Hello, please let me know if you need any help," says the shopgirl pleasantly.

"*Merci*," I respond while Roger nods.

We stroll through the section for newborns, and the

sweetest onesie catches my eye. It's made of super soft cotton and has a cartoon lion on the chest.

"Roger! Look at this! It's so adorable!" I exclaim.

He grins and holds a yellow one up to my bosom.

"We should have one made for you, Mama Lion," he laughs. "Then I can tuck all of you in bed like triplets!"

Our loud snickers cause the other patrons to glance at us and smile.

I notice one woman who appears to be shopping alone glimpsing at Roger every so often. I shake my head—thirsty girl. But when she accidentally brushes up against him as she passes, I growl.

"Back off!"

She jumps and scampers away. She doesn't dare to look at me.

Mama Lion doesn't play with her mate!

Roger chuckles and kisses my lips softly.

"Now who's the possessive one? Hmmm?" He teases.

I roll my eyes at him for repeating the words I told him last week. The caveman snarled at a guy who asked to pose with me for a selfie as Roger and I strolled along Rodeo Drive.

"Whatever. Blame the hormones!" I retort.

"THESE SHOTS ARE INCREDIBLE!" Lola says as she peers over the photographer's shoulder.

We're in Dubai, the last stop on the five-city global trip.

Luc returned to Paris after New York for meetings. The rest of us spent three of the seven days allotted to the United Arab Emirates' boutiques in Abu Dhabi.

I suggested we contrast the city's sea of desert with the turquoise waters of Dubai, The Empty Quarter Desert in Abu Dhabi serves as the first backdrop. The Bedouin noblemen see the world's largest sand desert as a vast ocean to travel across on their journeys.

We paid homage to their history with a twist. I portrayed a desert princess who captivated a desert traveler, Roger. Our steamy affair took place over the course of three nights in a lavish tent.

Lola outdid herself with the collection exclusive to her Lola's Coterie Abu Dhabi boutique. The vibrant colors, sumptuous materials, and sophisticated lines make for extraordinary pieces. Of course I requested a few sets of the lingerie and loungewear for our maternity line collaboration.

We've been sketching like mad since Lola told me about it. Our goal to maintain the sex appeal with pre- and post-natal functionality has our creativity with the materials and cuts keyed up. So far, the designs realize what we want to project. Roger concurs.

The six-hundred-foot megayacht we're using for the Dubai photoshoot is lavish and belongs to one of the royal family members. The impressive boat parallels the view. Spread out beyond the dazzling water with glittering ripples that reach across to the shore is the city's varied skyline.

Architectural marvels grow out of the surrounding desert. The contrast of the modern glass towers—some in unusual shapes—to the nature around it is remarkable. It provides the perfect scenery for the Dubai boutique's collection.

Lola incorporated the gorgeous blues and greens of the water with the earth tones of the sand for the color palette. Glittery Swarovski crystals embellish the bras, panties, slips, and evening wear pieces to mirror the glass structures.

This time Roger and I play the roles of dashing billionaire mogul and paparazzi-hounded celebrity. Our holiday is fraught with dodging photographers with high-powered lenses while on our megayacht to being chased through the streets after a night out. Not much different from reality...

"*Oui!* It's as though we're experiencing our everyday lives!" I giggle as I look over his other shoulder at the photos.

Roger grunts and adds, "Right. Well, if it gets as extreme as this storyline, you're getting security."

I open my mouth to respond. But Sebastian cuts in, holding up his hand to stop me.

"I agree with Roger completely. You are carrying the next generation of Steeles. And as the eldest of this line, it is my responsibility to protect everyone. Period."

Now I know how Lola must feel when Sebastian enacts his Alpha Dom. He's so commanding, I'm about to say, yes Sir!

I turn to Lola and she shrugs. Outnumbered and understanding their concern, I nod in agreement.

"Words, Pretty Kitty. I will have your words," Roger demands.

"*Oui*," I answer.

Roger and Sebastian reply excellent in unison, and Lola smiles as she wraps her arm around my waist.

"Get used to it, Hot Mama. There's nothing that will stop these cavemen from taking care of their loved ones."

Now I know how Haley feels with four older brothers. *Merde…*

* * *

WHEN THE CAMPAIGN IS COMPLETE, Lola and I round out this city's trip with marketing efforts. We host private viewing parties for the city's VIPs and dinners at STEELE Dubai. We take part in interviews with local fashion magazines and lifestyle television shows. Social media takeovers increase followers for the business and our personal accounts. The results satisfy the public relations and marketing teams.

Thankfully, we're on our way back to Paris. Roger and I sleep in the bedroom of his private jet while Starr stretches out on the sofa converted into an additional bed. Sebastian, Lola, and Blair head to New York City on his jet.

It exhausts everyone after the month of non-stop travel. But it was well worth it. The early shots are incredible as predicted. The sales team expects great numbers in revenue and an increase in brand awareness.

They hinted at Roger being a regular in the campaigns to keep the momentum up. He didn't comment. Although his response to a male model partnering with me was to huff a negative on that suggestion.

The next campaigns will be for the maternity collection. So, I would prefer my sexy fiancé to another man. We'll see—

"Stop thinking so hard, babe. Shall I ease your tension?"

Roger's husky voice along with his rock-hard cock poking my bottom as we spoon on the bed pulls me from my musings.

My body tingles in response. My nipples tighten painfully. My core throbs with desire.

Oh, well... Points added to the Mile High Club cumming up!

ROGER

"*H*ey, babe! Are you ready, yet? We needed to get going fifteen minutes ago!"

I call to Leonie, who's running late as usual. But not today!

It's been three weeks since we returned from the Lola's Coterie boutiques trip. I cannot believe how time passed so quickly. Nor how much Leonie's body has changed.

She's noticeably pregnant from the front and side with her belly poking out. Now, I can rest my hand on top and cradle her belly underneath. Her breasts are deliciously plump. Just thinking about suckling her tips makes me hard.

Every morning and night after we shower, I massage warm oil all over her belly and breasts to keep the skin soft and pliable. Then rub her back, legs—especially her calves and ankles—and feet to soothe the cramps and to prevent swelling. The sounds of Leonie's contented purrs as she writhes with pleasure on the massage table add to my desire for her.

MILF Alert for damn sure!

"Leonie! If you do not come out of that dressing room in five seconds, I will carry you out of here, to the car, and to Dr. Berger's office wrapped in a robe!"

Yeah, we're almost late for the big reveal. Are The Twins boys or girls?

Hopefully, we'll get to his office before they're eighteen years old and not eighteen weeks.

I run my hands through my hair and sigh. I make my mind up. I cannot wait any longer. As I storm towards the door of her dressing room, it opens.

Leonie walks out looking afuckingmazing.

Her ass-length hair parted in the middle cascades down her back in silky mahogany waves. The soft black cashmere mini dress skims her long legs mid thigh. While a fashionable take on cowboy boots in black leather reach below her knees. Her black suede shoulder bag and glamour girl shades finish her chic outfit.

The babies bump sticks out as a reminder she's pregnant and not *The Lion* megamodel prowling down the catwalk.

My mouth gapes.

She tucks a lock of hair behind her ear and giggles at my reaction.

"Roger, you boost my ego! I couldn't find anything that fit!" Leonie exclaims as she pats her belly.

So far she hasn't gone shopping. Instead opting to make

do with items from her vast wardrobe. Every day, designers send maternity clothing or pieces that can work with her new figure. Leonie combines them with her existing wardrobe and always looks stunning.

"Babe, you are hot as hell! Go shopping with Hettie or Anita or both. But right now... We're out of here!"

I grab her hand and rush from the room.

Fortunately, Eric has my Aston Martin DB7 Vantage pulled up. I help Leonie into the passenger's seat. Then race around to the driver's side as I thank him.

"Of course, Monsieur Steele. Best of luck!" He responds with a goofy grin.

Even reticent Eric is eager to hear the news.

I grin back and jump in the car. I need to something to keep me sane, so I opted to drive us to the appointment. A glance at my platinum Rolex Cosmograph Daytona confirms we have fifteen minutes to make a twenty-minute ride.

"Call Dr. Berger's office," I request to the built-in phone system.

"Dr. Berger's office."

"Good morning, this is Mr. Steele. Please inform the doctor Mademoiselle Beaulieu and I are on our way and will arrive five minutes late. Thank you." I say.

Leonie has the grace to appear sheepish.

But I don't make a big deal out of it. She's adjusting well and doesn't need a lecture. I simply accept her tardiness as par for the course.

"It's all right, Caramel BonBon. We'll get there soon enough," I say as I squeeze her thigh.

She brings my hand to her lips and kisses it softly. Then rubs her cheek against it, purring like a kitten.

"Yeah, yeah, yeah... I love you, too," I laugh.

We make our way through the bustling Parisian streets. I park in one of the two spaces Dr. Berger has reserved for patients. Then hop out to help Leonie from the low seat. Despite being pregnant, she loves to ride around in my "James Bond sexy spy car."

"Ready, babe?" I ask her, knowing she's nervous and pretending she's not to keep me sane.

"*Absolument!*" Leonie says with a brilliant smile that lights my heart.

We make our way through the double doors of the townhouse. The receptionist assures us Dr. Berger understands our delay and will be right with us. Just as we settle on a sofa, his nurse calls to us.

Once inside the examination room, Leonie changes. But this time she doesn't offer the flirtatious shimmy.

"Babe, it's going to be fantastic knowing their sex," I say as I rub her belly, then jerk away in surprise when I feel movement.

"Did you feel that?! Was that a kick?" I ask Leonie excitedly.

She glances up at me with wide amber eyes. She's just as shocked as me.

"Holy shit! That's incredible! The experts say when

you're nervous, it can give the baby a jolt of energy," I continue babbling in amazement.

"Oh, Roger! I can't believe it!" She responds with tears in her eyes now. "I can't wait to see them!"

A knock at the door interrupts our First Moment. Dr. Berger enters with the nurse and asks Leonie about her wellbeing. Following her examination, he preps her for the ultrasound.

Leonie grasps my hand as her eyes remain riveted to the screen. Smiling this time when she hears their heartbeats fill the quiet room. A tear slips down her cheek.

I bend over and kiss it away. Then nuzzle her cheek with my nose, inhaling her sultry perfume.

"Roger! Look! Look at them!" She exclaims as she points at the screen.

Two tiny faces appear. One with a thumb in their mouth and the other holding the umbilical cord. Their eyes are closed tight as though sleeping peacefully.

It's surreal that I made them from my seed jetting into Leonie's womb. My babies. Mine!

Obviously Dr. Berger learned from the last visit not to incite hysteria with frowns and shakes of his head. This time, he smiles broadly at us when he announces The Twins' sex.

"Congratulations! Two healthy boys!"

"Fuck yeah!" I shout to the heavens as I punch the air with my fist not being squeezed by Leonie.

"Are you sure? Everything is in place?" She asks anxiously.

Dr. Berger smiles and moves the wand over her belly slowly. He points to the monitor to show us exactly how certain he is in his pronouncement.

I beam as the proof appears without a doubt. Call me Big Poppa!

After the doctor and nurse leave, I pull Leonie into my arms. I bury my face in her hair as she wraps her arms around my neck. She presses her face against my chest while we take a moment to absorb the incredible news.

"Thank you, my love. You've made me the happiest man in the world. You and our baby boys are healthy. I love you so very much."

I murmur as tears fill my eyes now.

"Merci, Mon Cœur, je t'aime aussi," Leonie whispers as she holds me tighter. "Our little family."

* * *

"Tell us, *Mon Trésor!* Don't keep us in suspense any longer!"

Josy blurts out as Leonie and I walk into the Petite Salon at Apicius, the Michelin starred restaurant.

We're having dinner with both sets of in-laws. My parents flew in yesterday afternoon, eager to hear in person the sex of The Twins. Everyone wanted to come to the doctor. But we decided to have dinner instead for the big announcement.

Leonie chose Apicius for its modern French cuisine.

She favors the light, elegant and inventive dishes and teases the traditional bourgeois dishes fit with her father's ideals.

I love the architecture of the nineteenth century former residence turned hotel. The outdoor dining in the courtyard is enjoyable in the heart of Paris.

We selected the Petite Salon for its privacy instead of the Dining Room. No need to worry about people overhearing over conversation. Leonie and I want to keep the details of our babies under wraps for as long as possible. The media is already going wild with bump sightings.

"Oh, *Maman*! It's such wonderful news!" Leonie exclaims as they hug and double kiss.

"Shelley, *Maman Aussi*! I'm so glad you and *Papa* Steele came!" She continues as she hugs her second mother.

I smile whenever I hear Leonie refer to my parents as hers. They welcome the terms of endearment. My mother even teared up when Leonie asked if she could call her by *Maman Aussi*.

"Glad to hear it's good news, *fils*!" Guy says as he claps me on the shoulder in greeting. "You appear pleased."

I chuckle and nod as I return his greeting, "Very pleased indeed, *Papa* Beaulieu!"

"Josy's right. No need to draw it out, son," my father Morgan adds when we embrace.

I help Leonie into her chair. Then I sit beside her, taking her hand in mine and kissing the back of it.

She glances up to smile and nod for me to tell the news.

I turn to our loved ones gathered and grin broadly.

"Leonie and I are expecting twin... Drum roll... boys!"

My father rises from his seat and lifts Leonie to her feet. He kisses her cheek as he holds her hands.

"Well done, daughter! Congratulations!"

Leonie beams as she squeezes his hands. Her amber eyes dance with delight as she glows with pure happiness.

"*Merci beaucoup*! You'll be a grand-père to twin boys soon!"

We share more words of good cheer all around. The room is full of our laughter and predictions of their birth date. I remind them about the earlier expectation of twins, and they poke fun at me for being so responsible with my research.

Leonie pulls out her iPad to FaceTime Lola and Sebastian. Then adds on the rest of the clan. I put the iPad on the middle of the table so they can see all of us.

"Well??? What are The Twins?" Lola demands.

"Boys!!" Leonie cries. "See for yourselves!"

Dutifully, I pass out copies of images from the ultrasound to those gathered. While Leonie holds up one for the FaceTime group.

"Holy cow! You can see their faces and everything!" Harris exclaims peering closely from his iPhone.

Haley claps and adds, "They're absolutely incredible! Roger, they look like you!"

We laugh at the folly of her comment since they don't have true distinguishable traits yet.

"Fantastic, bro! We see what you made," Malcolm says, giving me a virtual high five.

"Mini Steeles in the oven!" Sebastian laughs, then

glances between Leonie and me. "In all seriousness, we're so happy for you both. Congratulations, Mommy and Daddy!"

Leonie and I thank them all.

Once it's quieted down, I turn to Leonie.

"My love, this is a day I want you to always remember" —I take a flat black leather case out of the breast pocket of my suit jacket—"this is for you."

Leonie peeks up at me, then presses the sapphire-studded closure. She kisses my lips and murmurs thank you against them.

I remove the platinum necklace and place it around her neck. The three large, pear-shaped sapphires styled like her *toi et moi* ring settle against her heart. The intense, velvety, deep royal blue colored stones are the rarest and most valuable—just like the three males in her life.

"Oh, Roger, this is beautiful. *Merci, Mon Cœur*," Leonie says as she fingers the sapphires sliding along the chain. "All three of my boys close to my heart."

Tears fill her eyes as she cups my face and kisses me. Then she wraps her arms around me to bury her face against my neck.

I rub her back soothingly as I murmur words of ever-lasting love.

"The heavenly blue of sapphires signifies the epitome of celestial hope and faith. Believed to bring divine insight, prosperity, and safe keeping according to the ancient and medieval world."

Guy's worldly knowledge sums up the reasons I selected sapphires besides their blue color represent males traditionally. Everyone comments on his words and the gift's beauty.

As planned, the wait staff enter with bottles of Taittinger Comtes de Champagne Blanc de Blancs. Under normal circumstances, it's Leonie's favorite thanks to James Bond in *Casino Royale*. But tonight they bring her iced lemon green tea in a flute.

Her laughter bubbles like the champagne when she spies her cocktail.

"*À votre santé!*" She says standing with her hand on her babies bump as she leans into my side.

"Cheers!" We follow, raising our crystal flutes in the air with hers, including everyone on FaceTime.

Lola has meetings in Paris. So she and Haley arrange to come together to see Leonie "live and direct." Harris tells us he'll create the best baby monitoring system ever with all the high-tech bells and whistles available. We chat some more. Then end the video call to eat.

"Yummy for my tummy!" Leonie says after swallowing a bite of her herb-crusted chicken and closing her eyes.

When her little pink tongue pokes out to lick leaked juice from the corner of her mouth, my dick twitches. I shift in my seat to adjust my suddenly tight trousers. We haven't had sex in two days since she's tired from the pregnancy and working on the penthouse renovation. It's nice to spoon at night and all. But damn if she doesn't keep me on the edge...

"Now you can plan the nurseries' color schemes. You should pick up on the blue in your sapphires."

Josy's mention of nurseries distracts me from my carnal needs.

"What a wonderful idea!" Shelley adds, clapping her hands. "You'll need one for each home. Paris for you, Josy, and me. Monte Carlo for your penthouse and Roger's villa. Positano for Villa Sogno. Manhattan for you and me and Steele Southampton—"

"Oh, Shelley, you have the child's head spinning! She need not think about all the homes now. The Twins won't travel for a bit anyway," Morgan admonishes her, chuckling as he places his finger against her lips.

She laughs and nips his fingers. His nostrils flare as his dove gray eyes darken.

Talk about live and direct...

My parents are a hot as hell couple. They may be in their mid-sixties and mid-fifties, but Dom Morgan and sub Shelley don't let age stop their love affair.

That's how Leonie and I will be. Forever committed to each other.

ROGER

"— *S*cheduled a bunch of appointments. She's a sergeant, I tell you!"

Leonie's laughter draws me out of my musings. When I frown, she rolls her eyes and repeats herself.

"Your mother Shelley scheduled a bunch of appointments for our wedding planning for this week. She's a sergeant who kept everyone on point with Lola and Sebastian's nuptials. My mother is proving to be just as bad!"

I join in her laughter as I recall Sebastian throwing his hands up in surrender. They only allowed him to plan the honeymoon and to select our formal attire. And that was only after he put his foot down and wouldn't budge. He didn't mind not having much say in any other part of the planning for his wedding…

I'm of the same mindset. Let them have their fun. But I decide on my fun with my new bride. Period.

"Well, remember, I get to plan our honeymoon. You

must block two months after The Twins turn 3 months old and can travel," I say.

"That's around six months after we get married," Leonie pouts, then rubs her fuller belly. "Thanks so much, Little Cubs!"

I laugh and kiss both sides of her belly.

"Now look what you've done. You've upset your *Maman's* honeymoon timing."

Leonie tsks at The Twins. Then reaches for her mobile as it vibrates beside our bed. She shakes her head when she sees the name on the screen and sighs resignedly.

"Bonjour, Maman Aussie…"

Leonie shifts on the bed to sit up. Ready for the day's marching orders.

I help her to fluff the pillows behind her back. Then head to the bathroom. Time to start my day.

"THE PROJECTIONS' estimates are above the recommended budget we provided last week. We must regroup with the contractors, finance, and marketing to generate an alternative plan…"

The weekly update meeting seems longer than usual. I keep glancing at my mobile for the time rather than being obvious, flicking my French cuff back to view the face of my Vacheron Constantin watch.

Leonie's words and discontent swirl in my mind. They overshadow the team's progress reports as it works to find a solution.

She's right that she has a lot to work on with our wedding plans, her hectic modeling schedule, renovations for our penthouse makeover project, and helping my mother with their new space. Not to mention her pregnancy. She insists on doing everything herself. It's ludicrous.

"—what are your thoughts... Roger? Roger, would you prefer we renegotiate the terms?"

I stop rubbing my top lip to glance up and find all eyes on me. Their questioning looks leads me to conclude they expect an answer. I will not bullshit them. I didn't hear a dam thing they said. I shift my gaze to the presentation screen. That's not the last slide I saw.

"I apologize. Would you go back to the slide on with comparison charts and go from there?"

They nod and proceed.

This time I pay attention for the rest of the meeting. Not a good look for the President of Residential Properties Division to ignore his team's work.

Fortunately, the meeting ends in another thirty minutes. My assistant of five years Françoise Faucher smiles as I return to my offices. She's in her mid-fifties and commands respect from everyone. In fact, she's one of the company's best employees. I value her as an integral part of my team.

"Mademoiselle Beaulieu called for you—"

"Is she all right?? You should have told me right away—"

I trail off as I rush to turn the knob on my door and pull out my mobile, propriety forgotten. Fuck!

"Are you okay??" I ask anxiously when Leonie answers on the third ring.

"*Oui, oui!* Nothing is wrong. I asked Françoise not to worry you since I knew you were in your weekly meeting."

I sag into my desk chair and run my hand through my hair as I lean my head back. I'm too wound up with worry. My mind clicks on the solution... We need a break. Now.

Babymoon floats to the surface of my muddled brain like a life preserver floats on the ocean to save a drowning man. That's the solution!

"Babe," I say, cutting into Leonie's sentence about food selection and paint colors. "Get you passport and be ready to go in an hour. I'll pick you up then."

Stunned silence.

"Babe, I've gotta call the pilot. We need a break. Be ready."

Leonie sputters, then agrees hesitantly.

"Whatever *Maman Aussi, Maman* Josy, the penthouse contractors, the wedding vendors, Lola's damn Coterie or the cosmetics company want from you, can wait until we get back next week. We'll return in time for your appointment with Dr. Berger. *D'accord?*"

"*Oui, oui! D'accord!!*" Leonie exclaims.

I hear her clapping and singing to The Twins how they're going on holiday with *Papa*.

That's what I want. The fun loving, easygoing Leonie who laughs and shimmies her happy dance.

Especially when said shimmy gets my cock hard as nails...

* * *

"OH, Roger! *C'est fantastique! Merci, Mon Cœur!*"

Leonie says as she bounces on her seat in the Mercedes-Benz G-Wagen when Lucien's lavish hillside Villa dei Fiori in Capri appears around the bend in the driveway.

Her much fuller breasts bounce right along with her, nearly spilling from the scoop-neck of the long-sleeved top. Leonie's black lace cups runneth over deliciously.

Yup very wise decision.

"It's good to see you so exuberant, my love," I respond, flicking her prominent nipple with my finger.

"Bad boy!" She giggles as she swats my hand away and peers through the windshield. "It's pink!"

The salmon-colored stucco exterior with white trim around the windows, columns, and roof lines blend beautifully with the lush greenery and stunning sea views from all sides. The sea-edge gardens, bountiful with camellias, magnolias, and palm trees prove as captivating as the impressive views of Mount Vesuvius, the Peninsula of Sorrento, the entire Gulf of Naples, and Anacapri. Its private swimming pool set in the grass of the side garden and its exclusive sea access with a second plunge pool below makes it a unique property.

Lucien bought it a few years back while studying with a chef on the isle. If it can make Leonie this excited, I'll buy it from him at whatever cost!

"Yeah, babe. It's the most luxurious and historical villa

in Capri. I knew you'd appreciate its design," I respond, grinning at her.

We stop in front, and the staff greets us and helps us to get settled in. Leonie, the gracious lady of the manoir, receives them with aplomb. As awed by her beauty as she is of the villa, they hurry to assist her, especially when they notice her babies bump.

"*Oh guarda il bambino! Bella ragazza!*" They exclaim.

Leonie giggles with glee. Then responds, "*Grazie mille! Ragazzi gemelli!*"

Fluent in English, Italian, German, Spanish, and of course French, Leonie easily converses with them. As do I since Italian is the third language I know besides French and English. Often we'll role-play scenes from a *Fish Called Wanda*. Just thinking about Leonie screaming my name with sexy Spanish phrases makes me want to carry her off behind one of the flowering shrubs. Instead, I wrap my arm around Leonie's waist and we head inside.

I've been here before and know to choose the sumptuous gold and red suite. It's on the second floor with expansive views of the Sorrentine peninsula and beyond. An anteroom and separate bath round out the large space.

"I love it!" Leonie declares when we enter. "My, my, my... The bed is massive..."

She sashays over to it with her maxi skirt swirling round her long legs. Then she sits down with her arms spread wide. With a wink, she beckons me to her.

"Kindly leave our bags. We're fine, *grazie*," I say, only moving my gaze from the siren for a moment.

"*S*", *Signor Steele*," the two porters respond.

The soft click of the door closing behind them is my signal.

I saunter over to Leonie, pushing the sleeves of my linen sweater to my elbows. I've got work to do. Without breaking our intense gazes, I kneel before my lover and cup her face. I tilt it to the perfect angle, then slant my mouth over her plump lips.

Leonie's mewls and purrs when I deepen the kiss harken me with a primal call. She's been so busy, her energy has been lower. Now she's recharged and I'm going to fill her socket.

"Open for me, Pretty Kitty. I need more room," I tell her as I rub the palms of my hands along her inner thighs.

She complies with a coy smile. Slowly, she spreads her legs to accommodate my broad shoulders. Then lifts her heels to elongate her limbs. With the tips of her fingers, she gathers her skirt to reveal she's sans panties.

A deep passionate growl falls from my mouth. I slip my arms under her thighs, spread her wider, and cradle her ass. Pulling Leonie to the edge of the bed, I dive into her moist pussy. A deep inhale of her tantalizing feminine scent lengthens my dick.

I nuzzle my nose against her folds, bumping against her swollen clit. When she wiggles her ass to move closer to my mouth, I spank her butt cheek.

"Be still or I'll bind you to the bed and edge you for the next two hours," I threaten with a growl.

Leonie whimpers.

I know she misses our lovemaking as much as I do. So I intend to make it last and well worth the time we missed connected as one.

Her sweet essence flows. My tongue laves and sucks at the juncture of her thigh and pussy, folds. I hold back on her clit and probing her channel until her body lets me know she's at the point of explosion.

Leonie writhes and whines as I increase my ministrations. One hand grips my hair, pulling the long strands from their roots to lock my mouth to her pussy.

"Roger, *Amoureux*, please..." she pants, tossing her head side to side.

Her pussy walls flutter when at last I fill her channel with my tongue. I lap up her juices, not wanting to miss a drop of her sweetness.

"Aahh... Aaahh... Roger... please!" Leonie cries. "Please... let me cum!"

I drape her legs over my shoulders. Then lift her ass off the bed, repositioning the tilt of her pelvis to allow me more access. My powerful arms and core hold her aloft easily. My thigh muscles tighten to stabilize my position.

Leonie uses one hand to balance and the other to continue her grip on my hair.

I coat my thumb with the juices on her upper thigh. Then my tongue prods the textured tissue on her upper pussy wall while my thumb thrusts into her bottom hole.

Leonie wails like a teakettle on full steam. She tosses her head back and bucks against my mouth and thumb. Her hand slips on the silk bedding. But I hold her higher as

I rise to my feet and slide her along the top of the mattress. Never moving my mouth or thumb.

"Rogeeerrr... Ooohh, Rogeerrr!" She wails as her body continues to convulse.

My cock presses to the point of pain against the zipper of my jeans. With Leonie positioned on her side, I free my aching weeping dick and settle behind her. She bends her leg at a ninety-degree angle and reaches for me greedily.

Happily, I oblige my siren.

"Fuuuck!!"

My eyes close and my breath catches as I sink deep within her pussy and her walls clamp on my cock.

"So fucking good, Kitten... Fuuuck. Me..." I growl as Leonie quivers around me.

I grip her hip with one hand and wrap the other around her body to hold her throat. Locked together, I rock in and out of her pussy, grunting like a feral animal.

Leonie meets each thrust with one of her own as she undulates her hips. She tenses when her orgasm nears and clenches my cock in a vise-like grip.

"Uh. Uh. Uh. Uh."

Her grunts echo mine as we ride each other over the edge.

"Cum for me, Pretty Kitty!" I command.

Her strangled cries of rhapsody push me to the brink. My spine tingles as my cock expands and pulsates to jet my seed within my mate.

"Fuuuck... Yeeesssss!!" I bellow.

White spots dance before my eyes and my mind blanks.

Working by instinct alone, my hips continue to pump my dick into Leonie until the last drop of my copious jizz coats her pussy walls.

As I collapse to the bed, I lift my arm around her waist and pull her to me. Still fully dressed and connected at our cores, we fall into a sated slumber.

* * *

"ROGER, THIS IS DIVINE," Leonie says as she floats in the mosaic tile lined swimming pool overlooking the Bay of Naples. "This was your best idea ever!"

I chuckle and slide my hands along her flanks as I bury my face in her neck, breathing in her heavenly scent.

"Mmm mmm. My 'best idea ever'... Really, babe?" I say, then nip the delicate shell of her ear.

She giggles and swats me away.

Reluctantly, I let her go and watch as she takes long, leisurely strokes to the other end of the pool. Her mahogany hair fans out behind her like a mermaid. The sun glistens on her toasted caramel-colored skin like diamonds on golden topaz. I'm entranced by her natural beauty.

"It's so tranquil. I never want to leave!" Leonie pouts as she peers past the palm trees to the sea beyond.

I make a mental note to send a text message to Lucien with an offer—what Leonie wants, Leonie gets, and more. Then dive under the water to swim below the surface. I pop up next to her and she splashes me. When she tries to scamper away, I catch her by the hips and hold on tight.

"Not so fast, Kitten," I growl.

Leonie twists her hips until she rubs her round ass against my crotch, activating my cock instantly.

I return her grinds with my own. Then trail the fingers of one hand around her hip to cup her red string bikini-clad mons.

"Mine!"

"*Oui*, only you *Amoureux*," Leonie purrs seductively as she continues her dick-awakening grind.

"You got that right!" I respond and push my thick digit inside of her tight pussy.

I flex and curl it, then add another to bring Leonie to a quick climax to prepare her for me. As she pants leaning heavily into me, I let loose my hard cock. Leonie braces herself against the rim of the pool as I slide home.

Fuck me. She feels so damn good. Words to describe the sensation escape me. So I don't bother to think on it. I just let our bodies do their thing to bring us a vision-stealing, mind-blowing orgasm at the same time.

I slip out of her warm heat and hold her close to my chest. The beats of our hearts matching in rhythm.

"I want us to stay…" Leonie whispers sleepily.

Now, lying in bed for the night, I think about how I'd like to stay, too. But tomorrow our week-long getaway ends. Back to business. But with revisions.

My Responsible side won't allow Leonie to drive herself crazy. She'll get an assistant for basic tasks and work with a wedding planner. Well, that is, if my mother will allow someone else to take over.

As the head of STEELE International, Inc.'s STEELE Foundation that builds and manages attractive, affordable housing for urban, lower-income families, Shelley grew accustomed to throwing elaborate galas and events. She's the family's go-to party planner. I'm sure Lola can convince Leonie it's best to leave Shelley to her task like Lola did with her wedding.

For the modeling, she's completed the bulk of her assignments. That whirlwind five-city trip exhausted me. So I know Leonie felt it, even days after we returned. That's done along with this year's campaigns for the cosmetics company.

As for the design side of her life, that will take some convincing. She's excited about the Lola's Coterie maternity lingerie collection. She stays up sketching pieces and talking with Lola at all times of the night since she's based in New York City now. They act like they're both still in Paris chatting instead of five hours apart.

The renovations for our penthouse and my parents' dominate most Leonie's time. I'm going to check on someone at STEELE who can manage the projects for her. Leonie will still have the final say. But she need not saddle herself with the day-to-day aspects, just the bigger parts.

Especially now that Shelley put the nurseries into

Leonie's head. It's crazy to think we need that many—nine. Give me a break. That will take more convincing...

"*Mon Cœur*, what are you thinking about? Your body is all tense."

The connection Leonie and I share astounds me. No matter what or where, we sense the other's thoughts and emotions. Tonight is no different.

"How we can keep this blissful feeling going after we leave tomorrow," I respond and kiss the side of her neck.

"*Bof!* Who says we're leaving?" She huffs with her Gallic shrug.

I zerbet her neck and she bursts into a fit of giggles.

We spend the rest of the night making lasting memories of our first holiday at Villa dei Fiori. Then a nod to those to come.

LEONIE

"*I*'m walking towards the elevators. I'll call you ba—Oh!"

As I'm jostled from behind, my Chloé Silverado bag falls off of my shoulder. Followed by my mobile clattering to the floor. I place one hand protectively on my babies bump while the other reaches out to slap the wall beside me.

Merde!

"Mademoiselle? Mademoiselle! Are you okay?"

I lift my eyes to the voice. A man holds my arm and gazes at me with concern. I peer over my shoulder to see Delia Shaw standing behind me.

Did she just push me??

Just as I open my mouth to ask just that, she speaks.

"Oh, Leonie. I'm so sorry! I didn't see you."

She pauses to glance pointedly at my belly. Then scans

my body from the tips of my Manolo's to my high ponytail with a smirk.

"Although... I shouldn't have missed you! You're very pregnant. Much bigger than before," she continues. "My bad. Are you all right?"

My mouth drops open at her audacity as my face flames. Is she serious with me right now??

"Wow! How does Roger, I mean *Mr. Steele*, feel about your... change? Oh, never mind. There's the elevator. Some of us need to work for a living. Not all of us are engaged to the boss. Nice seeing you, Leonie. Tootles."

With amber eyes blazing hot enough to set Delia ablaze, I watch the curvy brunette saunter to the open elevator. Then pivot and waggle her fingers at me as the doors close.

What the everlasting fuck was that all about?!

That brazen floozy... heifer... shrew!!

Delia. Fucking. Shaw.

I haven't seen my American former classmate and colleague in over four months, and I'm glad of it. She's been a pain in my ass for far too long. Today proves no exception. The gall!

First, Delia flirts blatantly with Roger when he guest lectured one of my classes at Paris American Academy. Then she accuses me of scoring the internship at STEELE Paris since I was "dating the president." Although in reality, I was at human resources for my *third* interview as a part-time junior designer on the Interior Design Team.

She and Antonio Vasquez—my former seat mate and, unbeknownst to me, interested suitor—were selected as the inaugural PAA interns at STEELE. An internship Roger had to create to make up for his gaffe of fighting Antonio at the PAA end-of-the-semester reception.

Roger, the possessive caveman, thought Antonio and I were kissing and punched him in the face. To make amends, Roger provided compensation for Antonio's medical costs and a generous sum of money in recompense. In addition, he had the STEELE human resources team put together an annual paid internship program for two students awarded in perpetuity.

Unfortunately, human resources and management chose Antonio and Delia. Antonio with the Technical Design Team since he's a computer wiz and specializes in AutoCAD software. They placed Delia on the Interior Design Team with me.

Despite working together, I successfully avoided both of them since I was part-time. Only the occasional interaction at team activities with limited conversation. Sure, they tried to play nice and invited me to lunch often. I declined. I trust neither of them, particularly Delia.

Roger told me about her incident in his office. She appeared unannounced and unexpected; her behavior just short of stripping and jumping his bones. Delia could bypass the stone wall of Françoise, his assistant, since she was at lunch.

Fortunately, she returned and promptly censured Delia for inappropriately entering the president's offices and trying to seduce him. Then Françoise escorted her to security and human resources like a rebellious student sent to the principal's office for correction.

How Delia accessed the executive floor in the first place is still a mystery. The security team found her STEELE ID programmed to include the twentieth floor. They assumed it was a fluke when it one of their staff originally set it since they control the computer software for all IDs. Sneaky hussy...

"Here, mademoiselle, let me help you sit down."

Drawn out of my ruminations, I turn to him as he hands my mobile to me.

"Mademoiselle Beaulieu! What happened?"

Françoise appears and bustles the man out of her way. She clutches my arms. Then she stares into my eyes before she glances at my belly to assess me carefully.

"What did you do?!" She demands of the man who helped me, her icy blue eyes glare at him with contempt.

Two security members approach and take the man by the arms.

"Oh! Wait, *non, non!*" I start as I lift my hand to stop them. "You misunderstand, he helped me."

Everyone turns to me and I notice other passersby have gathered. Some hold their mobiles out for photos and video.

Merde!

This is not what I need right now. Delia already made me to feel like a blimp. I don't need this scene splashed across the Internet. No fodder for the media.

"I'm fine. Really," I say as I straighten and take my mobile from the man. "*Merci beaucoup, Monsieur.*"

He nods and hastens away without a backwards glance once the guards let him loose.

"Shall we inform Monsieur Steele?" The taller security member asks of Françoise.

She turns to me and I shake my head. She declines their offer and leads me to the private elevator for the executive floor. Meanwhile, the guards disperse the crowd.

I pause at the elevator and look at Françoise, "*Merci* to you, too. But I need to go to the other elevator bank. I'm meeting with a few designers about the penthouses renovation projects."

Françoise nods, "Oui, I will have them set up in Monsieur Steele's private conference room. He's not in at the moment, and it would displease him if I let you out of my sight."

She raises her elegant brow and tilts her head. The woman is formidable. I give in without an argument.

She presses her ID to the plate and the doors open. Once inside, she types in a code on the keypad for the twentieth floor. The other floors don't have the feature.

"Hmm, that's new," I muse aloud.

"*Oui*, after Monsieur's unsavory visitor, Ms. Shaw, he had security add this feature as double verification," she responds with an expression of disdain on her face.

Smart move...

We exit the elevator and walk to the conference room. I smile at the receptionists and other staff members as we pass them along the way. Once inside, Françoise offers me tea or water. I accept a glass of water gratefully. Then return my disrupted call and assure my agent all is well.

Françoise uses one telephone to arrange the meeting relocation. When she finishes, Françoise glances at me expectantly.

"If you don't mind, please tell me what happened. Monsieur Steele will want to know details."

Of course, she would keep him abreast. I don't mind as she has my best interests in mind.

"The infamous Ms. Shaw jostled me from behind. Apparently, she didn't see me. Oh, but that was despite me being 'very pregnant' and 'much bigger than before' she told me…" I respond with a smirk.

Françoise's eyes widen before she collects herself to maintain her professional demeanor. But she can't help herself either.

"That Delia Shaw is a true troublemaker. I will let Monsieur Steele know immediately," she replies.

I shake my head and let her know I will speak with him later. I don't want to interrupt his off-site meeting. She agrees and we chat about my pregnancy progress and wedding plans while we wait for the designers.

When Clinton, his assistant, Brandon Eliot, and another designer arrive, Françoise excuses herself.

Before my hospital scare, I worked with Clinton as the design director on a new STEELE residential project, and Brandon was one architect. The other designer is a woman

I haven't met before. Perhaps they hired her after I, or rather Roger, put an indefinite hold on my position.

When he suggested I restructure my time to preserve my energy, I agreed with him. The renovations for our penthouse and his parents' take up most of my focus. My passion is design and the reason I switched from my highly successful modeling career of eighteen years. But I realize I can't do it all alone. Especially such extensive projects. Someone else from STEELE can manage them for me based on my ideas, and I'll make the final decisions.

The same is true of our wedding plans. My mother and Shelley were more than thrilled to take over. General Josy and Sergeant Steele to the rescue! They told me I will merely show up and chose from three options at the most —no stress for *Petite Maman*.

The bigger items, like my dresses, will wait until my body shows what it will look like closer to the date. I have sketches of exquisite gowns from Monsieur Valentino on standby. Lola, Haley, Blair, Billie, and Starr are in cahoots with their dresses as matron of honor and bridesmaids. Roger, his brothers, Lucien, and Luc will wear bespoke tuxedos.

The location was the easiest to decide—*Le Beaulieu Manoir*. The majestic home and picturesque grounds will serve as the backdrop to my fairy-tale wedding. My father was beyond pleased Roger and I chose my ancestral home for our momentous occasion. I'm super excited!

I told Roger I would schedule interviews for assistants vetted by Françoise. So far, she hasn't found suitable candidates. I'm not in a rush with everything else taken care of for now.

"Leonie! So good to see you!" Clinton says as he shakes my hand and double kisses my cheeks.

"How lovely you look!" Brandon adds, his arctic blue eyes glow.

The assistant and new designer nod in agreement and smile.

Well, at least they don't think I'm unappealing...

Clinton makes the introductions. Then we get down to business.

I was happy for an opportunity to work with him and Brandon again. So I suggested them to Roger, and he agreed they would do a superb job. Although he was hesitant about Brandon being a part of the team. He's a handsome man in his early forties and was a regular lunch mate of mine. Roger felt Brandon involved himself too much when I became ill at the office.

Oh boy, Possessive Alpha Male Alert.

The meeting goes well as expected. Their ideas blend seamlessly with mine. Plus, they offer alternatives I had not considered. We set a date for them to tour the penthouses. Then end with more congratulations and well wishes.

That checked off my to do list, I thank Françoise and make my way back to Eric who waited to drive me to another baby boutique. The highlight of my day!

ROGER

*D*amn. I'm running late for my meeting with the Interior Design Team. Although I have to say, the sweet taste of Leonie still lingering on my tongue was well worth being tardy. The greedy Kitten, I chuckle to myself.

Surreptitiously, I adjust my cock that decided to awaken at the thought of Leonie's delectable pussy that I left wrecked and passed out in orgasmic bliss on our bed. The jacket of my pinstripe Ermenegildo Zegna three-piece suit covers the bulge and hides my groin as I shift it.

"Oh, Mr. Steele!"

I glance over my shoulder mid-stride to my private elevator. Fuck. It's that intern from before—Delia Shaw. Since our last encounter, I reviewed her file hoping to uncover a reason to end her internship. Unfortunately, I found none.

"I am not available," I answer as I quicken my pace.

Undeterred, she speeds up and reaches me just as I place my ID on the plate.

"Yes, Sir. I understand. Just a question on the new project in the sixth arrondissement? If I may ride up with you to the meeting..."

I sigh and gesture for her to enter the open doors. Then press the button for the nineteenth floor. I fold my arms defensively over my massive chest and nod for her to speak.

She lowers her gaze to the floor as her creamy complexion blushes a rosy hue. The contrast to her brunette hair makes it more noticeable.

Delia is a curvy, sensual woman. Her straight hair falls down her back like a curtain made of silk. Fringed with long lashes, her moss green bedroom eyes can captivate a man easily. The Cupid's bow of her full upper lip begs for a kiss.

I take in the rest of her. The emerald green fitted suit jacket nips her tiny waist to flare at the swell of her hips. The tops of her tits peek out from beneath a flesh-toned lace camisole, high and firm. She's petite. But her shapely calves end in sky-high, fuck-me heels to add length and height. Although she still stands a good six inches shorter than my six feet, three inches.

"Mr. Steele?"

Her Demi Moore-like husky voice brings my focus back to her face.

A flicker of desire appears in Delia's eyes.

But when I blink, it's gone. Perhaps I was mistaken. I nod again, and she continues.

"Well, I reviewed the AutoCAD renditions and found—"

The elevator lights blink on and off.

I shift my gaze up to the ceiling. They appear normal. I look down at her and she appears distressed.

"It's fine, the power must have had a surge. Go on," I encourage her.

She rubs the back of her neck as she stretches it to the side to release tension.

"Well, uh…"

The lights go out completely and the elevator jolts to a stop.

I fall back against the wall and hear a thud.

"Fuck!" I grumble.

What the hell happened?!

The interior of the elevator is so dark that I can't see my hand in front of my face. Groping along the wall, I feel for the panel. My fingers find the emergency call button, but it doesn't activate. None of the buttons work. Damn!

"Aahh…"

The painful cries from the other side of the elevator stop my mutterings. Right, Delia.

"Are you all right?" I call out.

More pitiful moans fill the air of the noticeably warmer space. Not wanting to step on her, I inch closer to the sounds with my hands outstretched. The tip of my Oxford shoe bumps against soft flesh.

Another moan comes from Delia.

"My apologies. Are you standing or on the floor?" I ask, not moving forward to avoid hurting her.

Delia doesn't answer.

"Hey. Did you hit your head on the wall or something?"

This time I reach out and make contact with her body. The feel of it is soft and heavy. I jerk back, realizing it's her breast.

Fuck!

"Excuse me! I didn't mean to touch you inappropriately. I can't see—"

The full weight of her body falls into mine as the elevator drops several feet. With one hand, I grab a hold of what must be her waist to keep her from dropping to the floor. The other hand I reach out for the wall to gain purchase. Delia wraps her arms around my neck. The elevator cuts off again.

Disoriented, I continue to hold her. She presses her pillowy breasts against my chest. The hold around my neck tightens.

"I... I... I'm claustrophobic..." Delia wails, the sound of her voice muffled by my shirt and tie.

Gently, I pat her back to soothe her. This is not good at all. The elevator is going haywire, and she's scared. Great. Just fucking fantastic!

"Okay, it's okay. The building operations team will take of it," I offer as consolation.

Her fingers climb up into my hair, gripping it. Then musing it up as she pulls her hands away. They slide down my shoulders to my tie. She jerks on it as she falls backwards.

The movement throws me off balance, and we tumble to the floor. The sound of material ripping fills the elevator as her knee bends. I land half on top of her and half on the floor. My left hand takes the brunt of my fall as I try to avoid crushing her with my weight. It twists as it hits the floor at an awkward angle.

"FUCK!" I bellow from the pain.

"Ooomph!"

Delia lands on her ass with her legs around my waist. She still grips my tie in her fist and my shirt with her other hand.

I scramble backwards like a crab away from her as I clutch my hand to my chest. It throbs like crazy. The pain shoots up my arm in endless waves. I'm on my ass with my knees bent and my back against the wall.

Suddenly, the lights turn on and the doors open.

The difference from pitch black to bright white is blinding. I squeeze my eyes shut and stars dance before my eyelids. My head falls back against the wall.

"*Mon Dieu!*"

"Hey! What happened?!"

"Are you okay?"

"Isn't that Mr. Steele the President of the Residential Properties Division?"

"Yeah. Who's he with, though?"

I open my eyes. Once they adjust, the first thing I see is a red-faced Delia lying unconscious on her back, legs splayed out, skirt and camisole torn, hair disheveled. One shoe on her foot, the button on her jacket hanging by a thread.

What the fuck?!

My head swings to the crowd at the elevator doors. Security, maintenance, and members of the Interior Design Team stare at us. Some look aghast, others angry, all curious at the spectacle before them.

"Oohh..."

Delia's soft cries amplified by the now silence spectators.

Shocked, I realize my tie and shirt also tore and my hair tangles about my head.

What could only be minutes stretch on with everyone frozen in place.

The sound of heels clicking on the tile rapidly precedes Françoise. She surveys the sight, then moves past the gawkers. She doesn't enter the elevator. Rather, she galvanizes the security team to disperse the crowd and the maintenance crew to keep the doors from closing.

She punches a number on her mobile, and in a low voice she speaks in French. Satisfied, Françoise glances at Delia, then back to me.

"Monsieur Steele, is your hand hurt?"

I gather my wits and rise from the floor. I slide up the wall and get my feet underneath me to stand. My wrist feels like it's broken for sure. The pain is intense and unrelenting.

"Yes, I land—"

She holds up her hand for me to stop speaking.

"Nothing else, Monsieur Steele," she responds. "Mr. Perry is on his way."

I close my mouth and nod.

Françoise has summoned the STEELE Paris General Counsel?

Fuck. Me. It's worse than I thought.

My head clears immediately.

"Ms. Shaw? Can you hear me?" Françoise asks as she now turns her attention to Delia still without entering the elevator.

I glance at Delia, and my mind goes over the events. I did nothing to harm her. She looks like I have assaulted her.

FUCK ME!

LEONIE

*M*y poor baby has been beside himself for over a week after the fiasco with that conniving Delia Fucking Shaw...

Instantly, I knew something was wrong with him when he walked through the door. The sling may have been the obvious clue, but it wasn't the only one.

I was off center for over three hours. I couldn't put my finger on it. But I knew something was wrong. Call it my maternal instinct or the crazy connection that Roger and I share. It wasn't good.

"ROGER?" I ask. "Roger! What happened to you?!"

The water slides down my body as I rise from the bathtub. Careful to hold on to the sides, I place my feet on the slip-proof mat at the bottom firmly. I pay no heed to my body's reaction to its mate. My hardening nipples and the heat pooling in my lower belly go ignored after one look at Roger's tired face.

He leans against his vanity, but moves to help me one-handed step out of the bathtub. His gray eyes are hollow and dark circles visible below speak to his troubled countenance. Wordlessly, he wraps a warm bath sheet around me as I step into my terry slippers.

"Mon Cœur, please speak to me!" I implore, his silence too much to bear.

Roger nods, "First dry off. I want you to sit on the bed."

I protest. But he cuts me off with his fingertips to my lips, and he shakes his head.

With a sigh, I comply.

Once dried, Roger hands my floral silk Lola's Coterie kimono to me. He holds one side up to ease my arm's entry into the sleeve. Then takes my hand and leads me to our bed. He settles me on the bed with the pillows behind my back, toes off his shoes, and sits beside me.

I watch him as he leans his head against the pillows and closes his eyes. He winces as he adjusts the sling across his dress shirt. I notice his suit vest and jacket draped on the sofa. I take his hand into mine and stroke his cheek. I need to be closer to him. So I curl into his side and put his arm around me. I place my hand on his chest and wait until he's ready to speak.

Roger is home, and he's in one piece. So, I can be patient.

A few minutes pass and I wonder if he's fallen asleep. His breathing has evened out, and he's more relaxed than before. I lift my head to peek at him, and he opens his beautiful gray eyes. I scoot up and cover his lips with mine, hungry for my mate.

He opens his mouth to my probing tongue. I lick at his tongue, aching to taste him. On a groan, he grips the back of my head, fisting my long hair, and tilts me to an angle better suited for him to deepen our kiss.

Fiery desire ignites throughout my soul, flickering over my flesh with a flame set on high to make me combust. The urge to be one with Roger won't be denied. I know he needs me, too.

Right now.

I lift to my knees and around my expanded belly, fumble with his belt and the zipper of his trousers. He grunts when I free his turgid length. It grows ever larger in my hand. Impatient, I bring his bulbous tip to my already wet seam and lower down onto his dick, massive even though it's not fully erect.

"Fuuuck Leonieee..." Roger groans as his hand grips my hip.

He's so big I have to lean forward to position my pussy to take his entire length. I Rest my arms on his shoulders with my palms flat on the headboard. Then rock back and forth and circle my hips to get him inside of me. My juices flow and ease the slippery way.

I throw my head back when my ass lands on his muscular thighs bunched up with sexual tension. The feeling of warm wetness makes me cry out as Roger's mouth engulfs my puckered nipple as he latches on to it.

He suckles strongly, pulling on the sensitive bud and nipping at it. The sounds of his lapping and the combination of pleasure and pain drive me crazy.

I speed up my movements and ride Roger in wild abandon. I sense his need and it spurs me on. My mate is in pain and he needs me to comfort him, to take it away.

"Aaahh... Roger... Roger... Mmmmmm... Amoureux..." I cry as an orgasm rips through me.

"Fuck!" He grunts as my pussy walls clench around his cock.

He digs his heels into the mattress for leverage and wraps his arm around my back to grip my opposite hip. As he slides below me, Roger jacks his hips up to pound up into me.

I squeal in delight and tighten my thighs to lock him to me. My fingers twine in his hair at the nape, and I tug hard.

He responds with a bite to the side of my neck at the juncture with my shoulder. His mark.

I yowl and ride him harder as another climax hits me.

Roger is all grunts and growls. A feral beast in the throes of mating. His soul focus on satisfying our needs.

With his one arm around me, he lifts us up and shifts our position. I hang from his neck with my upper back pressed against the headboard and my legs wrapped around his hips, ankles locked at his tight ass. He kneels and pistons into me with a snarl.

Sweat coats his forehead and his hair hangs in his eyes, still squeezed shut as though fighting off an internal foe. Only our connection keeps him grounded.

The sensation of his enormous dick swelling and throbbing serve as my only warning before Roger throws his head back and roars his release. His hot seed shoots into my pussy, filling me, then spilling from my core.

I'm triggered by his intense climax and scream his name as another orgasm carries me to another level of ecstasy. On its own accord, my pussy convulses to pull out every drop. My mind drifts and my body goes limp. The last things I hear before sweet *slumber collects me are Roger's words of his everlasting love for me and me only. Incoherently I mumble I love you. Then surrender.*

* * *

LATER THAT NIGHT, he told me about the second unprovoked incident he had with Delia.

Trapped in an inoperable, pitch-black elevator for twenty minutes with her crying claustrophobia and him trying to help her. Only for the doors to open and the scene depicts one of an unwanted advancement witnessed by several STEELE staff members was unbelievable.

Once again, Françoise saved the day with her fast thinking. Preempting any negative talk with the General Counsel taking control of the situation and calling the medics was smart.

They were both taken to hospital. But not before the human resources team took photos of both. Roger treated for a badly sprained wrist that requires him to wear the sling for two weeks. Delia had a mild concussion sustained when she hit her head on the elevator wall.

As a precaution, Albert along with HR video recorded statements from both for the record. Roger gave a full account. Delia said she was frightened and nothing out of sorts occurred between them. She took a few days off to recover. Today was her first day back...

The building operations and security teams cannot account for the malfunctioning of Roger's private elevator.

Albert had multiple systems-check tests run by the internal maintenance crew and by two external companies. They added all reports submitted to the file.

Done and time to move on.

Now I wait for Roger at LEVELS Paris. I sent a handwritten invitation and a mask to him via Eric. Roger had a late meeting and Eric was bringing him home. Instead, he'll bring him here. It's Masquerade Night. Perfect for anonymity and a change of pace.

LEVELS Paris in the 7th Arrondissement Palais-Bourbon Le Faubourg inhabits the former Parisian home of a pampered courtesan to a French king. The magnificent *maison* on a tree-lined street sits behind duplicates of the original double carriage doors and features a spacious interior courtyard. They host grand soirees during the warm-weather months under the stars and strings of fairy lights.

The layout—the same as the other two locations—spreads across seven levels. The main entry foyer has two sides with two greeter stations for access to Dine & Dance levels and BDSM levels; 7th Sky Lounge, as with each club, the Sky Lounge offers a view of a nearby landmark for Paris a stunning view of the Eiffel Tower resplendent in lights at night, a bar, restaurant by day dance club by night, a coverable pool that's open for the summer, and a glass-retractable roof; 6th and 5th multilevel dance club with two bars and a lounge for food and drinks; 4th Level 4 Restaurant and bar open for breakfast, lunch, and dinner; 3rd has twelve private suites for members to continue their pleasure apart from the BDSM levels; 2nd Peepshow for

BDSM with seating alcoves, main stage, performance rooms, and a bar that serves non-alcoholic mocktails; below ground the Cellar BDSM dungeon with mocktails bar. The Dine/Dance members only have access to the party levels—Sky Lounge, Dance Club, and Level 4 Restaurant.

With it in my native city and its stunning architecture make LEVELS Paris my favorite of the three.

Roger doesn't want others to recognize me. So, we only go when members wear masks and play in the Cellar or act as voyeurs at Peepshow. At other times, we sneak in through the employee entrance and go straight to our private suite.

Tonight I'm in our suite. I had the Level 4 Restaurant set a decadent dinner of his favorite dishes—lobster bisque, steak frites, and a green salad. I'll be his dessert with strawberries, warm chocolate sauce, and fresh whipped cream. Yum!

The click of the door lock disengaging makes my heart flutter. He's here!

Roger strides in, looking more tantalizing than dinner. Behind the black mask, his dove gray eyes twinkle with mischief when he spies me sitting at the table. I'm naked except for a red mask and pussy bow around my neck. His full lips curve into a sensual smile as his gaze travels over my exposed body.

He slips his hand into his trouser pocket and cocks his head to the side. His intense stare pebbles my nipples and makes my pussy drip juices onto the leather seat. The increasing bulge of his dick adds fuel to my burning flame.

"*Bonsoir Monsieur Steele*," I purr as I rise to my full height of five feet, ten inches.

Roger watches me with hooded eyes sashay over to him. The sway of my hips tracked by his piercing gaze. I use all of *The Lion*'s grace and seduction to entrance him.

All thoughts of my being an undesirable blimp fade away each time Roger looks at me with unbridled desire.

That trollop won't take my man's or my happiness away from us.

Tonight, I plan to rock his world.

* * *

ROGER

It surprised me when Eric handed to me an envelope with Leonie's calligraphy-style handwriting on the front of it. The scent of her sultry perfume, Dior's Pure Poison, wafts around me as I sit in the backseat of my Cullinan. I close my eyes as I bring the envelope to my nose and inhale deeply to allow the scent of my mate to fill me, washing away the day's stress.

It's been a hell of a week.

From the crazy elevator ride to the shock of seeing Delia sprawled out to Albert's cover-your-ass plan. He encouraged me to go back to work as usual. So I did just that with meetings, being seen around the offices, events, and so on. Behave no different from prior to the encounter. Present the unflappable presence of their leader, a president of STEELE International, Inc. Be a Steele.

Then Delia returns from her sick time off today.

I had a meeting on the nineteenth floor, and she was a part of the team present. I was the polite head of the division—nothing more, nothing less.

Tension rose in the room as those gathered waited for something to happen or to words spoken. But I gave them no inkling of the irritation that ran through me at the sight of her.

Delia wore her hair in a severe bun. Her gaunt face on full display with dark smudges under her tired eyes. Her underdog demeanor and demure choice of clothing so opposite to her flirtatious self stood out. She whispered a hello to my greeting, but avoided any further engagement.

Later, Françoise, who attended the meeting purposefully, told me to be careful as she sensed Delia was up to no good.

I agreed and met with Albert before I returned to my offices. We connect with Sebastian to keep him in the loop via video conference. I tell them about the meeting along with Delia's appearance and behavior.

They thought it best to keep away from her and the team she's on. Her internship is over at the end of the month. Only four weeks and Delia Shaw leaves for good.

When I open the decadent envelope to find Leonie's invitation to LEVELS Paris, I knew I was in for a treat. I just didn't know it would be to this extent.

Leonie *The Lion* became every man's fantasy from the moment she simultaneously graced the covers of *GQ*, *Sports Illustrated Swimsuit,* and *Maxim* years ago. She's even hotter today. Her pregnancy enhances her beauty: glowing caramel skin, mouthwatering melons, and grip-worthy hips. No doubt my woman surpasses all.

My cock thickens and lengthens as she sashays her way to me with feline majesty. The purr of her greeting sends a zing down my spine straight to my balls. They fill with the need to claim and mate her.

I run the tip of my tongue over my bottom lip and stroke my growing cock with my unbound hand.

"Here, Kitty, Kitty, Kitty," I growl to Leonie.

She sucks the corner of her plump lip between her teeth as her amber eyes narrow. With ease, she drops to her hands and knees and keeps her ass high as she prowls towards me. Her hungry gaze never leaves mine.

Fuuuck. Me.

When she reaches where I stand salivating over her and not the delicious smelling dinner, Leonie nuzzles her cheek against my trousers leg as purrs rumble in the back of her throat. The bow around her long, slender neck adds to her pussy cat persona.

Leonie nudges my hand from my dick to rub her nose and open mouth against the front of my trousers.

A groan falls from my lips, then a hiss when she nips my weeping tip through the material. My head falls back as I close my eyes to enhance the sensations of her play.

With her teeth, she undoes my belt and zipper. She

buries her nose, mouth, and chin inside of my pants, showering my cock with kisses through my black silk boxer briefs. A long lick makes my dick jump.

Fuck this sling!

I pull my arm from the contraption and release my aching cock. My other hand grips her ponytail and wraps it around my fist to use as a handle to guide her head.

Leonie's muffled hums vibrate along my length as she takes all of me down her throat. Her gag reflex kicks in, and I groan.

"Yesss! Take every inch. Take… it… all…" I growl, thrusting my hips as I hold her head in place.

She drags her long fingernails up my inner thigh. Tendrils of desire swirl on my flesh. Leonie reaches into my trousers, then cups my sac and massages my tight balls. When her fingernails dig into the sensitive skin, I howl.

I lock her head in position with my grip and fuck her face like a madman.

"You're mine. Your mouth, your pussy, your ass, your heart. Only… mine…"

As my spine-tingling climax rushes headlong, my thighs shake and my eyes roll back.

No thoughts of Delia lying on an elevator floor as though sexually assaulted by me in front of STEELE staff. No concerns for negative aftereffects.

Nothing but a state of sheer euphoria surrounds Leonie and me.

The power of my release—not only physical, but mental —knocks my legs from underneath me. My cock falls from

Leonie's mouth with a pop, and she moans from the loss. I land on my ass and cradle her in my lap, burying my face in her hair.

Once again surrounded by her scent calming and centering me as I let it all go.

"I will love you always, Leonie," I murmur.

"Oh Mon Cœur, je t'aimerai aussi pour toujours," she whispers hoarsely as she wraps me in her warm embrace.

Before I follow Leonie into a stress-free slumber, I carry her to our bed. I slip her under the covers. Then strip and crawl in behind her, pulling her back to my front.

At last, I surrender to the peace.

LEONIE

"*O*MG! May I have your autograph?!"
"Can we take a selfie with you??"
"Even pregnant, you look ahmaaazing!!"

I laugh and do as requested of three young fans with British accents who cluster around the table of the outdoor café. They pepper me with questions about diet and exercise, skin tips, and fashion advice for an upcoming date night.

Their attention doesn't bother me since I enjoy sharing my time with girls and teens.

Twice a month I go to the center to meet with my mentees. It's a passion of mine I've done for over ten years now. My mentees trust me and find the center a safe space to open up. Even those I've mentored before often come back to meet with me and to talk to the new girls. It's so good to watch them grow up.

Besides their concerns about life and the state of the

world, we discuss their goals and what they want to do after they graduate from school. Just as important, they share their thoughts on body image and stereotypical misperceptions about women.

As someone who has worked hard my entire career to dispel models as dumb; only clothes hangers; only good enough to stand there and pose prettily, not think, I can relate. I've encouraged my peers to do the same.

My mentees and I also have fun doing makeovers and spa days. Several times a year, they attend my photoshoots and fashion shows. Several photographers and designers have joined our sessions and become mentors.

Today's fans breeze in and out. But I make an effort to leave them with a positive impression and positive memories. I wave as they go about their day, giggling at their mobiles. Undoubtedly posting to their social media accounts.

"You're good, girl."

"I'd say!"

Anita, Hettie, and I are having lunch at the historic Café de la Paix in Le Grand Hotel. We're on a break from our shopping spree. Our last stop was Galeries Lafayette across the street. So we popped over here for some of the café's tasty fare.

I finally followed Roger's advice to buy some clothes. At twenty-three weeks, The Twins have grown and so has my belly. No longer a bump, it's more of a mini beach ball! We just had our third appointment with Dr. Berger yesterday.

All is well, and we scheduled appointments with him every two weeks.

"Oh, I love talking with young girls and teens! Their perspective on life intrigues me. I learn from them as much as they learn from me," I respond.

"Would you have preferred girls instead of your twin boys?" Hettie asks. "You have such great handbags, clothes, and shoes! Your daughter would be lucky."

Anita nods in agreement, her jet black curls bob around her heart-shaped face.

"Yeah, like Diana Ross and Tracee Ellis Ross. She always wears her mother's fabulous clothes and looks fantastic!"

I shake my head as I rub my belly.

"No, I'm thankful for my boys. Perhaps in the future we'll have a girl. But all I care about is having healthy babies and a successful delivery."

We pause in our conversation as the server takes our order.

"I agree. When I found out I was pregnant, all I wanted was a healthy baby. We didn't learn the baby's sex in advance," Anita starts, then continues. "Norman wanted a boy—you know all testosterone. Not that it disappointed him when Antonia was born. He's a softie when it comes to his baby girl!"

We laugh at the thought of the former world heavy-weight champion nine years straight—eight by knockout—playing with a toddler. Anita entertains us with stories of tea parties where Norman wears pink feather boas and floppy hats and combs dolls' hair and dresses them up.

"The men he knocked out would pass out all over again this time laughing if they got a glimpse of him now!" Anita giggles.

Her words make me think of my little family. I envision Roger and our sons at *Le Beaulieu Manoir*. As they play hide and seek amongst the clusters of ancient trees. Ride ponies and a horse along the scenic trails. Dive in the waves on the private beach in front of the Steele Southampton Village family compound. Wonderful, I smile.

"What about you, Hettie? Do you and Joel want children?" Anita asks after the server places our dishes in front of us.

Hettie nearly chokes on her sip of Chardonnay as her sepia brown eyes bulge and her face flushes scarlet red.

Anita and I burst out laughing, and I start to snort. Other patrons glance at us and smile at our silliness.

"Ha. Ha. Listen, I just got the man to put a ring on it after dating for three years. I don't want to give him a coronary by mentioning little ones!" Hettie says, clutching her chest dramatically.

We laugh some more. Then dive into our food.

I'm so hungry these days. And horny. And moody. Good grief!

Roger teases me mercilessly or fucks my brains out until I can't take another orgasm or runs in the opposite direction, ducking for cover.

My yoga sessions with Anita keep me grounded and somewhat sane. She and Starr coordinated my new program. With all the yoga flows and now pre-natal

Pilates, my flexibility and core strength including my pelvic floor have increased. They agree the workouts will help with delivery. I'll take it!

"Joel mentioned you and Roger are going to London for a Lola's Coterie meeting. How is she doing? Is the maternity collection going well?" Hettie asks.

I nod and pull out my mobile to show them some of my sketches. Lola has prototypes to show me. Since Sebastian has business at STEELE London, Roger and I plan to meet them next week.

I'm excited to see my best friend in person. It's been forever...

After six years of living in Paris and working together, life has put us on separate continents. Now instead of hanging out at each other's penthouse with bottles of Lola's favorite Dom Pérignon Rosé Vintage 2005 or my Réserve Jean de Lillet Blanc, we FaceTime at all hours. She drinks the Dom P. while I sip iced lemon ginger tea in a Baccarat flute.

Another good thing is we've fallen in madly in love with brothers. So we'll always be close. Our families have expanded exponentially. We went from only children to two to being a part of the Steele clan of five siblings. Our children will be blood relatives. It's so incredible how life unfolds!

But I am thankful for Hettie and Anita. They're my new crew. We must go on one of Starr's international fitness retreats with the entire gang, including Billie and Blair. It'll be an epic Girls' Getaway!

My mobile chimes with a text message. I pick it up to find it's from Roger.

Hi, babe. How's it going? Did you get some agreeable things?

I text back: *Hi, all's good. We're at Café de la Paix. I picked out a few things. The stores will deliver them. We're not done, yet.*

Good! Anything I might enjoy? ;)

Naughty Boy! I will see you later xoxoxo

Bisou Bisou

When I glance up, Anita and Hettie are smirking at me. I shrug my shoulders and put my mobile back on the table.

"Don't hate!" I retort.

They snicker and roll their eyes.

We finish our meal and head to the Cullinan. Even though both women have cars and drivers, Roger insisted I ride with Eric.

"I'm not putting you and our Twins in the hands of any other driver. Would you rather I take you?"

I giggle to myself at Roger's overprotectiveness as Eric helps me into the SUV and ensures I buckle up. Hettie and Anita hop in on the other side. Then we're off to Rue de Rivoli.

I make a note to stop by Lola's Coterie Paris to pick up some new pieces for Roger to enjoy…

LEONIE

"*H*ere, let me see."

Roger reaches across the armrests to triple check my seatbelt fits securely, yet comfortably over my mini-beachball belly. After readjusting the buckle, he sits back in his leather chair, still eyeing my seatbelt. Satisfied, he nods and mumbles to himself about that should do it as he clips his seatbelt together.

We settled on board his gleaming charcoal gray Sikorsky S-92 Executive Helicopter bound for London. The one hour thirty-five minutes will pass quickly aboard the $17 million plus luxury aircraft. The decked-out interior features platinum silk wall treatments, charcoal gray carpet, dove gray leather seats, ebony wood tables, and steel accents. The color scheme is like the STEELE corporate offices in New York City.

I stroke his cheek and smile adoringly at my responsible love.

"*Merci, Mon Cœur.* You're so good to us."

Roger takes my hand and kisses my fingertips. He entwines our fingers as he rests our hands on my armrest.

The flight attendant steps into the main cabin to let us know the pilots are ready for departure. Roger informs her we're all set. She smiles before she disappears through the ebony wood door that separates the crew's area from ours.

Roger turns to me with his intense gray-eyed stare.

"Let me know if you feel in any way out of sorts."

I squeeze his hand and nod to reassure him.

The flight is as comfortable as ever, with the attendant serving us plenty of water to stay hydrated and my new favorite snack of honey graham crackers. I spend the time reviewing my notes for my meeting with Lola, Luc, and the creative and marketing teams for Lola's Coterie.

She wants to surprise me with the prototypes from the sketches we did together. The process has been exciting, choosing the color palette, going to the fabric houses, and thinking up ways to keep the sexy along with the functionality. I can't wait to see and try the pieces!

I glance over at Roger and admire the strong profile of his handsome face. He's let his five o'clock stubble grow in and he looks delicious. Except I miss being able to lick the cleft in his chin. He'll more than likely shave tomorrow morning, though.

"Are you peeping at me, Pretty Kitty?"

I giggle at being cold busted. Roger was so engrossed in his laptop I didn't think he noticed me studying him.

He rises to stretch. Then squats down in front of me with his hands on either side of my belly.

"Hello there, my babies. Your *Papa* can't wait to hold you in my arms for real," he croons as he rubs his thumbs along the sides of my belly.

His touch sends a thrill through me. Not the I want to fuck you until we pass out. But the you made these babies and are my mate.

I run my fingers through his hair, dragging my nails along his scalp.

Roger shivers. Then places two kisses on my belly.

When his gaze lifts to mine, the gray orbs darken with desire. As he stands, he leans on my armrests and slants his full mouth over mine. Our tongues dance as they tangle. He dominates the kiss and ends it with a bite to my lower lip as he tugs it when he rises to his full height, towering over me.

My hungry eyes stay glued to his and spark with intense need.

Roger chuckles darkly and sits back in his seat, shaking his head as he buckles up.

"Not now, Pretty Kitty. Not now."

He picks his laptop up and goes back to work.

I whimper and pout.

But he shakes his head and presses his index finger against his lips to shush me.

Merde!

With a huff, I snatch my laptop out of the side compartment and open it. Two can play this game. But I up the ante.

Feigning warmth, I fan myself and unbutton more of my pink Oxford maternity shirt to reveal the ruby red silk balconette bra. The lace trim designed to cover the nipples barely, reveal my aroused brown buds.

I pluck an ice cube from my glass of water and rub it along the back of my neck. With my hair piled atop my head, my long neck shows the trail of melted water. Once the ice reaches the side, I put it to my lips and suck on it with my eyes closed. A moan of pure bliss from the cool relief slips out.

The commotion of metal hitting metal and a growl draw my attention to Roger. In a blur, he's out of his seat, kneeling before me, and tugging the bra cups down. My much larger breasts spill out, and he latches onto my nipple with a growl.

My head lolls back against the seat as I enjoy the sensation of him suckling the sensitive bud. He alternates between them as he massages my heavy breasts. The ache in more core intensifies with each pull, sending a jolt to my engorged clit.

Roger's hands drop to the button on my maternity boyfriend jeans and rips it open along with the zipper. His thick digit slips inside my soaking pussy, then withdraws to have two others join it. He curls them to rub my G-spot, and I levitate off my seat.

"Oooh, fuuuck...." I groan, followed by a hiss when he pinches my clit.

With my hips lifted, Roger pulls my jeans down enough for him to duck his head between my thighs as they rest on his shoulders. He presses for the seat to recline, and he scoots my ass to the edge. As I lean back, he hunkers down to his premium on-board meal.

I lose myself in the sensations of his firm tongue sweeping my pussy walls, collecting my nectar. Roger laves and nips at my lower lips when his fingers return to my core. I'm so enthralled, I heft the weight of my breasts and tweak my nipples, tossing my head side to side.

My eyes pop open when the tip of his massive dick breaches my folds and drives into my pussy with one thrust. I'm so wet, he glides right in.

Roger allows my body to adjust to his girth. He lowers his head to my breasts, swatting my hands out of the way with one hand. The other slides in position against my ass to lock me in place.

As he moves, I match his thrusts pound for pound. I bite my bottom lip to keep my screams of ecstasy from erupting throughout the cabin. No need for the flight crew to hear my pleasure.

Roger buries his face in my neck to stifle his own grunts and groans as he continues to ride me like a wild stallion. His body tenses, and he sucks in a breath as his dick expands within me. His long middle finger slips into my bottom hole, and it's the catalyst to make us explode together.

Our bodies tremble as he slows his pace to bring our scattered pieces back together from the ether. The beat of our hearts and our labored breaths decrease. Roger holds me tightly until we rejoin the world, whole once again.

"Naughty, Pretty Kitty," he murmurs gruffly in my ear.

We watch as he pulls out of my pussy slowly. His dick slick and glistening from our combined arousal. He groans deep in his throat when he slips from my well-used pussy.

It's so fucking hot, I no longer need to pretend.

Roger kisses me, and goes to the water closet. He returns with his pleasure pole tucked away and his clothes neat. But his face is flushed and his eyes glow. He wipes me clean with a warm washcloth and helps me to redress.

The flight attendant announces we'll land in fifteen minutes.

"Right on time..." Roger says as he waggles his eyebrows.

"Mmmhhhmmm..." I murmur, stifling a yawn.

Roger laughs, "You brought it on yourself, Sleepy Head!"

I FEEL REINVIGORATED and ready for my meeting when we land on top of STEELE London's Tower.

Roger takes my hand to help me disembark, and with Eric we make our way to the entry for the stairs to the elevator. Even though he's going to Sebastian's office, Roger rides down with us to the lobby. Then walks me to one of the Sebastian's cars his driver left for Eric.

I slip inside the back of the sleek, gunmetal gray

Mercedes-Maybach S 650 Sedan. Roger leans in and buckles me in. I laugh.

"Thank you, *Papa*. Now go to work! Tell *Oncle* Baz hi."

"Have a good meeting and tell everyone I said hello"—he chuckles and gives me a kiss, then continues—"I'll see you at *Oncle* Baz and *Tante* Lola's later."

He shuts the door and raps on the roof to signal Eric he can drive me to Lola's Coterie London.

Roger and I wave even though a tint covers the windows. I watch until he's out of sight before I settle in the cushy leather seat. I've gone from one cocoon of luxury to another.

While we drive to Bond Street, I return emails and text messages.

Françoise found three candidates for me to interview as personal assistants. I skim through their resumes. Then I ask her to schedule them for next week. I need someone who's organized and companionable. So if Françoise likes these three enough to send to me, they must have the rest of the skills to handle the tasks.

The design team for the penthouses sent updates and revised plans. They're on track to meet Roger's timeline. We'll move in with my parents while the construction takes place. The *Manoir's* massive size affords plenty of space. Next week we're set to move into the East Wing with the entire section to ourselves. So again, I'm set.

My mother and Shelley have also eased my workload tremendously. They're like a well-oiled machine: vendors selected, invitations sent, menu and caked arranged. I answer a few of their questions and make some requests. Simple. All is good on that front, too.

We pull up in front of the boutique and Eric helps me to get out. Then he walks me to the door. As he holds it open, I thank him and stroll inside.

"Certainly, Mademoiselle Beaulieu. I'll be right outside," he responds.

Stylish, sexy shopgirls assist fashionable, gorgeous women and men. The boutique invites patrons to relax in an atmosphere of splendor and entices them to indulge their inner sexpot or to gift their lover with pieces.

They recognize me and wave as I pass through to the elevator to take me to Lola's office on the top floor with the atelier and business staff offices. When I step off the elevator, I skim the large white space for my best friend.

She's at a large table in the center with Luc, Blair, others, and Billie's face on a monitor via video conference. The table has portfolios on it and two racks of cloth-covered bags line up next to it. Lola's talking, but stops and claps her hands when she spies me. She rushes over with her hazel eyes shining and a huge grin on her face.

"Hot Mama! How gorgeous you look, Leonie!"—she exclaims as she hugs me and bends down to greet her nephews—"Hello to you, too! My have you grown, Little Ones!"

I rub my belly and laugh.

Luc and Blair stride over and embrace me, too.

"Leonie, you're glowing, *chérie!*" Luc adds as his

sapphire blue eyes take me in from head to toe. He nods his approval and gives way to Blair.

She double kisses my cheeks and smiles as she holds me by the arms to get a good look at me.

"I agree. Pregnancy has made you even hotter, honey!"

We laugh and head to the table. Billie waves and blows kisses, motioning to my belly. I greet the other familiar faces, and we start the meeting. The creative team starts with an overview of the inspiration, thought process, and initial designs.

I glance at Lola, and she's beaming at me, bursting to show the prototypes. I'm as eager to see them, and though I appreciate the team's efforts, I want them to get on with it already!

They must read my mind because one assistant brings a rack forward.

We gather around as they unveil the pieces one by one. Jewel-toned lace, silk, and satin bras, thongs, briefs, slips, and kimonos appear. A kaleidoscope of colors and textures blend beautifully before us.

I suggested the theme of precious stones and their colors since babies are a gift and come in a variety of skin tones. Soft materials to lie against sensitive skin. Easily removable cups for breastfeeding and built-in pockets for leak-proof pads serve as examples of functionality. While the cuts and structure amp up the sensuousness of a woman's pre- and post-natal body.

The collection impresses everyone and lives up to the Lola's Coterie brand. I'll take some pieces to try. Once Lola and I give final approval for the collection, it will go into full production.

The marketing team presents next. They share ideas for the campaign, the tagline, media focus, and timetable. They want to continue with Roger and me since the last round of campaigns scored the highest engagement and sales this year.

I smile to myself as I think of Roger's reaction. He'll grumble, but won't have any other male near me and his sons. So, I tell the team it's a good idea.

They're pleased and finish their deck.

The meeting rounds out with open discussion for feedback and ideas. Lola and I thank everyone for their skilled work, and we adjourn the meeting. Billie signs off with a promise to come to Paris next month.

Lola loops her arm through mine, and we go to her office with Luc and Blair.

"So, how are you doing? Does your progress please Dr. Berger?" Lola asks before the glass door can shut.

I smile at my best friend and reassure them all is well. They take turns touching my belly when one of The Twins moves, followed by the other.

Luc tries to cover the sadness in his eyes. Almost eight years ago, he tragically lost his wife Carole during the birth of his son and only heir Lucas, who also didn't survive.

I squeeze Luc's hand, and he nods at me gratefully.

Blair places her hand on his arm, and Luc glances down at her with a smile. He pats her hand and shakes off the sadness. Clapping, he turns back to me.

"I have a surprise for you!"

He gestures to the sofa and table where a beautifully wrapped box sits.

I smile and take his arm as he leads me to sit. Like a child at Christmas, I rip into the paper and pull the top off. Nestled amongst tissue paper is the complete collection of *Winnie the Pooh*—the first editions. My eyes fill with tears as I read his touching note.

Luc offers his handkerchief to me and puts his arm around my shoulders.

After I gather myself, I thank him and promise to read to The Twins every night.

We spend the next couple of hours catching up before we leave. Luc and Blair have a gala to attend. Lola and I drive to her home with Eric—not even Sebastian's driver is good enough for Roger...

We arrive at their palatial estate in the ultraexclusive Kensington Palace Gardens. Like The STEELE Tower in New York City is on Billionaires' Row, their West London home is on Billionaires' Boulevard. Lola tells me the mansion has at least forty rooms over five floors—including the attic.

"Yeah, and my first time here, we christened each room over the three days we stayed!" She giggles.

"Well... the Steele men certainly don't lack stamina!" I add joining in her laughter.

We burst into guffaws that turn into a fit of snorts. I nearly pee on myself. We laugh even harder when I tell

Lola. By the time Eric opens the doors, tears roll down our cheeks, and our faces flush bright red.

Lola loops her arm through mine and we walk up the steps, still in tears from our jokes.

The ornate wooden door opens to reveal Roger and Sebastian. They take one look at us and panic.

"What the fuck happened?!"

"Who the hell bothered you?!"

I look at Lola, and we crack up.

Roger and Sebastian exchange glances, shake their heads, and bring us inside.

"Okay, private jokes… Got it," Sebastian smirks.

"Come on, Giggles…" Roger adds as he takes me by the waist.

I burrow my heated face in his side to muffle my snorts.

We walk past elegantly decorated rooms filled with sunshine streaming through the floor-to-ceiling windows. Priceless antiques blend with modern art against a muted palette of pewter, platinum, and cream with marble floors covered in handwoven Aubusson rugs. We pause in front of an elaborate, double-story twin staircase.

"Come, we'll take the elevator to your suite so you can change. After, I'll go to mine," Lola says as she takes my arm again.

I glance at Roger and note he and Sebastian wear sweatpants and long-sleeved t-shirts with soccer slides. Nice and comfy for our slumber party. I'll do the same. I give Roger a kiss on the cheek and go with Lola.

We turn to an alcove with a door. While Roger and

Sebastian go beyond the stairs towards the back of the home. Lola presses for the third floor, and she fills me in on the layout.

Once the elevator opens, she leads me down the hall to the end where a set of double doors stand ajar. She pushes them to show the first room. It's large with a sitting area before a fireplace, desk by one wall, and two chairs on the opposite for reading. It's well-appointed and welcoming.

We step through to the bedroom. It features an over-sized four-poster bed with antique furnishings. Lola points out the marble bathroom and separate dressing rooms. The maid unpacked my bags and placed my clothing and toiletries in both.

I turn to Lola and smile.

"This is a gorgeous home, *Chérie*! I can see the touches you've made already," I say as I point to her favorite prints on the wall above the fireplace.

She smiles back and adds how Sebastian said the house needed a woman's touch to make it a home. Lola hugs me and goes to their suite on the second floor. We'll meet on the first floor by the elevator in fifteen minutes.

I return to the bathroom to take a quick shower. After I change into a white tank top and matching pink cashmere kimono and lounge pants with slippers, I ride the elevator to the main floor. Lola is already there, sitting on the steps.

She points at her wrist exaggeratedly as she shakes her head.

"Yeah, yeah, yeah.. I move slower these days, you know," I answer pointing to my belly.

"Sure, whatever you say!" Lola laughs. "You've never been an on-time person, Leonie... Pregnant or not!"

I help her up, and we head in the same direction as the boys. The delicious aroma of Indian food fills the air and grows stronger as we near what must be the kitchen.

Lola pushes a door open and my mouth waters. Not only from the table laden with dishes. But from the sight of Roger and Sebastian shirtless flexing their arms and chests à la Arnold Schwarzenegger.

They're super fit from boxing and MMA training, respectively. So one isn't better than the other. Even five years older than Roger, Sebastian is hot as hell. No disrespect to my bestie. But it's the truth!

Lola and I stand by the door unbeknownst to them. We listen to them debate the benefits of their preferred disciplines very seriously. It's a glimpse into them as children—super competitive, unmoving in their beliefs, ridiculous.

When they notice us finally, they don their shirts and agree to disagree.

"Give us a break! Mine is bigger than yours. Blah, blah, blah!" I tell them as I make my way to the table—*Maman* is hungry.

Lola laughs, "Right, you big babies! Sit down and eat!"

Their egos mollified, Roger and Sebastian join us at the table. We fill our plates with vegetable samosas, tandoori chicken, vegetable biryani, dal makhani, and paratha. It's a full-on smorgasbord. And I'm in heaven.

"How did the prototypes come out?" Roger asks between bites.

I take a sip of my iced lemon green tea—Lola had a fresh batch ready for me—before I answer.

"*Fantastique!* Even better than I imagined them! The details, the sumptuous materials. They're as sexy as the regular collections."

"Yes! Leonie's designs capture the needs of the moms with the allure for the dads," Lola adds waggling her eyebrows at Roger.

We laugh and I assure him he'll experience the pieces firsthand. Lola had them packed up for me to take back to Paris when we leave in two days.

"How were your meetings?" I ask Roger and Sebastian.

They fill us in as we finish dinner.

Afterwards, we stretch out in the entertainment room to watch a movie on the big screen and chill. I miss the easy camaraderie and fun Lola and I have together. It's so good to have days to catch up. No need to go anywhere. Just hang out all weekend like old times.

The new times are wonderful, too, I think to myself as I snuggle against Roger between his legs on a double chaise. He holds me tighter, twining our legs, and kisses my head. I glance over at Lola and Sebastian cuddled up similarly. He's whispering in her ear as she fidgets, locked in his embrace.

I nod. Yup, even better.

ROGER

"*W*hat the fuck?? You've gotta be fucking kidding me!!"

I bellow as I lose control completely. Responsible Roger takes a back seat in the face of this absolute bullshit.

The papers flutter in the air as I throw them at the conference table in my office. Security escorted a man who insisted upon speaking with me personally up to the executive floor. He bypassed Françoise to hand a manila envelope to me. Then he left in a hurry five minutes ago.

Curious, I opened it and withdrew a sheaf of papers. One glance at the heading and I lost it.

Delia Shaw, Plaintiff,
    vs. Roger Steele, Co-defendant
    STEELE International, Inc. Co-defendant
    Petition
    Civil Claim

Unfuckingbelieveable!

After I read enough of the document to make my blood boil, I fume and pace my office. Thoughts of how the hell did this spin out of control swirl in my mind. Delia Fucking Shaw!

A knock on my door stops me. I pivot to snarl at the invader. But it dies on my lips.

"Roger?"

Leonie stands in the doorway with her hand on her belly protectively as she eyes me cautiously.

"Fuck!" I throw my head back and roar at the ceiling.

I run my hands through my hair and tug. I cannot believe that conniving woman dropped a bomb on my life just as it's going so well.

Fuck. Me.

Small hands placed on the middle of my back tenderly and over my heart calm me instantly. Leonie presses her hands towards each other and leans into my side to still me. I drop my hands from my head and wrap them around her, letting her comforting presence seep into my every cell.

I take deep inhales and slow exhales as Starr taught me to settle my soul. Only, I know this is way beyond the scope of pranayama.

Another knock and I groan into Leonie's hair.

She pats my back and turns to the door, angling herself between me and the outsider. My *Lion* protects me now.

"Oui?" She asks brusquely.

I glance over her head to see Albert. They've never met.

I squeeze her once more, then stand tall. Time for Roger *The Responsible* to take over.

"Bonjour, Mademoiselle Beaulieu. I am Albert Perry, STEELE's General Coun—"

"Ah, *oui, oui*. Forgive my bluntness. *Enchanté*, Monsieur Perry," she interrupts as she extends her hand to him.

"Albert, please," he responds, shaking her hand. "Now, what has happened, Roger?"

He turns to me, and I gesture to the sofa and club chairs for them to sit. I gather the lawsuit petition and civil claim from the conference table. Then hand them to Albert as I take a seat beside Leonie on the sofa.

She takes my hand in hers and squeezes as she flicks her concerned amber gaze between Albert and me. After a few minutes of silence while Albert reads, she shifts to face me.

"Please Roger, tell me what's in those papers?"

I bow my head, pissed and ashamed.

I have to tell the woman I love, will marry in a month, and carries my sons another woman accuses me of sexual assault and harassment—the elevator and office encounters combined. Said woman feared for her safety since I attacked Antonio Vasquez at the Paris American Academy end-of-the-semester reception. She wanted to wait until after her internship ended in case I retaliated and fired her, a blemish on her career. The whole thing is surreal.

Leonie sits for a moment, quietly searching my face after I tell her.

Fuck! If she doubts me, I'm truly fucked. Not with the legal ramifications, but with her lack of trust in me and in us. I'd never cheat on Leonie, ever. Period. She's my every-thing and has to know it.

"Leonie—"

"Roger, we need to make some moves right away. I will have Françoise get Morgan and Sebastian on the line immediately."

Albert rises and strides to the door.

The whole time he spoke, my eyes never left Leonie's. I put every bit of emotion into mine to convey my love for her and my unquestionable faithfulness.

She closes her eyes. Her breasts rise and fall with a deep, even breath. She holds it a moment and exhales as she reopens her eyes. A fire burns within them and ignites that spark we share. Leonie grips my hands and with fierce determination tells me we will get through these nasty accusations and come out more powerful and united than before.

Tears burn at the backs of my eyes. She is an incredible woman. I am forever humbled by her.

Albert returns and I close my eyes to gather myself. Leonie squeezes my hands and sits forward to face him.

"Let us sit at the conference table. Françoise will have them on video conference shortly," he says, taking the peti-tion and claim with him.

She enters and hands Albert a sealed file. Then leaves with a nod of support to Leonie and me.

I help Leonie stand, and we join Albert. The screen fills with my father and eldest brother, the former and current CEOs of STEELE. Shame floods me once again. But with

Leonie unshakeable beside me, I know we'll get through this. Not to mention the fact I'm innocent.

"Give it to me straight, Shaw," my father demands, the original Alpha Dom in full effect.

Sebastian nods as he runs his thumb over his lower lip. He's in profound-thinking mode.

Albert recounts the petition and monetary damages. Then he reviews the cover-your-ass file he created with human resources. My father and brother listen and wait for him to lay it all out. Their questions for him and for me hold no judgment. Neither is unfamiliar with inane cases brought against them. It goes with being multibillionaires and people wanting money.

They agree with Albert there's no basis for a case. But we must go through the motions. They want assurance the damages to STEELE and to me are minimal.

Albert will put together his best team and handle the situation quickly and efficiently. He doesn't expect any obstacles to clearing my name.

We end the impromptu meeting with plans to regroup tomorrow after Albert briefs his team.

Once he leaves my office for his own, Morgan and Sebastian encourage me to go home and rest with Leonie. But return to work in the morning. They reiterate: present the unflappable presence of their leader, a president of STEELE International, Inc. Be a Steele. Business as usual.

Morgan shifts his attention to Leonie.

"Now, young lady, do not allow this ridiculous claim to upset you in any way. You have yourself to see to and Baby

Steeles to nurture. If at any time you need to speak with someone, call me or *Maman Aussi*. Do you understand?"— he pauses for her words of confirmation before he continues—"My son is innocent. The two of you will carry on as usual."

Sebastian agrees and says he'll have Lola call Leonie once he thinks we're settled at home.

Leonie and I thank them and end the video conference.

"I am so sorry, my love. Are you okay with everything?" I ask, cupping her face so I can stare into her eyes directly.

With no hesitation, Leonie places her palms on the sides of my face and pulls me down to kiss her. I cover her mouth with mine and devour her with a kiss so passionate, her toes must curl. She whimpers in response and wraps her arms around my neck, clinging to me.

We kiss until we need to catch our breath. I lean my forehead against hers with my eyes still closed, breathing our mingled air.

"Only you, Leonie. I have never loved nor wanted a woman the way I need you. You are my life. Only you, my love," I murmur, my voice thick with emotion.

"Oh, Roger, I love you more than you'll ever know. I trust you and have no doubt of your innocence, *Mon Cœur*," she whispers in response. "Let's go home. I need you inside of me. I need to be one with you."

My soul soars at her words.

LEONIE

"*Merci beaucoup*, Nanny Grace! These are so lovely!"

I hold one of the two hand-crocheted, navy blue cashmere blankets up and admire the fine stitchwork of the intricate design. The center panel has an entwined B and S for Beaulieu and Steele, surrounded by a twelve-inch border of swirls and whorls. The matching beanies and booties complete the sets. They're the perfect addition to the nursery in the East Wing of *Le Beaulieu Manoir*.

Because of the hullabaloo caused by that woman who shall not be named, I forewent an assistant in favor of a nanny. I can handle the work of my everyday life now that the other aspects are taken care of by my helpful wedding planning *Mamans* and design team. Plus, the maternity collection is in production and doesn't require as much of my attention as before. I sketch new pieces, but nothing too time-consuming.

A nanny is a better addition to our household. Françoise found the agency the überwealthy and celebrities use to hire their nannies, nurses, and governesses. Their training is top-notch in everything from changing a diaper to language lessons to disarming a would-be kidnapper. Although Roger has a security detail at the ready...

Grace Hart presented as the best candidate. Besides being appropriately trained and smart. She fits in with my personality, has the stamina to handle twin boys, and is a widowed, early forties, mature woman. Not a trollop and has zero interest in my man.

Roger warmed to her just as I did. My mother and Shelley met with Grace, too. They grilled her in their demand for only the best for their grandsons. My father and Morgan ran separate extensive background checks on the agency and on her. All are suitably pleased.

Yesterday, Roger and I completed our move into the East Wing. We'll stay here for the next two months or so while our penthouse reconstruction completes. We took over my former bedroom suite.

The rest of the wing comprises several bedrooms and bathrooms, kitchenette with eating area, library, art studio, media room, and living room. In essence, it's a house within a house and was all mine before I bought my duplex. It's where I stay when I visit my parents. The maids maintain it. So it only required the arrangement of our personal items and clothing.

Now I'm decorating one of the nine nurseries Shelley and my mother insist we need. The number may seem like overkill or an extravagance. But they want The Twins to have the comforts of familiarity in whichever home they're in. After I thought about it, I agree. And hell, why not?

Roger and I combined two of the other bedrooms into one as their nursery to afford plenty of space. They finished the construction last week with the cream, aqua blue, and platinum palette in place. Sunlight streams through the windows and the balcony doors. We had hidden blackout shades added to keep the light from disrupting their sleep. Or causing them to wake up before Roger and I do!

Rather than purchasing all new furnishings, we opted to combine items from both families to fill their room. Shelley gave us the matching cribs she had made for Harris and Haley—acknowledgment of them being the first set of twins. The cribs made from mahogany wood stand on Sheraton legs, have carved head- and footboards, and feature sides cut in one-dimensional shapes of the legs. Musical mobiles with new colorful animals hang above each in the same style. They're simply stunning.

Once our penthouse renovation completes, we'll move the cribs to The Twins' nursery there. We want the gifts to be their main beds. We'll replace them with bassinets we found in the attic here that are being refinished.

The rocking chair and ottoman used by one of my

paternal relatives sits near the window. It is mahogany, too. We reupholstered the pieces in pewter suede with a cream silk pillow. Then had a reproduction made for Roger to sit on. One would never guess they're from different time periods.

The rest of the furnishings, including the dressers, changing table, and storage selected to complement the chairs. They blend seamlessly.

Harris made good on his promise and created state-of-the-art baby monitors for each nursery. He installed the set here last week while he was in Paris on business. He will do the others when the rooms are ready. I told him he should market them. The Steeles and their money-making ideas.

The nursery is near the suite of rooms Roger and I share. While Nanny Grace's room will be down the hall. For now, she's staying in her flat until The Twins are born. Then she'll also have a room at the penthouse.

Although Grace will have rooms at each of our residences, she'll only stay until Roger gets home or when we go out. She will travel with us, too. But we plan to be hands-on parents who have the help of a nanny. We'll raise our children, thank you very much.

"You're so welcome! My hobbies have been crocheting and knitting since I was a little girl. I stitched these up in no time."

I turn my gaze from the soft, cuddly blanket to smile at Grace. The twinkle in her eyes shows her love of her craft and sincerity.

"The Twins thank you, too!" I respond.

"They are lovely indeed, Nanny," My mother adds as she admires the beanies. "You did a beautiful job."

Shelley walks over from where she was putting the bedding in the linen closet to peer over Josy's shoulder.

"I agree, very nice and thoughtful of you. They're heirloom quality," she nods.

She and Morgan flew over with Sebastian and Lola last night. They came to help us get adjusted and to check on the status of the legal claim. The men are at STEELE Paris meeting with Albert and his team, then finishing the workday. We're meeting them for dinner later.

"Hhhmmm. Have you ever considered using your skills for fashion?"

I make a face at Lola.

"Don't you even think about wrangling my babies' nanny away from them, Lola Steele!"

She laughs and puts her hands up, palms forward in surrender.

"Just asking, *Maman Lionne!*"—she peeks over her shoulder at Grace and winks—"Crochet would make an intricate trim or cups in my new collection."

I throw a ball at her, and she catches it laughing. Wagging my finger at her, I continue.

"Last warning..."

"Okay, okay! Just teasing. I'd never poach your nanny. She's the one I liked the most for The Twins, remember." Lola says as she puts the ball in the antique toy chest.

Working as a team, we finish organizing the nursery

faster than expected. We take a survey of all drawers, closets, bathroom cabinets and agree it's ready for The Twins. Then head to the solarium for lunch. Nanny Grace joins the staff to eat before she goes home.

"*Mon Trésor*, I am so proud of you! Next month you get married and just over two months and you'll have our grandsons!" My mother says as she clasps my hands in hers and kisses my cheek.

I tear up, and she gives me a hug. When I sit back, Shelley reaches over and pulls me into her embrace.

"Oh, hugfest time!" Lola says as she wraps her arms around both of us and beckons to my mother for her to join in.

My tears stop and I squeeze them each in turn.

"*Merci, merci, merci! Je vous aime tous!*"

* * *

"How did you make out with nursery number one?"

I glance up at a smirking Roger and laugh. Right!

"It's even more beautiful than I imagined it would be from the sketches and in my mind!" I respond with a laugh. "One down, only eight more to go!"

"Uh… make that nine! *Tante* Lola and *Oncle* Baz need one in New York, too," Lola says.

"Right next to our own?" Sebastian asks pointedly with his eyebrow raised and a glance to Lola's flat stomach.

She swats at him and rolls her eyes with a huff.

Everyone laughs at their antics. It's a known fact Lola is

resistant to having a baby so soon after they married. Even though it's been a year...

We're having dinner at Guy Savoy the three Michelin star restaurant famous for its mixture of true luxury and ultimate simplicity in both decor and dishes. In the chic *sixième* Île-de-France region of Paris.

Mr. Valentino sent an assortment of dresses that would fit my growing belly. Tonight I wore a pink mini dress. I fell in love with the off-the-shoulder neckline trimmed with a scalloped ruffle. It's such a pretty, feminine touch—especially with all the testosterone floating through me. The body is unencumbered and flows away below. The sky-high strappy sandals add length to my legs and makes me feel glamorous and sexy.

Roger smiled appreciatively when I walked up to him waiting at the bar with my father, Morgan, and Sebastian. It sent a thrill through me at the desire in his gray eyes.

Now he squeezes my thigh under the table as he smiles at me again.

"My baby can have as many nurseries as she wants," he winks.

His lighthearted mood makes me hope the meeting with the legal team went better than expected.

We weren't so optimistic since the tabloids somehow got wind of the story. From the grocery store checkout racks to the Internet gossip sites and social media, word spread rapidly. A photo of Roger scowling at some random time splashed across the covers alongside a shot of Delia looking terrified. They even dragged up a photo of me yelling at Roger to stop fighting Antonio. Nothing of substance, pure sensationalism to add fuel to the fire.

Even as we walked through the dining room, I noticed a few people turn to gaze as we passed them by. Some with open curiosity, others skeptically. These types of patrons are used to scandal. But the world being the way it is with the MeToo movement, everyone questions the truth. Except in this case, Roger is innocent. I'm glad he doesn't notice. No need to ruin our evening.

Damn that she who shall not be named!

I grin at Roger and kiss his lips.

"*Merci, Mon Cœur...*"

The conversation turns to our wedding, teasing Roger about the late honeymoon, and life. It's fun and lively with no one giving any thought to the legal situation. We enjoy a regular family dinner.

"Pardon me while I go to the restroom before we leave," I say as I push back from the table.

Roger rises to help me and Lola says she'll go, too.

We giggle like two schoolgirls going to the bathroom on break as we make our way through the tables. While in my stall, I hear two women enter the room chatting. At first I don't pay them any attention. But the words rapist and Steele catch my attention.

Merde!

I hasten to fix my clothing and open the door.

Lola also rushes out with a look of anger directed at the pair. The petite spitfire has always been my protector from unwanted attention at clubs with guys trying to get to handsy. So her blazing hazel eyes and fierceness don't shock me.

"How dare you?!" She demands. "You have no clue what you are speaking. Yet you have the audacity to judge an innocent man?!"

"Right! My fiancé is not guilty of any wrongdoing!" I add resting my left hand protectively on my belly as I pin them with an icy glare.

The women blink and widen their eyes in surprise at our vehemence. They flick their gazes from Lola to me to my very pregnant belly with my enormous engagement ring shining in the light. Speechless, they flee the restroom.

I reach for the counter, light-headed suddenly.

Lola grabs me, and we slip to the floor. I bury my face in my hands and weep. I've held in the stress of the entire ordeal and get myself busy with the move, the nursery, the design work. But hearing their nasty comments out loud is too much for me to bear. I just can't take it anymore.

"Hush, Leonie. Don't let them upset you. They don't know what they're talking about. Roger is innocent and the truth will come out. I know it has to be hard and you being pregnant makes it tougher to handle. But know you have the support of our family. We love you and Roger very much and won't allow anything to hurt either of you."

Her words soothe me. But I don't have the energy to get up just yet. So we sit a while longer.

The door bursts open and Roger and Sebastian rush inside. Roger drops to his knees before us and clutches my arms with an expression of panic. Sebastian pulls out his mobile and makes a call.

"What happened? Are you all right?" Roger asks, scanning me from head to toe.

I nod, and Lola responds.

"She's fine. These two wo—"

I put my hand up to stop her from speaking. I don't want to upset Roger and ruin our evening. But she shakes her head forcefully.

"No, Leonie. He needs to know."

She turns to Roger and continues to tell him about the encounter.

I watch dismayed as his face reddens and his eyes darken. I can feel the anger coming off of him in waves. It reminds me of his initial reaction at his office upon receiving the paperwork. I hate it and my heart aches for him.

I place my hand on his cheek. But it takes a moment for him to register my touch. Slowly, he turns his gaze to me. I see such anguish in the depths of his eyes it hurts my soul. This is so unfair.

"Come. Let us go back to the *Manoir*," Sebastian says authoritatively as he lifts Lola to her feet, then me.

Roger hangs his head and takes a deep breath before he stands too. Sebastian claps his shoulder and pulls him close to whisper in his ear. The words have the effect of making Roger stand tall and straighten his jacket.

He nods and claps Sebastian on his shoulder in return. Then faces Lola and me.

"Lola, thank you for supporting us and for helping Leonie. My love, I am so sorry I put you in a position to experience such behavior. I do not want you to get upset, and we will call Dr. Berger to meet us at the *Manoir*. Sebastian is right. Let us go now."

"It's all right, *Mon Cœur*. However, you are not to blame. Once we reveal the truth, we can all rest."

We nod solemnly and leave the restroom.

I avoid making eye contact with anyone as we bypass the dining room to head to the entrance. I'm not sure what I'll do if I see those women gawking at us.

My mother and Shelley have anxious expressions on their faces. While my father and Morgan are in a serious discussion. When they see us approach, they bustle my mother and Shelley out the doors. We follow and get into the cars.

It's silent except for Roger's conversation with Dr. Berger. He agrees to meet us right away. Satisfied, Roger strokes my cheek, then my belly. I rest my hand on top of his. We ride the rest of the way, each in their thoughts.

"Leonie, you go change and wait for the doctor in your rooms—"

I start to protest my father's directive once we're in the foyer of the *Manoir*. But he lifts his hand to stop me.

"Do not argue with me, Leonie. Your wellbeing is of the utmost and I will not allow you to suffer. We will change and wait in the East Wing's living room. If he says you and The Twins are fine, then you may join us."

I glance up at Roger for his opinion, and he nods.

"I agree with your father, Leonie. It is best for us to hear Dr. Berger's assessment."

With a sigh, I nod, and Roger leads me to the elevator. I want to argue I'm not a child. But I know it concerns everyone, and they want nothing to happen to me or to The Twins. So I give in.

Roger helps me to undress and kisses the top of my head once he has me settled on the bed with a cashmere blanket tucked around my legs. He goes into his dressing room and emerges in sweatpants and a long-sleeved t-shirt. Just as he sits beside me and holds my hand, there's a knock at the outer door.

"Come in," he calls.

Dr. Berger and our parents enter the bedroom.

"*Bonsoir, Mademoiselle Beaulieu,*" Dr. Berger says as he strides to the bed. "Let's get your vitals and see how you feel."

He checks me and finds my blood pressure elevated slightly. So he recommends I rest for the rest of the night in bed.

I ask if I can join everyone in the living room and sit on the chaise. Roger sits forward to object. But Dr. Berger gives in when I offer my most pleading puppy eyes.

"She'll be fine as long as she relaxes and keeps her legs up," he says with a smile.

I smile and thank him. Then kiss Roger on the cheek as I lean into his side.

Our parents nod and walk out with the doctor. Both *Mamans* cast worried glances over their shoulders at me.

But I give them the thumbs up and swing around to get up. They nod and smile.

"Are you sure, my love?" Roger asks after the outer door closes. "I don't want you to feel compelled to put on a brave face. I realize that's what you've been doing, and I ask that you be honest with me."

I hang my head this time. Then peer up at him through my eyelashes before I respond.

"You're right. I just didn't want to upset you. You have enough to worry about without me adding my concerns to them."

Roger shakes his head and cups my face, lifting my chin to bring our eyes in line.

"You are my number one priority, Leonie. I am the one to take care of you. I appreciate you wanting to protect me. But no one could protect me from myself if something happens to you. Promise me you will keep nothing from me," Roger responds.

I nod.

But he cocks his head and raises his eyebrow.

"Words, Pretty Kitty. I will have your words," he demands.

"*Oui*," I answer.

"*Bien*," he says as he kisses my lips.

I sigh with contentment and melt into his loving embrace.

We'll be just fine.

ROGER

"*B*ro, this shit is fucking insane! I almost knocked the teeth out of some paparazzo on our way in."

I look up to see my second oldest brother Malcolm striding into my office, followed by Harris. Sebastian is in a meeting in his offices down the hall.

He, Lola, and my parents have been here for the last two weeks to support Leonie and me. Malcolm, Harris, and Haley arrived this morning. They'll work from their offices here, too. However, Haley will work remotely from the *Manoir*. She wants to stay close to her sisters.

I'm thankful for their love and support. It's typical of the Steele clan to drop it all to rally behind one of us. This time, it's me.

Fuck!

It's been a nightmare. More negative media coverage.

More comments from "sources close to" blah blah blah. More absolute bullshit.

Malcolm's experience isn't the worse of it. I had to implement the security detail for Leonie when a reporter harassed her after leaving a baby boutique with our mothers. Eric had to intervene and knocked the reporter to the ground for pushing her in his eagerness to get a shot of her in distress.

I lost my shit and had the reporter arrested and threatened to destroy the newspaper if any photos surfaced.

Now Leonie avoids going anywhere but to the penthouses to check on their status or for her prenatal visits every two weeks. I insist she only leave the *Manoir* with her full detail present. She's being honest with me and hasn't had another fainting episode. Thank God!

Guy hired additional security for the *Manoir* since some paparazzi scaled the wall to get photos of us on the grounds and in the mansion. Fucking drones circle overhead at all times of the day and the night. Federico Fellini said it best in his interview with *Time*: "Paparazzo... suggests to me a buzzing insect, hovering, darting, stinging." How apropos. It's an invasion of the worse kind.

The team includes foot patrols with giant guard dogs trained to attack on command. We reinstated the guardhouse at the front gate instead of just the intercom; a man approves entry. Harris worked with the security company to update the surveillance system and the control room. It's twenty-four-hour, seven-days-a-week coverage.

I even upped the ante at STEELE Paris. Obviously to no

avail based on Malcolm's encounter. Before I respond to him, I call the vice president of security to update him and to request additional precautions. When I ring off, I nod at my brothers and go to the drinks cabinet for some waters.

"It's a pain in the ass. These fuckers are like sharks with one drop of blood in the vast ocean," I say as I toss them bottles.

We stretch out on the sofa and club chairs while I fill them in on the latest developments. Just listening to myself makes me angry. I still can't get over the fact that my woman, sons, and family are being treated like they're criminals. If the media would only focus on me, fine. But to include them is merciless. Particularly since Leonie is visibly pregnant. They don't give a fuck.

It makes me wonder what's happening with Delia Shaw. I truly doubt she's receiving this treatment since her legal team has gone out of their way to make her appear as innocent as a newborn baby...

She's doing the press junket with interviews on talk shows and with magazines and newspapers in Paris and in the United States. It's global coverage since we're both American and the encounters took place in France. Because the legal claim involves STEELE International, Inc. and a Steele makes it sensational. The media can't get enough of it. I heard they offered her a book deal for millions of dollars.

Fuck. Me.

The atmosphere at STEELE Paris varies with each new headline. Some days it's quiet and on others there's a buzz in the air—the tension palpable. Of course it gets hushed when I come around. Human resources noted an increase in the number of time off requests or "concerns with managers." Full investigations prove no validity to the claims. It's just a domino effect.

But as they have advised me, I continue with business as usual and move ahead. Françoise has been a rockstar. She's shut down the executive floor except for upper-level management who have offices here. No one gets to me without her approval first. I made a note to increase her salary and send her on a two-week, all-paid trip to anywhere in the world. She deserves my thanks and more.

The ringing of my mobile interrupts Harris' comments. It's Leonie's ringtone. I stride to my desk to retrieve it. Every time she calls, I brace myself for some new shit. I take a deep breath to avoid stressing her out with my concerns and answer.

"Hi, babe. What's up?" I ask as evenly as possible.

I physically sag when I hear the tinkle of her laughter as she's saying something to Haley in the background. No crisis, after all.

"Ciao! You didn't tell me Haley and Blair were coming! I'm so happy to see my girls! They said Malcolm and Harris are with you?" Leonie says.

"Yes, they're here, and they wanted to surprise you. Surprise!" I laugh, a genuine one.

Leonie claps and I can envision her shaking her hips and dancing around as she does her shimmy—just a little slower...

"It's wonderful! Plus, Hettie is here, and Joel is joining us for dinner. Ow... And Luc, too! Okay, okay, Blair!" She adds laughing.

Obviously Luc and Blair are still going strong. I'm sure she came to support her friend. But the added benefit of being with her lover must rank just as high.

I shake my head as I think back on Luc's expression when I asked him about the two of them. I chuckle, thinking how I ruffled the unflappable French aristocrat.

"Well, gotta fly! *Je t'aime beaucoup!*" Leonie exclaims as she ends the call on a laugh.

"It's good to see you smiling, bro."

My gaze shifts from my mobile I was staring at with I'm sure must have been a goofy grin to Malcolm.

He smiles just as wide and tips his water bottle to me in salute.

I return his gesture and amble over to talk some more with my brothers.

The cure to the blues: family and friends.

ROGER

"*R*ight, that sounds doable. What about the portion where—"

As I swivel in my desk chair, my gaze goes beyond the glass wall and door of my office to the outer office and the floor beyond. The sight of my father, Sebastian, and Albert striding with purpose to my offices breaks my concentration on the conference call.

Fuck.

"Listen, I must get back to you…. Right, sounds good," I say to the vice president on the new build in Manila.

Françoise glances at me from her desk on the other side of my door, then back at the trio. She stands to greet them, more than likely to offer them coffee.

From the solemn expressions on their faces, I'm sure we require a more potent brew. I take a cleansing breath and brace myself as I round the desk to open the door.

My father's gray eyes are stormy as he pins me with an

intense stare. He never breaks eye contact until he passes me and heads to the conference table. He doesn't speak a word until everyone takes a seat.

"Roger, they set the date for a preliminary investigation conducted by a pretrial judge for a month from now. Since she filed the petition with a civil claim, the magistrate may proceed with the investigation. Albert confirms it is a routine part of the judicial process."

Morgan delivers the news with aplomb. But I don't have the same self-confidence.

This shit is so fucked up.

"Albert also said they didn't have enough for a case to move forward," I snap.

I can't keep the snark out of my voice as I stand abruptly and pace.

"What the fuck?! I did nothing to that lying witch! She damn well knows it true! This shit is all about money! That slimeball Antonio got paid. Now, she wants some..."

While I rant and rave, Sebastian rises and goes to my desk. He presses the buttons to lock my office door and to darken the glass. No need for anyone to see me lose it. That will only add fuel to this fucked-up situation.

They allow me to run out of steam.

I drop into my desk chair and swivel to face the Paris streets. My thoughts turn to Leonie. How will she take this fresh development? She's thirty weeks along now and doesn't need the stress of a pretrial investigation. I know she believes me. But it must be a strain for her. We promised to be honest, so I have no choice but to tell her.

I lift my gaze to the heavens and send a silent prayer for her and The Twins' wellbeing, strength, and guidance. Along with another cleansing breath, my head clears. I return to the table with renewed confidence. I'm determined to get through this and to come out stronger as Leonie said weeks ago.

"Father, Albert, forgive my rude behavior. I appreciate all that you're doing for me."—I lean forward and lock my intense stare on Albert—"Tell me, what do we do?"

We spend the next two hours speaking first as our group, then Albert's team joins us. Françoise orders lunch for everyone delivered so as not to disrupt our discussion. She also clears my schedule for the rest of the day and tomorrow. As always, she proves to be indispensable.

Albert summarizes the procedure for the criminal felony charge. Since an inquisitorial system serves as the basis of the French criminal procedure, the pretrial judge takes an active role in investigating the facts of the case. Therefore, the judge may investigate any violations related to the application and proceed to further inquiry people who may have involvement as witnesses or who may have evidence.

The proceedings conducted in writing or made into a written record immediately afterwards. If the pretrial judge determines the case should go to prosecution, they will refer it to the district court of appeal for prosecution rather than directly to the court.

Albert leaves it at that stage with acknowledgement of the case going to felony court if they determine prosecution. He says he's optimistic it won't proceed as far as a full trial. His team agrees.

I turn to my father for his opinion.

"I trust Perry. We will move forward with his recommendations, posthaste. The sooner we get beyond this bullshit, the better for you and for STEELE. Understood?"

"Yes. I agree and will proceed as planned," I reply.

Sebastian asks a few questions, then concurs.

After we review next steps, Albert and his team leave to handle their side of the case.

"I'm going to the *Manoir*. With all the 'leaks' and 'sources,' Leonie needs to hear this from me as soon as possible," I tell my father and Sebastian. "It may also be an opportune time for her to get away for a few days with her girls. Not just a spa day. I can fly Starr and Billie over, too."

"She may insist on staying here and not leaving your side. But it's worth a try. I'll ask Lola to encourage her," Sebastian says.

Morgan nods, "It would de her good. However, the wedding is in ten days. What are your plans?"

Fuck! Me!

I totally forgot, being all caught up in this bullshit. The last thing I want is for this scandal to overshadow Leonie's fairy-tale wedding and our memories.

The media is already going crazy. This pretrial will make them worse. Forget blood in the water—it'll be an all-out feeding frenzy. They'll use any excuse to tarnish whatever comes in contact with me.

I won't let them ruin our wedding day. I'm taking control.

My father and Sebastian agree it would be best to postpone until after this entire thing concludes. With the pretrial in a month, I can't imagine the proceedings taking more than a month. So on the upside, we can marry shortly after The Twins are born and be closer to our honeymoon time.

Yeah… I'll keep trying to convince myself it's a logical, necessary course of action and will go over smoothly.

This is going to piss Leonie off.

"WHAT?!?!"

As expected…

"You cannot be serious, Roger?!" Leonie shouts.

She was quiet and understanding—braver than I expected—when I told her about the pretrial. She reminded me she has unwavering trust in me and knows we'll prove my innocence.

The wedding postponement… Not… calm… at… all.

Leonie turns into a ferocious feline and rises from the sofa quickly, considering her belly has grown a lot. When I try to help her, she slaps my hands away and stands on her own, albeit awkwardly.

Her amber eyes flash; the gold specks explode like sparklers.

Note to self: do not twist *The Lion*'s tail… Damn.

It is the most withering glare I've ever seen in my nearly

thirty-three years. If I were a weak man, my balls would shrivel up and my dick disintegrate.

Instead, I stand to my full six feet, three inches, and crowd her space.

A lethal lion never backs down, especially when cornered. And Leonie is no exception. She lifts her chin and continues to glare at me in defiance of my dominance. Her own blazing through.

Fuck me if my cock doesn't twitch.

Okay, *Queen of the Jungle...*

I growl deep in my chest; the rumble vibrates out of me. My eyes darken to slate in an instant. My wolf is ready for you.

"Don't you even try it, Roger Steele!" Leonie snarls, widening her stance like a cage fighter. "You want to give in to that sneaky trollop? Let her take more of our joy? Well, I say *non!*"

She folds her arms under her bountiful breasts. The action causes them to sit up even higher, pushing against the thin material of her silk tank top.

My gaze drops to the tops of her mounds. They've doubled in size and are more than a mouthful.

The nipples poke through the lace of her Lola's Coterie maternity bra and beg for me to draw them between my lips. Her breasts have gotten sensitive again. Dr. Berger says it's because of her body preparing for milk production.

Well... Let me get some chocolate chip cookies.

Unconsciously, I run my tongue over my salivating mouth.

"No you do not, you beast! How can you stare at my tits at a time like this?!" She screeches.

Slowly, my eyes glide up her body as though touching every bit of her exposed skin. Her chest is flushed red and her jaw set. Those luscious lips pout and her eyes bore into mine.

When she notices my hooded expression, her body reacts instantly. Her chest rises and falls. No longer from her anger. But from her burning desire. Her nostrils flare, and her eyes match mine, full of lust. Leonie can't resist our magnetic pull no more than I can avoid it.

I refuse to answer her with words. I let my body speak for me to hers. Each likes what the other offers. The whiplash change in mood elevates the erotic tension swirling around us like electricity in the air.

My fingertip retraces the path taken by my eyes in reverse. I tweak her nipple, and Leonie moans as her arms drop away, opening her body to me. My *Lion* bows before her Alpha mate.

"Pretty Kitty, you say you trust me. That you know I do what is best for us. Yet you fight my decision to postpone our wedding day," I growl in her ear.

My other hand reaches around to give her ass three rapid spanks. Leonie mewls closing her eyes as she rises to her toes gripping the lapels of my suit jacket.

"It was not a simple decision to make. But it is for the best. With the media frenzy this pretrial will cause, I will allow no one to ruin your fairy-tale wedding and to tarnish the memories of our cherished day," I continue as I drag my lips down the column of her neck to suck on the juncture at her shoulder.

Leonie purrs, then hisses when I increase the pull to leave my mark on her smooth skin.

"Once this scandal is behind us, I promise we will celebrate our nuptials immediately"—I say with the whisper-soft touch of my lips to her throat—"And go on our honeymoon as planned."

I cup her ass then squeeze it as I press my rock-hard dick against her soft, curvy hip.

"You will be all mine sooner than you think, Mrs. Roger Steele... Mine!"

Leonie yelps when I sweep her off her feet with ease to carry her bridal style to our bed. She burrows her face into my neck as she wraps her arms around it.

"It's just so unfair, *Mon Cœur*. Why must we suffer while that lying cow parades around garnering sympathy and painting you as some giant monster? I hate it," Leonie says miserably.

My heart sinks. She's been on the damned Internet again. I try to tell her it won't do any good for her peace of mind if she keeps reading the tabloids and gossip sites. I won't address it. Instead, I kiss the top of her head.

I know what's best to remedy this situation, too...

· · ·

"*Ооон... Oh, mon Dieu! Tu as.... Tu as raison! Ooohhh,*" Leonie screams.

Her body trembles from her third successive climax after I kept her on the edge for the last thirty minutes—one for each ten. Sweat coats her flushed skin. Her chest heaves and her eyes flutter close with exhaustion as she sags against the pile of pillows.

"It pleases me you finally see I am correct. Now, it is my turn, Pretty Kitty," I murmur as I wipe my soaked mouth against her quivering inner thigh.

I extricate her fingers from my hair and sit back on my haunches as I survey my handiwork.

Leonie is absolutely gorgeous splayed before me. Her glowing face is serene with satiety. The enlarged nipples taut from my eager suckling—proof of my goal to drink her soon-to-be-ready milk. The fullness of her belly nurturing my sons amps my ego. Her long, toned legs so powerful from all the yoga sessions felt like a vice around my head when she came.

I lift one of her feet and massage the arch with my thumb, then rub the other.

My cock jumps at the sound of her contented purrs and the sight of her wiggling hips. I stroke my aching length as I lift to my knees between her legs. Unable to resist, I lave her swollen nipples with one stroke of my tongue.

Leonie writhes beneath me, and my dick thumps her belly. She moans and grips it, stroking from base to tip, smearing the pre-cum over the bulbous head. She repeats the motions, increasing the pressure and speed as I buck in her hand.

The tingle in my spine zings my heavy balls. I close my eyes and thrust my hips repeatedly, chasing my climax. My ass, eight-pack abs, and muscular thighs tighten as my release nears.

Blinded by the intensity, I bury my face in the hollow between her breasts. Then groan as copious amounts of my cum spurt onto Leonie's belly. I roll onto my back, spent.

With a seductive purr, she rubs the viscous essence onto her round stomach and ample breasts. Then staring at me with her feline eyes aglow, Leonie licks her fingers clean one by one and releases them with a pop.

It's the hottest thing I've ever seen.

MINE!

LEONIE

"Oh, Leonie! Cheer up! Think how much nicer your wedding will be once this shit is over! You don't want to reminisce and have a cloud of negativity shrouding your big day, do you?"

I glance over at Lola and raise my eyebrow.

"Hey! I'm not taking sides. But Roger *The Responsible* is right," she adds. "That's the best solution. Now you can wear your choice of gowns without a big ole belly bump!"

She balls up her Hermès beach blanket and puts it under her tunic. Then grabs mine and includes it to make her pseudo-bump larger.

I roll my eyes and walk faster towards the chaise lounges. But can't help laughing when she waddles past me, pretending to walk down the aisle.

"I hate you, Lola Steele!" I call after her.

She puts her hands on her lower back and exaggerates

her movements even more than before. Her snorts of laughter trail behind her.

"Some best friend, huh?"

I shift my gaze from Lola to Starr, who loops her arm through mine. Despite her attempt to maintain a serious expression, her sorrel-brown eyes twinkle with mirth. When Lola sumo squats to sit on her chaise and the towels fall to the sand, Starr bursts out laughing. Her dimples deepen in her angelic face.

Although she's acting the devil now...

"Oh, don't tease her—so badly," Billie chimes in as she cracks up.

Haley nods, "Well, you know Roger, he'll do what he thinks is best no matter what. However... I most definitely agree with his decision. For once, one of my overbearing older brothers is correct."

Hettie, Anita, and Bair stand firm with my Alpha male fiancé, too.

At first, the level of my upset was incredible, and it disheartened me Roger decided unilaterally that we would miss our day. I mean, ten days before the ceremony and boom! They announce the pretrial date. Talk about bad timing.

It pissed me off. But I changed my mind, albeit grudgingly. Roger's wily ways in the bedroom softened the blow —damn, he's a fantastic lover! After I awoke from my multiple-orgasm-induced slumber, my mind cleared.

Reality set in. No, I don't want to look back on our wedding day and have the stigma of a criminal investigation of sexual assault and harassment overshadowing our union. It's taken us over two years to get this far. A few more months won't make a significant difference.

Although I know I'll appear phenomenal in my gowns now or then. Big ole belly bump and all!

I also know Roger arranged this Girls' Getaway to make up for the delay. It's so incredible how we went from only Lola and me to Blair and Billie, then Starr, and now Hettie and Anita. He knows how close I am to my crew and the comfort they provide me. Not to mention the laughs, like Lola's hijinks...

"Ha, ha, ha, Loser Girl!" I say as I lower myself down onto the chaise next to hers.

"Remember to engage your pelvic floor, Leonie," says Anita.

I nod and do a few Kegel's before I put my legs up. Roger appreciates the newfound strength of my inner muscles. His groans of rapture are a source of inspiration when I just don't feel I can take another squat. I giggle to myself and do two extra squeezes.

At thirty-one weeks, Dr. Berger told me during my last visit the prenatal yoga and Pilates sessions were beneficial. The backaches and circulation improved with the movement and stretching. Even my balance is better. I sleep well when I mediate before I go to bed to ease my brain activity and any tension from the day. Seven months and counting. I can't wait to hold my babies in my arms and not just in my belly.

"I can't believe I've never been here before after all these years of living in France. It's spectacular!"

Hettie's exclamation brings me back from my musings.

Roger didn't want me to go too far—no more than an hour's flight time from Paris. So my father suggested the seaside resort town of Arcachon on the southwest coast of France, known as the *Côte D'Argent* or the Silver Coast. Off the Atlantic Ocean, the luxury spot is south of Bordeaux's Haut Medoc vineyards and famous for its delicious oysters and seafood. Unfortunately, being pregnant, I can't partake in either...

But the stunning unspoiled sandy beaches, like the one we're on, still make the getaway worthwhile. The magnificent villa we rented sits on the seafront and is only a brief ride to this beach.

Roger insisted Eric and a STEELE driver along with my security detail escort us. They drove from Paris in our and Sebastian's Cullinans ahead of the girls and me. Then met us at the heliport. Roger refuses to take any chances with The Twins and my safety.

We arrived last night and just chilled at the villa. It's a marvelous architectural piece of history. The slate tile roof and stone facade with pale blue trim are ornate. With three floors and a large parcel of land on the seafront, it's a sizable property. Each of us has a suite of rooms with private baths.

After changing into Lola's Coterie loungewear, we met in the eat-in kitchen for a simple dinner prepared by the chef. She made several platters of freshly caught seafood, herb chicken, and roasted vegetables. We ate the tasty dishes buffet style around the table.

Later we stretched out in the media room and watched a movie while we stuffed ourselves with the variety of pastries the chef made from scratch. The girls enjoyed aperitifs, and I had my iced lemon ginger tea. We spent more time chatting than we did watching the latest chick flick. The drama in our lives proved more entertaining than the anything the characters faced!

This morning we headed to the beach. I chose a baby pink gingham pattern bandeau bikini with a fluttery ruffle on the top. It's so cute and feminine. The girls teased that if I didn't turn to the side or face them, they would never know I had a giant beachball for a stomach. Nice compliment... I guess.

Once settled on my chaise, I put a pillow behind my back and Blair helps me to put another one under my knees. Then I sit back and take in the view of the white sandy beach and deep blue-green Atlantic Ocean. The air is crisp with the saltwater scent as seagulls call out to each other. The sun is warm on my skin. Its warmth is a luxurious sensation after being in clothes for so long. I tilt my head back against the chaise and close my eyes as I absorb my surroundings.

Peace and serenity.

"Great idea! Let's have a five-minute meditation session," Anita says when she spies my hands formed in a mudra on my thighs.

"Yes! Wonderful way to embrace all of this natural beauty," Starr adds.

I open my eyes to find everyone gathered around, settling on to the two chaises on either side of me. I smile and make room for Anita to sit at the foot of my chaise. We face each other cross-legged.

She leads us through a guided meditation that reflects on our connection with nature. Her melodic voice enchants us as we're led on the mind-body-surroundings journey. She ends with a chant and namaste.

When I reopen my eyes, my thoughts are clear and I feel lighter. So far, so good.

"Tomorrow morning we should come down and do a flow class on the beach. I'd love to start my day with a sunrise session," Billie suggests.

Starr nods, "I have a new sequence I'd love to share with you. Leonie, I can modify it for you. Although I must say, your strength shows in your movements. You can probably teach it!"

I laugh and thank her for her words of encouragement, but decline.

"I'm not ready for prime time! I'll leave the teaching to you and Anita, *merci!*"

"Well, I'm all for morning yoga tomorrow. But right now, I'm getting in that glistening water!" Haley announces as she stands and takes off her Missoni tunic.

"Me, too! I can't wait to dive in," Hettie adds as she takes off her Norma Kamali sarong-style midiskirt. "I won't say last one in is a rotten egg because you smell nice, Leonie!"

Everyone laughs, agreeing I would be the last one in the water. I must admit I'm not my usual quick moving self these days. Lola helps me to my feet and links her arm through mine as we walk to the water's edge en masse.

My security team keeps a distance. But stay near since the beach is busy with other visitors, vendors with trinkets, and waitstaff. They're discreet in swim trunks and t-shirts. Only their clear earpieces hint at their purpose.

I acknowledge them with a slight nod.

When we reach the water, the girls dive and jump in. I waddle... I mean wade right behind them as I giggle thinking about Lola's antics. The buoyancy makes me feel even lighter than the mediation session.

"The water is perfect! I'm so glad your father recommended Arcachon. Who knew France had Caribbean-style beaches!" Blair says as she floats over to me.

"We used to come often when I was younger. A simple trip my parents enjoyed since you get the beaches, the wine region, sailing lakes, and pine forests. The variety of activities kept us busy. The visits increased my interest in architecture with the historic homes of Ville d'Hiver," I respond, smiling at the memories.

Yeah, Roger is right. I want to look back on our wedding with a smile like I'm reminiscing now. It's just the fact she who shall not be named interfered with our plans.

C'est la vie.

"I know it's early. But I can really go for some more of those oysters. They were delish last night!" Anita says. "They made me miss Norman!"

She adds with a wink.

Unfortunately, I couldn't partake of the aphrodisiac. Although Roger put it on me so good before I left, I'll be fine for the next four days!

"Why are you grinning like the Cheshire Cat?" Billie asks as she raises her elegantly arched eyebrow.

I laugh out loud at being so busted.

"Oh, let me guess... That fine ass man of yours and oysters?" Billie says grinning.

"Maybe, maybe not!" I respond, then duck away, feeling my face flame from the carnal thoughts of Roger's lovemaking.

"That's a definite maybe!!" Yells Billie at my retreating form.

The others giggle and taunt me.

We spend the rest of the time enjoying the sun, sand, and surf for a relaxing day at the beach. When we return, I check in on the penthouses then take a nap while the girls go about their business. Lola, Blair, and Billie get in some work for the boutiques. Starr and Anita record Instagram videos for their thousands of followers for a crossover challenge. Haley geeks out on her computer where she's working on some top-secret project she's cagey about when asked. Hettie works on some cases for her clients. We're Independent Women who work hard and play harder!

"Lead the way to the baccarat table, *merci!*"

Starr replies when the general manager for the Casino D'Arcachon greets us and asks for our favorite games. Her eyes twinkle in glee as she claps her hands in anticipation of a night of gaming.

We decided to glam it up big time tonight in all red outfits. Starr wears a cutout crystal-embellished crepe mini dress that reveals a sparkly sequin and crystal-embellished bra cup. Lola flaunts her toned legs in a smock exaggerated pussy-bow hammered silk mini dress with ruffled shoulders and elasticized cuffs on the breezy sleeves. Haley goes for the sparkle with a crystal and paillette-embellished tulle mini dress. Blair picks a new piece from Lola's Coterie evening wear collection, a contoured lace-up satin mini dress with contrasting lace-up detail and underwire cups. Billie's elegant outfit of a strapless filigree-like appliqué crystal-embellished mini dress. Hettie goes for a 90s style in a slinky, open-back chain-mail mini dress. Anita does a take on the classic tuxedo with a crystal-embellished satin-trimmed halter-neck mini dress. I rocked my babies bump in a stretchy, one-sleeve ruched mini dress with an asymmetric skirt detailed and adjustable drawstrings on the shoulder and hem. We're all flowy hair, tan skin, and high strappy heels!

"*Absolument mademoiselles!* Please follow me," he says with a chuckle at her enthusiasm.

We walk through the 19th-century Château Deganne, where the casino is located. The impressive Neo-Renaissance-style mansion on the edge of the beach harkens to the grand times the area experienced. It's elegance similar to the Casino de Monte-Carlo reminds me of a James Bond from the time.

"I'm going to try my hand at blackjack," Hettie announces when we pass the table.

Anita nods, "Oh, me, too! I love pushing as far as possible without going over twenty-one."

Blair and Billie join them as the rest of us set up at the baccarat table.

A crowd gathers around our table to cheer Starr on her winning streak. Our laughter rings out above the excited din of the rooms.

"This is such a blast! Who would have thought this little gem of a town would have a casino?" Haley giggles as she picks up her winnings from another bet. "This may become a regular spot for me!"

Lola and I nod in agreement.

"STEELE should open a property here or take over this casino. I'm sure Malcolm would take it to the next level," Lola whispers so only Haley and I can hear.

Starr, too absorbed in the game, doesn't pay us any attention. Her laughter when she wins yet another round makes us laugh, too.

"Girls, I'm on a roll! You better put your money down and get in on this streak!" She turns to us and says with a wink.

"Hey, I'm all in on this one!" I answer, putting my chips on the table. "What's the saying, 'Mama needs a new pair of shoes,' right?"

They laugh as I rub my belly in emphasis.

"*Oui, mademoiselle.* But your shoes seem more than good to me."

I glance over my shoulder, then tilt my head back to meet the eyes of the stranger. He's around Roger's height, handsome with aqua blue eyes, and a smooth baritone voice. His smile widens when our gazes meet.

Is he flirting with me?

Uh, *non…*

"*Merci, monsieur.* How kind of you. My fiancé would agree," I say as I rub my belly with my left hand, the giant stone shooting sparks in the light.

The stranger glances down and nods slightly.

"Lucky man, your fiancé," he replies. "Well, I shall leave you to enjoy your evening."

He bows and strides away just as my security detail moves into position behind him, ready to handle the situation.

Lola bursts out laughing, "Okay, MILF Alert! Roger better be careful!"

Starr, who paused her game to face the stranger, nods in agreement.

"He needed to go. I don't want any bad vibes around my game!"

We crack up and get back to baccarat.

After a late dinner at the casino, we call it and head to the SUVs. The night is full of wins and losses, but all fun.

* * *

"HEY, why aren't you guys dressed yet?" I ask as I walk into the villa's living room to find the girls lounging about.

"Oh, don't you look lovely!" Lola says sitting up. "Can you do me a favor and hand me my tote from the foyer?"

I frown and cock my head questioningly.

Lola raises her hand to stop me from speaking.

"Come on, Leonie. You're already standing, and it's just around the corner. Please?!" She says with puppy eyes.

I roll mine and about-face, grumbling to myself.

It's our last night and we're supposed to go out to dinner at this great restaurant the house butler recommended. Now these girls haven't even dressed. We're going to be later than expected—considering I'm ten minutes late as it is…

I wanted to look extra nice since it's the night of my wedding had we been able to have it. It's also the one-year anniversary of Roger and I being back together. They know I was feeling down today, and now they're puttering around in pajamas!

Meanwhile, I'm all glammed up in a white stretchy, pointelle-knit halter neck mididress with a subtle diamond pattern. It's designed with a flattering ribbed waist and gold buttons along the arms for a little flair. I took care with my hair flowing in silky waves past my butt and a little makeup with shiny nude lip gloss. The white looks fantastic against my sun-kissed caramel complexion.

I guess I'll just change and hang out with the gang eating ice cream out of the tub…

"Hello, Kitten."

My eyes jerk up from the floor and land on Roger, who's standing in the middle of the foyer. I gasp and put my hand to my heart, shocked by his unexpected appearance. The emotions—and hormones—swirl through me. Tears fill my eyes.

"Oh, sweetheart, don't cry. I wanted to surprise you. I know today is technically our wedding day and our anniversary. How could I leave you alone at a time like this?" Roger says as he pulls me into his powerful embrace.

"I love you, Leonie, so much. I promise all will turn out well, my love," he croons against my hair.

I loop my arms under his and over his shoulders to hold him closer as the sobs rake over me.

He lifts my chin and kisses the trail of tears, then my lips.

At once, I'm engulfed in the flame of our intense love. The heat of our passion ignites the stoked embers.

Roger deepens the kiss and heat races through every cell of my body. He feels it, too, and groans against my lips.

"I miss you, too, Kitten," he starts, then pulls away gently. "But we have reservations for dinner first."

He presses his forehead against mine.

"Okay," I sigh softly. "Let me just rinse my face."

When I return to the foyer, Roger kisses my hand and leads me out the door.

The Girls' Getaway just got even better!

ROGER

"*O*kay, Steele, get with it now or I'll kick your sorry ass all around this ring. We don't have time for bullshit, man!"

Norman just landed his second blow to my flank, and I never saw it coming.

Fuck! That shit hurt for real.

He's not joking at all.

I'm grateful he didn't hit me in the head with that hammer fist of his. I shake my head and bounce on the balls of my feet for a few seconds to get my mind back in the game.

Another week passed, and we're two weeks away from the start of the pretrial investigation. In preparation, Albert's been grilling me and with the legal team he's been going over every possible scenario and angle to clear my name and STEELE. They're still confident of a positive outcome. We just have to get through the process.

Sebastian and Lola returned to the United States two days ago. Sebastian has some business in Chicago, and Lola plans to visit her Beverly Hills and Las Vegas boutiques. They'll return in a week or so.

Malcolm flew to Greece to look at some private island options for a new resort. Harris and Haley are still in Paris, working from their offices at STEELE or at *Le Beaulieu Manoir*.

My father and mother left the *Manoir* to move into their penthouse yesterday. They won't return to New York City until after the pretrial ends. Morgan says it's best to show a united front.

In the meantime, they're pleased with Leonie's designs and decor choices. Shelley is super excited about the completed nursery. She's beside herself in anticipation of "little babies puttering about again." Morgan is just as enthused with the continuation of the Steele family line.

Our penthouse is ready, too. But Leonie isn't ready to move back in as of yet. The media hanging around STEELE Paris would keep her trapped inside. I agree it's best to stay at the *Manoir* until after this complete fiasco is over and done. That way she can stroll outdoors or relax in the gardens. No need for her to stress out over getting some fresh air and direct sunlight.

It thrills Guy and Josy we're staying. Even though it's not for the happiest reason. It was Guy's idea to wait, and I thanked him for their hospitality. He merely laughed and told me we're family and that's what families do. Besides, the East Wing affords so much space and distance from his and Josy's wing.

Most nights we have dinner together and whoever is in Paris will come over for Josy's now famous Sunday brunch. Lucien has become a regular, too. He and Josy spend a lot of time in the kitchen making dishes from her family's recipes. Tonight we're going to the opening of his latest restaurant where he's debuting some of their pairings.

"Are you with me, Steele, or what?"

Norman's voice and the sound of his fists hitting each other bring me back to his training facility. He's staring at me like I'm nuts for getting distracted while in the ring with him. And he's right.

I shake my head once more and punch my fists together, signaling I'm back.

"Good! Now, let's get at it!" Norman responds.

We spar for another hour. Then follow up with a few laps in the heated pool and a dip in the ice bath. After a shower, I'm ready to start my day.

"Bonjour Monsieur Steele," Françoise says as I pass her desk.

"Bonjour, how are you?" I respond.

Her expression stops me cold. She looks crestfallen.

"What's the matter?" I ask.

Françoise picks up a paper from her desk and stands, indicating my office.

I nod and gesture for her to go ahead of me. This can't

be good. I hope she's not resigning. She's an asset I can't afford to lose, especially now.

Once I close the door behind me, Françoise hands the paper to me. I skim the words, then have to resist crumbling the summons in my fist.

Fuck!

The pretrial judge called her as a witness. Ordered to appear and to offer evidence, Françoise has no other choice but to do so. I wonder if they summoned others, and if so, what they'll say. It was pretty damning when the doors to the elevator opened and they saw Delia sprawled out with me next to her.

I shake my head, pissed already, and the day only started.

"Thank you for letting me know, Françoise. I don't want you upset. We'll get through this," I start. "Do you mind if I call Albert? He needs to be aware of the pretrial judge's actions."

Françoise nods, "Of course. Also, the vice president of security and the head of building operations told me they received summonses, too. They said to let them know what you need them to do. We don't know of anyone else being summoned."

I thank her and call Albert. He and his team ask for Françoise and the others to meet him in his conference room in ten minutes. I'm to stay in my office.

Next I call my father and Sebastian on three-way. They're not surprised, as we expected they would order some STEELE staff to take part in the investigation. We talk some more, then ring off.

I have meetings all day and will not allow myself to get distracted from the tasks at hand. I can't sit around and wonder what will happen, who will say what, how did this come about. No. I'm a Steele and Roger *The Responsible* Steele to boot. I have work to do, and I'll do it. Period. End of.

My mobile vibrates and I see Leonie's beautiful smile as I pull it from my trousers pocket.

"Hello, gorgeous. Can't get enough of me?" I tease.

Leonie's laughter lifts my spirits. It tinkles over the line straight to my heart, pushing the negativity out of my mind.

"Oh, you! Ha, ha! Actually… I wanted to remind you we're having dinner tonight at Lucien's new place. He just changed the time to seven instead of eight so we can go to the VIP cocktail hour," she says.

"Sounds good. I have a late meeting, so I'll meet you there," I respond. "You can ride with your parents, right?"

"*Oui*, no need for you to come out here to go back to the restaurant. I'll be fine riding with them," Leonie says. "My mother is super excited! She can't stop talking about it. Oh… Listen, I have to go. She's calling for me. I love you, *Mon Cœur.*"

We end the call, and I get to work.

· · ·

"—DON'T know what to think. He's always been a stand-up type of guy. Plus, he's engaged to that hot as fuck super-model. Why the hell would he want the intern?"

"Who knows? She's a desirable piece of ass. Always down to go for drinks after work. It's fucked up either way."

"Yeah. I'd say—"

The two male employees enter and leave the restroom, unaware I'm in a stall. Their comments must be like what others must say. It's interesting to hear their unfiltered thoughts. It's a good thing they said nothing disrespectful about Leonie, I muse.

After I left my last meeting, I stopped in here since my next appointment is on this floor with the design team Delia was a part of. No need to go to my office. I'm glad I didn't.

Now let's see how the team reacts. I'm curious to know if any of them received notification from the judge. I doubt they'd say, and I'm not asking. The last thing I need is for someone to complain I harassed them, too...

I make my way to the conference room. As I pass offices and cubicles, I get the district sensation of being watched. I shrug it off and keep my head held high. I'm not guilty, and I'm no wuss.

"Good afternoon, Mr. Steele."

I turn to the right and see a young woman smiling at me.

Oh, brother. Here we go...

"Good afternoon," I answer as I keep it moving.

"Oh, sir?"

Her question stops me, and I glance back at her.

She hurries over, and in a clear voice for all in the vicinity to hear, she speaks.

"Mr. Steele, I want you to know the majority of us believe in you and hope you are successful in getting past this ridiculous accusation. I've been an employee at STEELE for over six years, and never once have you or anyone else behaved inappropriately. We support you, Mr. Steele!"

I blink, taken aback by her decree. Then look around us at the other staff members who nod in agreement or who simply stare. She's right, more of them are on my side than not. Their loyalty warms my heart.

I return my gaze to her and nod.

"Thank you. I appreciate your support." I say sincerely.

"You're welcome, Mr. Steele," she smiles and nods before she returns to her desk.

I acknowledge the rest of the staff, then I continue to the conference room. My step lighter than before.

"*Toutes nos félicitations, Josy et Lucien!*"

"Cheers!"

"Congratulations! Well done!"

We toast Josy and Lucien after we gather for the VIP cocktail hour.

The red carpet was full of media and guests. Leonie and I could run the gauntlet without any major disturbances.

She looks sensational in an Azzedine Aläia black jersey, jumpsuit with a sleek high neck, long sleeves, and body-hugging fit. Her embellished black sandals lengthen her mile-long legs and add sparkle to the ensemble. Her hair flows behind her like a cape, adding to her superwoman appearance.

"I'm so glad *Maman* found someone to carry on the tradition of our Tunisian family's cooking. I certainly couldn't do it!" Leonie laughs as she raises her glass of iced mint tea to Lucien in salute.

He raises his flute of champagne.

"And I thank you for allowing me to adopt your mother as my second *Maman!*"

We laugh at their banter and continue with the round of toasts.

After a while, we take our seats and the rest of the guests join us.

The aroma tantalizes and makes our mouths water. The food as we expected is scrumptious, rich in flavor with exotic seasonings. The blend of French and Tunisian traditional dishes round out the menu. Satisfied sounds fill the air as much as the din of conversation and laughter.

"How was your day, *Mon Cœur?*" Leonie asks between bites.

"It was good. A couple of surprises. But all is good. Let's enjoy our dinner and I'll tell you later," I respond.

Leonie eyes me skeptically.

"It was fine! No bad news." I say. "I promise, Caramel Bonbon."

She nods and turns to Luc, who whispers something in her ear. They laugh and get back to eating.

Josy's delicious double-chocolate soufflés are a hit for the desert. No one can resist the tasty treats. Including Leonie, who gets a dollop of fresh cream on the corner of her mouth. Without hesitating, I kiss it off and kiss her lips when she laughs.

Her amber eyes glitter in the low light, just like her namesake feline. Her beauty captivates me. I'm not a wuss. But Leonie makes me weak.

As if reading my thoughts, she turns to me and winks.

LEONIE

My Adonis is a piece of art that rivals Michelangelo's sculpture of David. One chiseled arm thrown over his face to block the morning sun coming through the windows. Its rays of light slant across his powerful chest and eight-pack abs, highlighting the happy trail of dark hair. Even lying flaccid and against his thigh, his massive dick with its bulbous head, veins, and heavy balls makes my mouth water. His thick thighs and muscular calves stretch out beneath the silk sheet.

I satisfy myself by sketching his sleeping form. So peaceful and at rest. No concerns for the pretrial investigation to worry him in his slumber.

One more week and it starts. I know he's stressed by it. But keeping high spirits to avoid me worrying. I've resolved myself to the fact we can only do what we can and not allow a negative thought to disturb us. Roger is innocent. That's my focus.

For now, I'll take advantage of his rest to capture his beauty.

The five o'clock shadow along with his mussed, collar-length hair emphasize his sex appeal. His sensuous full lips and long eyelashes make any woman jealous. Balanced out by his sculpted cheeks and jaw add a decidedly masculine edge to his features. No mistaking Roger is anything but all man.

My charcoal pencil flies across the sketch pad. I want to note as many details as possible before he awakes. I plan to make a painting as a gift to him for our wedding. We can hang it in our bedroom. My eyes only—mine!

I'm so distracted by my task of getting the draping of the sheet just right, I don't notice him lift his arm and open his eyes. That is until in one swift move he swoops over and zerbets my neck. I swat at him with the pad to no avail.

When his no longer flaccid dick bumps against my belly, I know I won't finish my sketch today. I drop the pad to the floor and give in to his ministrations with a sigh of contentment.

"Good morning, Pretty Kitty," he murmurs, his lips tickling my sensitive skin. "What were you doing?"

His sudden nip to my neck makes me squeal in pain and pleasure.

Merde!

"Ahhh… Nothing," I moan.

"Wrong answer, Pretty Kitty!" Roger says.

He begins to zerbet and tickle me.

I laugh and try to fight him off fruitlessly. He's relentless. I surrender and let him have his way with me.

The zerbets turn to open-mouthed kisses and the poking fingers begin to prod my core. I'm already wet for him. My sexual needs have increased once again. I could complain. But why, when it's so worth it?

"Is this all for me, Pretty Kitty?" He asks, slipping two of his long digits deep inside of my pussy. "Have you been thinking about me all this time?"

I gasp when he flicks my engorged clit, then pinches it.

His baritone voice thrums in my ear, "Answer me, Pretty Kitty."

Without hesitation, I answer yes. My reward, Roger begins to finger fuck me in earnest, driving his fingers in and out. Each thrust brushes my G-spot and I lift my hips for more friction. My orgasm is within reach. I just need—

"*Non! Non!*" I wail when Roger removes his fingers and sits back on his haunches.

He tilts his head and stares at me as he puts his drenched fingers to my lips. He raises his eyebrow in silent demand.

Immediately, my little pink tongue darts out to lick each finger. I moan at the sweet taste and musky scent of my pussy juices. Once they're clean, I suck on them one by one, challenging Roger with an intense, seductive stare of my own.

He reacts by stroking his swollen cock with his other hand, rubbing the pre-cum over the tip.

"You want something to suck, Pretty Kitty?" He growls, squinting at me with darkened slate-gray eyes.

I nod and murmur yes around his fingers.

He pulls them free with a pop. Then stands on our bed holding the trellis canopy as he looks down at me.

I rise to my knees, then sit back on my heels with my palms on my thighs. His throbbing dick at level with my mouth.

Roger nods and taps my lips with his tip until I open up. He glides to the back of my throat. Then withdraws. Lazily, he repeats the movement as he watches my reaction. When I moan for more, he increases his pace and proceeds to fuck my throat.

I take every inch and beg for more with moans that vibrate along his length.

Roger throws his head back and roars his release.

Thick jets of his cum shoot down my throat, straight to my stomach. So turned on by his climax, I stroke my clit and drive my fingers into my sopping wet pussy as I seek my release. His last thrusts culminate in an orgasm that rips down my tingling spine and makes my toes curl. I get off as much from my climax as I do from causing him to explode. Roger's dick falls from my mouth as I wail in wild abandon.

He drops to his knees and kisses me passionately. Our tongues seek the other out and tangle as the kiss deepens.

Still recovering from my mind-shattering orgasm, my body trembles and I whimper.

Roger cups the back of my head with one hand and my

ass with the other, locking me in place. We kiss until our lips swell and we fall apart, panting for breath.

He smiles at me and brushes a lock of damp hair out of my eyes.

"Good morning, my love," he murmurs as he strokes my cheek, his gray eyes full of love.

I close mine and lean into his magical touch.

"LEONIE, you're doing well, and The Twins are growing at the appropriate rate. They'll gain more weight each week from now until your delivery."

I'm too busy watching our boys blink to pay attention to Dr. Berger. Their activity seen on the monitor beats whatever he's saying. I chance a glance at Roger and see him grinning from ear to ear at his sons. I squeeze his hand and he smiles down at me and kisses my forehead.

"You're in your thirty-third week or eighth month. So I want you to get your rest, move slower to avoid clumsiness, and continue your pranayama to help with shortness of breath. Do you have questions for me?" Dr. Berger asks, glancing between Roger and me.

"No."

"*Non.*"

We answer in unison and everyone laughs.

"All right, then. I'll see you in two weeks. Just monitor yourself and call me should you have any concerns," Dr. Berger finishes before he and the nurse leave the room.

Then he turns at the door.

"I'll leave some pamphlets for you with the receptionist. They offer significant information on breastfeeding and ways to connect with your babies before they're born," he adds.

Roger and I thank him, and they leave.

"Well, *Maman*, only a few more weeks to go! Are you ready?" Roger asks as he helps me get down from the examination table.

Once I'm on my feet, I cup his face and smile.

"I am so ready! *Et toi, Papa?*" I ask.

He grins again and responds, "Absofuckinglutely! It's time I hold them after you've had them for so long!"

We laugh, and I get dressed. With my sizable belly, it's all about Diane von Furstenberg silk wrap dresses and Lanvin wedge heels—classic and chic.

On our way out, we pick up the pamphlets. We settle in our new Rolls-Royce Phantom Extended. Roger custom ordered it since I had difficulty getting in and out of the too high Cullinan and too low DB7 Vantage. I felt like Goldilocks trying different automobiles until I found one that fit!

I skim through the pamphlets and stop at the one on naming your baby. We hadn't discussed names yet. At first I was nervous thinking about my mother's experiences. But now that I'm so close, it's time we decided on names for The Twins.

I hand the pamphlet to Roger and watch for his reaction.

His eyes widen as he reads the title. Then he shifts in his seat to look me directly in the eye.

"Are you sure?" He asks with a hopeful expression on his handsome face.

"Absofuckinglutely!" I mimic his earlier word choice.

He kisses me and flips through the pamphlet.

"What do you have in mind?" Roger questions as he holds my hand in his reassuring grip.

I take a moment to think about it. I'm the last of my Beaulieu family line. I'm sure my father had hoped for a son to carry on the name. After their difficulty in conceiving, then not being able to have more children, it left him with a girl. When Roger and I marry I intend to take his name. So Beaulieu will drop from my name, too.

An idea forms.

"I'd like their middle names to be Beaulieu. A symbolic way to carry on my family's name," I respond.

Roger tilts his head in thought. Then he focuses his intense stare on me for what seems like forever.

"That's a wonderful way to honor your father and to keep your family's name going," he says smiling.

Relief rushes over me, and I relax back into the cushy leather seat.

"What about first names?" He asks. "I was thinking something French would remind them of their heritage. They'll have the Steele name, so it would be respectful to have a name from your family, even beyond Beaulieu."

Tears blur my vision—damn hormones—at his suggestion. Roger is an Alpha male who's confident in himself so much he doesn't have the need to force his dominance in the naming of our sons.

"Aw, babe, I didn't mean to upset you. Don't cry," he croons as he leans over the armrest to cup my face. "Think about it. We can speak with your parents for their input. Okay, my love?"

I can only nod, too caught up in the emotions of seeing my babies so lively and being so close to term.

Roger's soothing voice murmurs words of love all the way back to the *Manoir*.

"I LOVE the idea of Beaulieu as their middle names. But you could name them Beau and Lieu, too!"

My mother cracks up at her own joke, and I join in.

We are so similar as we sit next to each other on the sofa in the living room in our East Wing. My parents spend more time here, so I don't have to walk so far to get to the bedroom should I need a nap.

We just finished lunch and shared the latest ultrasound images and our ideas for The Twins' names.

"*Mais non*," my father responds with a grimace. "Not at all."

He mutters about the destruction of our family's name and shakes his head.

"Do you want them to have the same first letter or similarities of some sort?" Shelley asks as she holds a set of images. "They are too cute!"

I cock my head to the side as I ponder the question.

Deep in thought, I bite the corner of my lower lip. Then I shake my head.

"Not necessarily. I don't want them to get confused. They need their own identities, too. That's what the pamphlet mentions on twins," I respond, handing the pamphlet to Shelley.

"Guy, do you have family members you'd like to honor?" Morgan asks as he glances over her shoulder at the pamphlet.

We talk some more about the names. Different ones pop up along with their meanings. Guy means wide. Leonie means brave as a lion. My parents named me that since they said I looked like a lioness with a head full of mahogany hair when I was born and because I was so brave to make it to full term. Beaulieu means lovely place. So meanings are important to us.

I rack my mind thinking of the best names. Inspiration hits when my gaze meets Roger's intense gray eyes.

"Rodolphe *et* Gaspard!" I shout.

Everyone turns to me, surprised by my outburst. Then they laugh.

"Ooookay… And why those names?" Roger asks between chuckles.

"Well, we should include you in some way, as should I since they come from us. So, Rodolphe means famous wolf; I call you *Mon Loup*, my wolf. And Gaspard means—"

"A treasure bearer, *Mon Trésor*!" My father claps his hands and rises to hug me. "So thoughtful, Leonie!"

"Rodolphe Beaulieu Steele and Gaspard Beaulieu

Steele!" Roger declares as he kneels before me and kisses my belly.

As if in response, two kicks or punches poke me, and Roger laughs when he feels them, too.

"You like your names, my sons?" He asks, stroking my belly on both sides.

They respond with more movement as I laugh. Dr. Berger wasn't kidding when he mentioned strong fetal movement at this stage of my pregnancy. They feel like David Beckham going for the winning goal during the World Cup Finals!

Roger peers up at me with such a heartfelt smile, I feel it in my very soul.

"Thank you, my love," he says in earnest. *"Merci beaucoup."*

ROGER

"*R*oger! Why did you sexually assault Delia Shaw?"

"No means no!"

"Roger Steele! *Honte à toi!*"

"Leonie! How can you marry a monster?"

"Leonie! This way!"

Fuck!

This is a damn media circus combined with a protest that's beyond fucked up. And this is only day one…

Albert and his legal team take the lead up the steps of the pretrial courthouse. Their mood is no nonsense and all business. They set the tone for us.

Sebastian and I flank Leonie, holding her arms as we move through the crowd held back by our security detail and the police. I feel her stiffen at the insults and accusations thrown at us. However, she keeps her head high and her back straight. My woman is no shrinking violet who simpers in the face of opposition. She's a fierce *Lion*.

The rest of our family and friends follow us. All Steeles; Guy and Josy; Lachlan and Lucien Jackson; Luc; Joel and Hettie; Blair, Billie, and Starr; Norman and Anita came out in a full force of support. Françoise, along with several other STEELE staff members join us in solidarity. Their presence is as much a comfort for me as it is for Leonie.

No one speaks while we proceed to the courtroom. The halls are full of people who turn in our direction as we pass. Our pace doesn't slow. We want to get in and settled quickly.

A flash goes off to our left. Followed by more as the media within the building take notice of our group.

More catcalls fill the already tense air.

Leonie squeezes my hand to reassure me when I bristle at a particularly offensive comment.

These people have zero knowledge of facts. Yet they judge and condemn me. The state of the world today assumes the man is guilty automatically. Some may be. But I am not. The immediate castigation angers me. I'm more determined to prove my innocence just to shut them the fuck up.

Finally, we reach the doors to the courtroom. More police officers stand guard to maintain control and to prevent overcrowding. They allow us to pass with nods.

Upon entering, the first person we see is Antonio Vasquez standing behind the claimant's table. He glares at me and places a supportive hand on Delia Shaw's shoulder. She shifts in her seat to glance at him. Then faces us when he indicates with the tilt of his chin our entrance.

For a brief moment, the real Delia shines through with a sneer directed at Leonie. The fleeting expression reveals her cocksure attitude and devious intent. In a blink, it's gone, replaced by a chaste, eyes downcast countenance. Then she widens her eyes and covers her mouth on a sob before she turns away slowly. Antonio pats her shoulder comfortingly and whispers in her ear.

If I hadn't seen her glare at Leonie, Delia's performance would have been believable—and the Academy Award for Best Actress goes to...

Sebastian huffs in response to Delia's dramatic behavior.

I agree, but remain silent, as does Leonie.

After I help her into her seat on the bench between her parents and mine, I join Albert and the legal team at the defendant's table. Not once do I glance at the other side. Instead, I maintain a neutral expression and face forward.

Game on.

At the call to order, the din of voices quiets and everyone stands. When the judge enters the courtroom, the solemnity of the situation hits me in the chest like a Mack truck.

Inwardly I curse the day I fought Antonio Fucking Velasquez. That slip in my control led to the creation of the damn internship program and subsequently to his and Delia's hiring as the first interns. A moment of weakness becomes a period of hell. Not just for me, but for my loved ones.

I have to force myself not to glance over my shoulder at Leonie and all who gather behind me. I know they believe in my innocence. Nonetheless, the embarrassment to my family and to our multigenerational multibillion-dollar company makes for a hard pill to swallow.

The proceedings start with an opening statement presented by Judge Favre as a summary of the claim and the parties involved. The magistrate outlines the timeline for the proceedings. He plans to convene eight times after today on alternating days over the next month. Today will give both sides the opportunity to make opening statements. With the investigation set to begin next week.

Delia's legal team presents their opening statement. They drone on to paint me as a sex maniac who preyed on Ms. Shaw—an innocent, trusting university student who earned her position as an intern. Her only mistake was being in the division run by a monster...

Her appearance would support her claim of purity with a navy blue conservative skirt suit, severe bun, and no makeup. Her curves no longer on display and her vivacious personality hidden behind a sorrowful persona.

It's hard to get a read on the judge. He sits stoically on his bench. Periodically during the claimant's statement, his eyes flick to me with an analytical stare. It's as though he can reach deep within me to find every bad thing I've done since childhood.

Damn. And I thought I had an intense gaze.

However, I don't flinch or change my facial expression. I know how to play the game, and I will not lose my control. Judge Favre can't pique me.

Rather than listening to their lies and get my blood pressure up, I focus on how my family and friends will celebrate the end of this farce. I envision us at the penthouse drinking Taittinger, then having dinner catered by Lucien with Josy's dishes and double-chocolate soufflés. I'd love to go to back to Capri and stay at our new villa—Lucien drove a hard bargain, but no price is too high for Leonie. However, in four weeks' time, she'll be too close to her expected delivery date to travel.

The thought of my sons increases my determination to finish this quickly. I don't want a blemish around their birth, no more than around our wedding. With Leonie at thirty-four weeks, she's close. Dr. Berger mentioned twins can arrive earlier than expected.

I tried to convince Leonie to stay home and not stress herself out being in the courtroom. But to no avail. She insisted her presence would make a difference: pregnant fiancée supports me despite the nasty accusations. Plus, she's famous and will have her supporters, too.

Her followers on social media constantly send direct messages and leave comments of encouragement. It's incredible the power of social media and the influence of those popular on it. Albert agrees it's a good idea for her to be present. As does everyone else.

Her parents' concerns mimic mine in that we don't want her to stress out. Leonie promised me she wouldn't overexert herself, and if she felt tired, she would return to the *Manoir*. Her health and our babies outweigh "appearances."

Albert rising from his seat cuts into my thoughts.

He presents our statement in a succinct, factual manner. Unlike the claimant's attorney, Albert completes his opening remarks in less than fifteen minutes. Even the judge seems to appreciate the brevity of Albert's words as Judge Favre's face relaxes a fraction.

He thanks both sides for their opening statements. Then he reminds everyone we will re-convene next week. He rises from his bench and exits the courtroom as we stand.

We wait until Albert and his team gather their paperwork before we leave. I walk past Delia. I refuse to pay her any attention. And it's obvious she's the type that lives for attention.

Leonie kisses me on the lips in full view of everyone. The sound of cameras clicking fills the room. She knows how to play the game, too.

We make our way back out to the waiting cars. Sebastian and I flank Leonie again as we move through the crowd. More insults and questions come at us from all directions. I squeeze Leonie's hand, and she nods slightly in acknowledgement. Sebastian mutters, "Assholes."

At last we get inside the four Mercedes-Benz Sprinters and pull away from the courthouse in formation. Albert suggested we lease the souped-up vans instead of driving our personal vehicles since strangers would view the license plates. We certainly don't want stalkers finding our homes. The damn drones and paparazzi are bad enough. We take a roundabout way back to the *Manoir* to avoid being followed.

I'm relieved today was a relatively short time. I reach for Leonie's hand and bring it to my mouth to kiss her fingertips gently. She smiles and takes off her glamour girl shades. Her amber eyes are tired. I curse to myself. She does not need this bullshit!

As if sensing my thoughts, Leonie offers a smile and strokes my cheek.

"Don't worry, *Mon Cœur*. We're all right"—she rubs her other hand across her belly—"No need to look so grave!"

"Leonie, next week you need to stay home—"

"*Non! Non!* I will not let you face that trollop's shit without me by your side! We are in this together, Roger Steele! I mean it!" She roars with her amber eyes flashing sparks, no longer weary.

The Lion will not back down.

"Fine, but you have to promise me truly you will not stay if you need to rest. If not, I will lock you in our bedroom..." I respond.

But Leonie only laughs at my threat, knowing it's an empty one. Although I would tie her to our bed with only enough length to get to the bathroom.

"Good luck with keeping Leonie away, Roger!" Lola laughs from the back row. "Her maternal instincts are on high right about now!"

Everyone joins in her laughter, including me. She speaks the truth.

We wait until we reach the *Manoir* and sit in the living room before we discuss the investigation. Albert gives his feedback along with his team. They pulled a report on the judge and found him to be stern and only interested in facts, not emotions. The statement made by Delia's legal team was full of emotion. While Albert's was all facts. He says it's a score for us.

My father and I ask more questions. But there's not much to go on at this point. The real action will occur next week. Albert suggests we enjoy the weekend, rest, and return ready for the tough part. He and the team leave, declining an offer to join us for an early dinner. Françoise also leaves and offers words of encouragement before they go.

The rest of the group heads to the dining hall—the larger eating area that harkens back to *Le Manoir Beaulieu*'s days of entertaining royalty in the larger space. The staff serves the meal prepared by their chef. Josy cooks on the weekends when she gives them the days off.

We dine on the scrumptious dishes and wines from their ancient cellar. No one discusses the proceedings. We opt to have a normal conversation with Harris teasing Haley about some mysterious project she's working on, and Hettie recounting Joel's time at their cake tasting with his allergic reaction to almond paste. Norman regales us with stories from his most renown matches, and Anita tells how he's a softy for their daughter Antonia. It amounts to a good time with loved ones.

* * *

"Nothing beats a stroll through the Bois de Boulogne on a sunny day," Leonie sighs.

We entered the park from a side gate of *Le Beaulieu Manoir* not detected from within the park. The *Manoir* is on the westernmost part of the outskirts of Paris in Neuilly-Auteuil-Passy. It's a majestic property with manicured park-like grounds, stables, tennis court, swimming pool and cabana, and a palatial mansion. They built the hamlet between the thirteenth and seventeenth centuries. Later, during the reign of Louis XV, it became a fashionable country retreat for French elites. The Beaulieu's twenty acres of land border Bois de Boulogne with parts of the acreage awarded to their ancestors by the monarch.

"It's a beautiful day. But not as lovely as you," I respond.

Leonie rolls her eyes at my sappy remark, and I laugh.

"Okay, okay! So, I'm not a poet. You've gotta give me some points for trying!" I add with a smirk.

She kisses my cheek and rests her head on my shoulder as we stop at the pond.

Children float sail boats on its surface while actual row boats glide by. The tranquil scene offers a respite to the bustling Paris streets.

Unconsciously, Leonie rubs her babies bump.

I can tell she's thinking about Rodolphe and Gaspard. I

move behind her and place my hands on top of hers as I lean my cheek against the crown of her head.

We stand in silence as we watch the children play and listen to their squeals of laughter. Their joy in the simple act of their boats skimming the water reminds me to just let go and allow the tide to take me.

Today, I can enjoy the ease of being with my love and taking time to connect with her and our sons. A simple stroll on a sunny day is just what I need.

LEONIE

"*L*eonie, you have a noticeable increase in your blood pressure. It's not from your pregnancy, as you have no other signs. It's stress related. How are you holding up with the investigation?"

I lower my gaze, upset with myself for letting the pretrial stress me out after I promised Roger I wouldn't. It's just been more than I expected, with the constant taunts and barrage of questions. And that's before we even get inside the courtroom where the real inquisition takes place.

Roger had to be in court this morning.

At this stage, it's super important I keep my prenatal appointments. So Lola came with me. I avoid her eyes when Dr. Berger announces my blood pressure and voices his concerns.

I just get so pissed seeing that fake ass hussy pretending to be so innocent! How can she cause all of this drama when there are women who actually face sexual predators and the women don't get an opportunity to be heard? Or they're not believed. It's not right on any level.

Sure, people have said I wasn't there, so how can I know for sure. Well, I wasn't there. But I know Roger. Yeah, that's what they all say... My response remains the same: I believe him and I trust him.

Delia, not at all.

She's flirted with him from the start in class and at his office. Then tried to castigate me for being Roger's girl-friend. All along she wanted him, and my relationship with him rankled her.

That nasty sneer she threw at me on day one in the courtroom was hardly the first time she hated on me because of Roger. Delia did the same thing when we were at human resources. She had the nerve to insinuate they hired me because of Roger.

Pathetic witch.

Now she's using the courtroom as her stage to play out this obsession across France and the United States. All because Roger doesn't want her.

It's just confounding how they ended up on the elevator together. No one can figure out what happened with the elevator controls no more than they could her ID badge accessing the executive floor.

That puzzle piece keeps me up at night. If only we can solve those issues, we would be in a better place.

So, yes, my blood pressure is elevated because of stress. Whose wouldn't be??

"—Leonie... Leonie?"

A tap to my shoulder disperses the turmoil swirling in my mind. I glance up at Dr. Berger, the nurse, and Lola. They're watching me expectantly.

"*Excusez-moi*. Please repeat your question," I say.

"For your health and the wellbeing of The Twins, you must not return to the courthouse," Dr. Berger says with finality.

I deflate and burst into tears. The emotions are overwhelming. I cover my face as the tears stream down my flushed cheeks.

Why? Why is this happening? Why now?

I HATE THAT HUSSY!

"I'M FINE, *Maman* and *Maman Aussi*. Really I am," I say as I lie in my bed at *Le Manoir*.

Lola insisted I return right after the prenatal visit. She sent text messages to my mother and Shelley. They left the courtroom and met us at the front door. The three of them promptly escorted me to my bedroom. Then they undressed me, put a nightgown on me, and tucked me in bed with pillows fluffed behind my back and legs.

"How's Roger? Did he see you leave?" I ask concerned their departure upset him.

My mother shakes her head, her ebony curly bob sways.

"*Non*. He didn't notice, and we didn't tell him. Only Your father, Morgan, and Sebastian know you're here."

Shelley takes my hand and nods.

"Don't worry about Roger. We need you to focus on yourself, Rodolphe, and Gaspard. High blood pressure is not good for any of you, especially so close to term," she says with concern in her chocolate brown eyes.

I nod and stroke my belly as I lean back against the abundance of pillows. My body calls for me to sleep. I let my eyelids drift close.

"How long has she been asleep?"

"It's been two-and-a-half hours. It exhausts the poor baby. Come, let's go to the living room so as not to disturb her rest."

"But is she all right??"

I shift my position towards the voices. They sound like Roger and Shelley. His voice laced with apprehension. I force my eyes open so he doesn't worry.

They're headed to the bedroom door.

"Roger," I call out softly.

He pivots and rushes to my side.

"Baby, how do you feel?" He asks as he sits on the bed and takes my hands in his firm grip.

I promised him I wouldn't lie. I glance away sadly because I am tired and I need a break. My mind wants to be strong for him, for us. But my body wins, and it demands I rest. No wonder I slept for so long.

Merde!

"Hey, it's okay, my love"—he cups my face to bring my

gaze back to him—"You, Rodolphe, and Gaspard need to take it easy."

I nod as tears fill my eyes.

"I told you once before, and I will repeat it again. You mean everything to me. You are irreplaceable, my love. Call me selfish. But I will not live without you, Leonie. And if you keep going on stressed and your blood pressure continues to elevate... I do not want to think of what can happen. I cannot lose you, ever."

Roger finishes his sentence in a husky whisper, his voice clogged with unshed tears. He leans his forehead against mine and closes his eyes as he squeezes my hands.

We sit in silence, absorbing one another's breath and gathering strength from our love.

"*Je t'aime aussi, Mon Amour,*" I whisper.

Roger sits back enough to look within the depths of my eyes. As he searches for any hint of me going against his wishes, I ease his fears.

"I promise I will stay here and rest. I won't return to the courtroom until it's time for the judge's determination," I say as I hold my hand up to stop him from interrupting me.

"I will be there on that day only. I will not leave you to face his decision without me," I finish.

Roger considers what I said. Then he nods.

"Fine. But you will use the rear entrance to avoid the craziness at the front. And no matter what he decides, you promise to stay calm?"

I nod.

"Words, Leonie. I will have your words," Roger demands.

Without hesitation, I respond.

"*Oui*, Roger. I promise, *Mon Cœur*."

"Good," he says, kissing my fingertips.

* * *

"Your numbers have improved exponentially, Mademoiselle Beaulieu! Monsieur Steele will be very pleased."

I smile at Nanny Grace.

As part of the deal of me staying at home, Roger insisted I have a nurse. I wasn't up for interviewing potential candidates. But then I remembered: Nanny Grace is a trained nurse.

She agreed to start earlier than the birth of Rodolphe and Gaspard. She comes over in the morning and stays until the evening. Throughout the day, Grace checks my vitals and records them in a log. Then she forwards them to Roger.

It gives him peace of mind. So I don't argue. He has enough to deal with the investigation and maintaining STEELE business as usual.

The company receives backlash in the media constantly. It's as though they can't wait to destroy the man and the company before they have any proof of wrongdoing. It's all based on speculation.

Being privately owned, it doesn't impact them as

severely. They pull on their deep roots and impeccable reputation developed over generations to overcome the image the media attempts to create.

Their marketing and public relations departments began campaigns to thwart any negativity. They highlight STEELE Foundation's work to build and manage attractive, affordable housing for urban, lower-income families led by Shelley. Their other philanthropic activities reinforce the company's connection with the community. Multiple interviews with prominent individuals and businesses fill the networks and publications on both continents daily.

As a result, STEELE hasn't lost partnerships. Some may have held off until after the decision. But contracts that were pre existing continue.

So if Roger isn't at the courthouse, he's at the office. Norman keeps him training to avoid him burning out and losing focus. "Don't lose your head, Steele!" Norman tells him. Roger still joins me for some of my mediation and yoga nidra sessions with Anita in my studio at the *Manoir*. All the disciplines blend to keep his mind and body at optimal performance.

I remind Roger how he insists I stay healthy, then he has to do the same.

"Yes, it will thrill him, Grace," I respond, just as pleased.

It's just the two of us here today. Everyone is at the courthouse. I told both sets of our parents to stand by Roger since I can't be there. Their presence is the closest I can get to supporting him at the moment.

"So what would you like to do now?" Nanny Grace asks as she puts away her log.

I consider my options: paint Roger's portrait, sketch more designs for the Lola's Coterie maternity line, or crochet another pair of booties—Nanny Grace taught me.

For years I've had such a busy schedule traveling all over the world for photo shoots and commercials, my interior design schoolwork, and events. I'm not used to being so still!

In the end, I opt to paint. While Roger isn't here, I can get more of it done without fear of him seeing it. He's forever surprising me with gifts, I want to do the same for him.

"I'm going to my art studio until it's time for lunch. Would you come and get me then? Once I start painting, I lose track of time," I answer.

Nanny Grace agrees and says she'll be in the library.

We part ways at the door to my sitting room.

Once in the art studio, I turn on my Seductress playlist for inspiration. The sensual songs combined with Roger's enticing form on the canvas and sketch pad get me going in no time.

The door chime cuts into my playlist—Harris outfitted it so I wouldn't miss a knock when I play music loud.

I glance at my mobile and notice three hours passed.
Wow!

The painting is nearly complete. Roger's likeness is unmistakable. My eyes roam over his beautiful body. I lick my lips as my gaze lands on his massive dick. So lifelike, I want to lick it all over. Yum!

Not wanting anyone to see him, I re-cover it with the tarp and call out for Nanny Grace to enter.

"It's time for lunch, Mademoiselle," she says.

Then she raises her eyebrow when she sees me stretching my neck.

"Have you been sitting still this whole time?" She asks.

"*Non*, I've moved around and did some stretches and leg pumps," I respond.

She nods and we leave the studio for the kitchenette's eating area.

My stomach growls as we near the tantalizing aromas of grilled wild-caught salmon and roasted vegetables. Dr. Berger wants me to eat salmon twice a week to increase my omega-3 fatty acid intake. The fish oils help with early development and postpartum depression. So I'm all for it.

After we eat, we head outdoors for a walk through the grounds as exercise. We stop by the stables and feed the horses some apples. I can't wait to see The Twins riding on the trails like I did as a child. They'll keep their ponies here and can have lessons. Maybe they'll take up polo.

Nanny Grace and I return to the main house. Along the way, I point out some memories from my childhood to her. She laughs at my clipping all the roses to make the biggest bouquet ever for my mother on Mother's Day. Instead of getting angry I botched her prized rose bushes, my mother smothered me in kisses and hugs.

That's what I want with my children. Wonderful

memories full of love and happiness. And I will be damned if I allow she who shall not named to ruin it!

I make up my mind to be extra careful over the next week and a half so I can be in tip-top shape to face that cow in the courtroom.

I can't wait to tell her, "Bye, Bitch!"

ROGER

"*A*ll rise... This court is now in session. The Honorable Judge Favre presiding. When each witness goes to the stand. Please state your name for the court."

Another day of testimonies by witnesses. Who knew so they would call many people before the judge for an incident that occurred between two individuals over less than twenty minutes in the dark?!

It's been weeks, and it drags on and on. Delia's legal team has a flair for dramatics as much as she does. They take hours to interview people. Drawing out answers. Recross examinations take place. Requests for additional time to review evidence. It's ridiculous.

It's also apparent they're in it for the money. Part of her petition involves monetary damages, including her legal fees covered by STEELE and me. It's obvious her attorneys plan to rack up billable hours, no matter how absurd they appear in the process. The circus extends beyond the frenetic scene outside to within the courtroom.

Although it feels more like the nine rings of Dante Alighieri's *Inferno* than the three rings under The Big Top of Ringling Bros. and Barnum & Bailey Circus...

The judge has to ask his questions. It takes time. But at least he's concise and the ringmaster.

Albert also stays within a reasonable amount of time. He's extremely thorough and puts doubt in any attempt by her team to paint me as a sexual deviant.

We've called character witnesses to support my defense. Business associates, leaders from nonprofit organizations, and STEELE staff have willingly come forward to dispute any claim of me being an aggressive predator. My reputation in business and in my personal life is impeccable.

Judge Favre interviews them, and his line of questioning is unbiased. Yet one can tell it's going in my favor. Delia's team is failing to provide suitable evidence for a prosecution determination.

Now it's time for the two of us to take the stand for questioning. It's the last step in the process before the judge announces his decision.

Albert and my legal team are confident it will be a positive outcome. I certainly hope so.

Leonie has been a real trooper. She's kept her promise to stay at the *Manoir* and rest. And it shows. Once again she's radiant and relaxed. It's as though a light switch flipped on within her. No longer are the golden flecks in her amber eyes flashing in warning. They're bright with happiness.

Next week she'll be thirty-six weeks. I can hardly believe it. Although her much larger belly proves she's close to the end of her pregnancy.

I'm pissed I missed her last prenatal visit with Dr. Berger. Thankfully, Lola went with her and heard his concerns about Leonie's blood pressure. If I had noticed my mother and Josy left the courtroom, I would have left too. I wouldn't have given a damn what the judge or Albert said.

The doctor's words scared Leonie more than anything I've said. So she's taken it to heart and keeps calm. Nanny Grace sends accounts of Leonie's vitals to me daily. The proof of her following doctor's orders keeps me sane. One less worry in my overcrowded mind.

Thoughts of getting back to Leonie, hearing about her day, and feeling my sons' movement make these long as fuck hours in the courtroom bearable.

When this is over, I swear we're taking a long vacation.

"ALL RISE... This court is now in session. The Honorable Judge Favre presiding. When each witness goes to the stand. Please state your name for the court."

Once the judge takes his seat after a break in the proceedings, he announces the witness testimony of Delia.

I ensure I plaster my most impassive expression on my face. No matter what she says or does, I will remain apathetic. My mantra of "I am innocent" runs on repeat in my mind. I take a cleansing breath and settle myself.

Delia, of course, came just as prepared as me.

Today she wears a somber charcoal gray skirt suit with a boxy fit and a crisp white shirt, black stockings, and basic black heels. Her brunette hair pulled up in a French twist draws attention to the trepidation in her eyes. Little to no makeup on her face. A simple pair of pearl studs adorn her ear lobes.

All she's missing is a book, and she'd look like a mousy elementary-school librarian.

Give me a fucking break. I nearly break form and snort in derision.

When Delia reaches the witness stand, she faces the bailiff and states her name softly with her eyes downcast.

He asks her to repeat her name louder, and she does a fraction.

I want to roll my eyes.

Delia takes the oath to tell the truth, then takes her seat. Her eyes scan the crowded courtroom. When her gaze lands on me, she flinches and sits back in the chair. Her gaze lowers to her lap where she wrings her hands anxiously.

"Are you all right, Ms. Shaw?" Judge Favre asks as he stares down at her from his bench.

She glances up from beneath her eyelashes and nods her head.

"Kindly speak your response, Ms. Shaw," the judge requests.

Delia responds yes, and he turns to his paperwork.

Great… Here we go.

"Mademoiselle Shaw, kindly tell us how it came about you were with Monsieur Steele on his private elevator?" Judge Favre inquires.

Once again she flinches, this time at my name, and darts her eyes in my direction.

"I… I was going…" Delia's voice trails off as she falters.

The judge peers down at her. Then tells her to take her time.

She responds how she's nervous, and the judge encourages her to take her time. She nods, then takes a moment before she continues in a somewhat stronger tone.

"I was on my way to the weekly Interior Design Team meeting. That morning, I… I had just found a discrepancy in the AutoCAD renditions for the new project in the sixth arrondissement," Delia starts.

She pauses to take a sip of water.

"They had the potential to ruin the structure of the building—"

Just like her legal team, Delia drones on about the computer-generated drawings instead of getting to the point. She takes what seems like forever to answer Judge Favre's question.

"—when I saw Mr. Steele in the lobby. I caught up with him, and he invited me onto his private elevator."

Delia shivers and sips more water.

That lying, scheming…

Like hell I "invited" her onto my private elevator! I tried to avoid her. Even going so far as to say I wasn't available!

Albert's hand opens and closes on his yellow legal pad atop our table.

Fuck!

It's his signal I need to check my control. I must have reacted in some way to Delia's blatant lies.

With a deep breath, I resettle myself and repeat my mantra.

Inhale, I am.

Exhale, innocent.

Pause.

Inhale, I am.

Exhale, innocent.

Pause.

"What exactly did Monsieur Steele say to you as an invitation?" Judge Favre asks after he takes notes.

Delia nods.

"He said, 'You can ride me. I mean ride with me... on my private elevator.' His words exactly, Your Honor," she responds, then glances down at her hands.

Murmurs fill the room as the crowd of spectators, media, and protestors react to her words. Or rather, my false ones.

I cannot believe her bullshit is going to fly! More fucking lies! And she's under oath!

Albert doesn't lose his cool. He merely makes a note on his pad. Then continues to listen to the inquisition.

The judge also writes on his pad. He maintains a

neutral expression the entire time. He sets his pen down and returns his gaze to Delia.

"Mademoiselle Shaw, kindly tell us what occurred once you were on Monsieur Steele's private elevator," Judge Favre inquires.

Delia swallows visibly. Then she reaches for the water pitcher to refill her glass. As she does so, her hand shakes, and water sloshes onto the railing around the witness stand. She emits a soft cry and searches around for something to wipe up the spill.

The judge calls for a five-minute recess and indicates the bailiff to get paper towels. He returns and helps Delia to clean up.

She's all "I'm so sorry" and "I'm just so nervous" that I want to dump the whole pitcher over her head.

Give me a fucking break already!

We resume, and Delia recounts the encounter. Or rather, her version that's full of more damning lies.

"Mr. Steele followed me onto his private elevator. I could feel his breath on the back of my head, he was so close... Before I could speak, he stared at me from my head to my toes. I felt as though he were undressing me... It reminded me of the time I was in his office—"

Delia shivers and clutches her arms.

"I felt uncomfortable. But you see, I was an intern, and this was my chance to prove myself worthy of a full-time position! So I just ignored his creepy stare and told him about the AutoCAD renditions. Suddenly the lights went out! I thought he did it on purpose, so I backed away from him. When the lights came back on, he was closer to me..."

Again she trails off and glances down at her hands, now pale in a death grip. She stops speaking.

"Ms. Shaw, do you need a moment?" Judge Favre asks.

Delia shakes her head and wipes her nose as she sniffles. When she raises her head, her eyes have tears in them.

What the fuck?!

"Judge Favre, Your Honor?" Her lead attorney calls out.

The judge glances at him.

"Judge Favre, my client is under duress. The events traumatized her when they happened and continue to plague her with nightmares. As you can see, she's shaken. We would like to request a recess for an hour, Your Honor," her attorney requests.

The judge turns to Delia and asks, "Ms. Shaw, do you require some time before we proceed?"

She nods tearfully, then answers verbally when he cocks his head.

"The court will resume in one hour," Judge Favre proclaims.

"ALL RISE... This court is now in session. The Honorable Judge Favre presiding. When each witness goes to the stand. Please state your name for the court."

Delia takes the stand again, and the bailiff reminds her she's still under oath.

Like that does any damn good...

"Mademoiselle Shaw, the question again is that you kindly tell us what occurred once you were on Monsieur Steele's private elevator," Judge Favre reminds her.

Delia takes a deep breath and sits taller. Then she turns and points at me.

"Roger Steele tried to rape me."

Fuck the rings, all hell springs loose.

The room explodes in a melee of shouts from the protestors calling me a rapist to the clicks of photographers' cameras to the spectators' shocked gasps. The commotion draws the attention of the police stationed outside of the courtroom.

They rush in from all doors and take command as Judge Favre and the bailiff shout for order in the court. More officers enter and start to remove protestors, the loudest and most violent in the crowd. My security detail stands at the gallery railing to prevent anyone from harming my family and me.

I glance at Delia.

For a second, our eyes meet. The hateful glare she throws at me sends chills through my body.

This bitch is out for revenge. She doesn't give a damn what lies she tells or who she hurts in the process.

In a blink of an eye, the expression disappears from her face. Then she brings her hands up to hide behind them.

My resolve for proving my innocence hardens further.

Albert tells me to remain seated and not to look at Delia or her legal team. He stands beside me on alert.

Half an hour later, the courtroom gallery clears of

everyone except for the people present to support Delia and me.

Judge Favre calls for the proceedings to continue with Delia expounding upon her accusation. He asks her to recount what happened and not for her conclusion. He explains the difference to her, and she continues.

Delia puts a negative spin on every action that took place:

The lights come back on; I'm on top of her.

I reach out to help her; I groped her breast.

I try to prevent her from falling when the elevator plummets; I slammed her against the wall and made her hit her head.

She holds onto my neck; she scratched me to make me let go of her.

I try to comfort her since she claims to be claustrophobic by patting her back; I tore her camisole to feel her up.

She fingers my hair and pulls it; she fought me off and yanked my hair out.

She falls backwards yanking my tie and pulling me off balance to fall with her; I pushed her to the floor and ripped her stockings and skirt in a frenzy to fuck her.

I use my left hand to brace my fall and sprain it; she used a self-defense move to bend my wrist backwards.

I scramble away from her; She kneed me in the balls to stop me from raping her.

She's sprawled out on the floor of the elevator; the impact of the blow I inflicted when I slammed her head on the wall caused her to suffer a concussion and lose consciousness.

Then her legal team jumps in with "evidence" collected at the hospital: my hair and pieces of my skin beneath her fingernails; one of my shirt buttons in her hand; bruising on her inner thighs consistent with force used by a knee to separate her legs.

By the time Delia's testimony and her attorney's questioning conclude, I doubt my damn myself.

Shit, did it happen that way for real?

Hell to the fuck no!

Again, Delia has it in for me, and she's going to the extreme.

It's my word against hers since the cameras failed along with the functioning of the elevator. Besides, it was dark. They're not programmed with night vision capabilities.

I can't believe this bullshit.

My face heats. My armpits tingle. My head pounds with an instant headache caused by the tension that racks every cell in my body.

This is beyond fucked up.

Despite it all, I maintain my stoic expression. I've trained my sense of control for years, and I rely on every lesson to keep my shit together. I cannot crack.

Judge Favre asks Albert if he wants to question Delia. He does.

"Ms. Shaw, would you like a moment before we begin?" Albert asks her while he sits at our table. "Perhaps a sip of your water?"

Taken aback by his kind offers, Delia's eyes widen and she glances at her legal team.

I don't follow her gaze. Rather, I look straight ahead.

"Uh... No... Er... Thank you," she responds, eyeing him warily.

"Fine. Ms. Shaw, I do not wish for you to relive the encounter. But I do wish for you to clarify some comments you made," Albert says.

Then he turns to the judge, "Your Honor, I would like to hand this deposition transcript to Ms. Shaw."

The judge allows Albert to approach the witness. She takes the document, and he points to a page.

I realize it's from the cover-your-ass file Albert insisted we create immediately following the incident.

He swiftly and summarily refutes all of her statements with her own words. He plays the video testimony from both Delia and me as further evidence of the encounter. By the time he's through, Delia's face is the one that's red.

Albert thanks her for her time and returns to his chair.

Thank fuck!

Judge Favre calls for a thirty-minute recess and exits the courtroom.

UPON HIS RETURN, the judge calls me to the witness stand.

I state my name and take my oath in a clear voice.

Once I'm seated, Judge Favre peers down at me. Then he asks me to recount the encounter from Delia approaching me in the lobby to the elevator doors re-opening. I answer honestly and succinctly. My tone remains even and strong.

I do not waiver. Not even after her attorney attempts to draw my anger by insinuating I wanted Delia because I was no longer attracted to Leonie because of her pregnant state. I nearly laughed as I recalled we had incredible sex right before the nightmare with Delia occurred!

Albert however was having none of it. He demands Delia's attorney censured for his obtuse line of questioning.

Judge Favre agreed.

Of course. Leonie could be pregnant with sextuplets and any man would still want her.

When Delia's attorney finishes his questions, Albert begins.

Once again, he quickly points out errors in Delia's testimony through answers I provide in response to his questions. He makes an exceptional case for my defense and ends in less than fifteen minutes.

Judge Favre calls for closing arguments.

Delia's attorney speaks first, and he lasts as long as his opening remarks. Then Albert presents a summation on par with his Harvard Law School Juris Doctor degree —superb.

Judge Favre announces he will make his determination at our last session in two days' time. Then he adjourns court for the day.

I take a cleansing breath and repeat my mantra.

Inhale, I am.

Exhale, innocent.

Pause.

Inhale, I am.

Exhale, innocent.

Pause.

Thankful to head home to Leonie and my sons at last.

LEONIE

*R*oger tosses and turns all night.

I tried to persuade him to stay in bed with me. But he didn't want to disturb my sleep. Well... I guess he doesn't realize I can't sleep if he can't.

Instead, from our bed, I watch him on the sofa. His long limbs are not at all comfortable as he flips from one side to the other. At one point, his blanket falls off. I wait a moment to see if he will reach for it. But he doesn't. So I pick it up and drape it back over his sleeping form.

I sit on the chair and watch him for a while. I must have dozed off because I awake in bed, and Roger isn't on the sofa. With a groan from the pain in my achy back, I get up and follow the sound of water to the bathroom.

Roger stands at the vanity, shaving his face. I lean on the doorjamb and watch my man. When he nicks his chin for the second time, I go to him.

"Hey, babe. I didn't know you were awake. It's early, you

need to go back to sleep"—he raises his hand to stop me from speaking—"And the chair is no place for you to get your rest."

He quirks his eyebrow at me, and I roll my eyes.

"Nor is the sofa for you, Monsieur Steele. You have a big day today. You need your rest, too."

I take the razor from his hand and push him away from the sink. I squeeze between him and the counter.

Roger lifts me and settles me on top of it.

"Now, allow me, Monsieur Steele," I say as I shave his face.

Roger closes his eyes and rests his hands on either side of my hips.

Silently, with a steady hand, I remove the morning's stubble from his cheeks and chin. Careful not to nick him, I rinse the razor and apply fresh shaving cream each time. When I shave all the hair, I put a warm wet cloth over his face. Then pat it.

Roger rinses the rest of the cream off his face and kisses me on the tip of my nose.

"*Merci beaucoup*, Kitten," he says with a smile, his gray eyes shine like liquid platinum in his gorgeous face.

I cup his chin and pull his lips to mine. *Non*, a peck on the nose will not do. No, sir!

Roger covers my mouth with his and takes control of the kiss as he angles my head just so. Our tongues dance, and I moan in appreciation.

"What do you want, Pretty Kitty?" He asks huskily.

"You, Roger, I want you, *Amoureux*," I purr, tilting my

neck to give him better access as he kisses from my ear to my collarbone.

"Mmmmmm... Then you shall have me, Pretty Kitty," he growls.

Roger grips my hips and moves my ass closer to the edge. He slides his hands up my thighs, taking my silk negligee with him. He lowers his mouth to my puckered nipple and suckles it until I writhe on the counter.

He chuckles against my skin.

"Eager are you?"

I huff and put my fingers in his hair to pull his mouth back to my sensitive bud. Then I groan when he nips it into his wet mouth.

"Yeeesss," I hiss as I drop my head back and lean on my other hand.

Roger continues to lavish attention on my breasts.

My pussy clenches on air with each tug. I need more! I sit forward and cup his heavy balls in the palm of my hand, kneading them.

He growls and thrusts his hips in sync with my motions. Roger loosens the tie on his black silk pajamas, and they slip down his hips to the floor. He takes the base of his dick in hand and shifts me forward until he impales me with his massive shaft.

We groan in unison as he enters me. Then take a few breaths as my pussy stretches to accommodate his girth.

Our rhythm is slow and deep. We allow our bodies to connect and speak for us. Only our moans fill the air along with the scent of our lovemaking.

Roger's cock swells, and I squeeze my inner muscles to draw out his release. With a shout he cums, and I follow right behind with a strangled cry.

"I love you, Leonie," he murmurs against my neck.

I shiver and bury my face in his hair.

"I'M READY!"

This is the fastest I have ever gotten ready in my nearly thirty-three years of life. Today is the determination day, and I refuse to be late! I will be by Roger's side to face that trollop once and for all.

I even went to see Dr. Berger yesterday to provide proof to Roger that I listened and stayed calm. My vitals and the stage of my pregnancy impressed both. At thirty-six weeks or nine months, The Twins have dropped and my waddle has increased.

And I'm going to waddle my ass to that courthouse and strike a fierce pose for that bitch.

Maman Lionne is ready for you!

My parents turn in surprise at my sudden arrival.

To accommodate my larger belly, I opted for a three-quarter-sleeved knit mididress in gray—the color of Roger's eyes—and a patterned silk Hermès Giant Scarf over my shoulders. A pair of gray Lanvin wedge heels and my hair in a sleek low ponytail round out my outfit. I pull my glamour girl Tom Ford shades from my Himalayan Birkin and head for the front door.

"Now, Leonie, you must promise to let us know if you get upset," my father says once we're in the Sprinter.

"*Oui, Mon Trésor*, no matter what happens, you must remain calm!" My mother adds. "The Twins are close to term. *Oui?*"

I agree and smile brightly at them.

No need to mention how my lower back has been bothering me since Roger and I made love earlier. He was gentle. So, I'm sure it's nothing to worry about.

Eric drives us around the back of the courthouse. Roger is right, the crowd stays in the front. He left an hour ago with everyone else to serve as a distraction. He didn't want the crowd's jostling and catcalls to bother me.

My security detail scans the area before we exit the Sprinter. Once they give the all clear, we climb out of the van. My father holds my arm as they escort us up the flight of steps. The police officers at the doors allow us entry.

A few people stand about the hallways as we cross through to the courtroom. But it appears the majority are inside or on the streets since it's the last day of the investigation. Everyone wants a front-row seat.

Whispers follow us. But I keep my head held high. There's no way I'm letting them get me upset, especially before I can get to Roger.

We keep as brisk a pace as we can considering my new runway walk...

Finally, we arrive at the doors. The guards open them and we step through.

My eyes go directly to Roger's table. He faces forward with his back ramrod straight.

The change in the crowd's murmurs at my appearance and the whispers of my name make him shift in his chair.

Our eyes lock. Everything and everyone fades to the background. Only Roger matters now.

I smile at him, and he smiles back.

Antonio also turns to look my way. I give him a withering stare, and he shrinks.

Asshole.

I spot Delia next.

She sits at the claimant's table attempting to look prim in a navy dress and bun.

Yeah, right, honey. I know you.

Delia must sense my stare. She glances over her shoulder, and our eyes connect. Hers widen at the sight of me since I hadn't been here in almost two weeks.

Rumors swirled that I left Roger; I gave birth and left Paris; Roger dumped me... Utter garbage. I wouldn't doubt it if she and her legal team started the lies. From the bit Roger shares with me about the investigation or I glean from Lola, Delia lied through her teeth during her testimony.

Non, hussy! I'm here and not going anywhere!

"Leonie, come sit here, sweetheart."

I shift my gaze from the liar to Shelley.

"Merci, Maman Aussi," I answer as I double kiss her cheeks in greeting.

In my periphery, I notice Delia frown and face forward.

Good!

As I take my seat between my parents and Morgan and Shelley, I wave at our family and friends. Lola, Sebastian and the rest of the Steele clan, the Jacksons, Joel and Hettie, Norman and Anita, Luc, Blair, Billie, and Starr, and Françoise and some STEELE employees gather in support.

Moments later, the bailiff calls the court to order, and the judge enters the room.

My stomach flips with worry. I close my eyes and send a silent prayer for Roger and STEELE cleared of these false claims.

Delia just wants attention and money. None of what she said holds an ounce of truth.

I glare at the back of her head. Then shift my focus to the judge.

He's unreadable. His eyes scan the crowd as he waits for silence. Once the gallery is quiet, he gazes at Delia, who squirms, then at Roger, who sits tall.

My mother and father take my hands in theirs and squeeze.

I don't realize how tense I am until I startle at their touch. My eyes stay riveted on Judge Favre as he reads his summation of the case.

He's so slow.

Mentally, I push him to read faster. Just give us the answer already!

"Because of the testimony provided by both the plaintiff and the defendant, the evidence brought forth, and of my careful deliberation, I determine Roger Steele and STEELE International, Inc. should—"

"AAAH… *MON DIEU!!*"

* * *

Roger & Leonie's Story Continues: *Justify My Desires*

Turn the page for the Steele Family, Author's Note, and Preview of *Justify My Desires*

THE STEELE FAMILY

STEELE INTERNATIONAL, INC

Multigenerational, multibillion-dollar business luxury real estate development and management corporation

Headquarters & Family's Primary Residences:

The STEELE Tower, New York City

A modern, gray-tinted glass fifty-seven story mixed-use skyscraper on southwest corner of Fifty-Seventh Street and Fifth Avenue within Billionaires' Row

Global Offices:

- The United States of America (New York City, New Jersey, Chicago, California, Miami, Las Vegas)
- The Caribbean (St. Maarten, St. Barth's, St. Lucia)
- The French & Italian Rivieras (Nice, Cannes, Positano, Capri)
- Monaco (Monte Carlo)
- The United Arab Emirates (Abu Dhabi, Dubai)

STEELE FOUNDATION: A STRONG AND SUPPORTIVE HOUSE

Builds and manages attractive, affordable housing for urban, lower-income families

Available for download at **bit.ly/STEELEFamily**

Author's Note

Thank you for reading Part II of Roger and Leonie's sexy, sizzling romance! I hope that you enjoyed the continuation of their passionate love affair. If so, I'd love to hear your thoughts, please share a review at **bit.ly/ CLBooksSI4Review** and tell your friends.

Click below for the stunning conclusion for this darling duo:
Justify My Desires Roger & Leonie Part III

At **CharmaineLouise.com** take the *Four types of lovers. Which are you?* **Quiz** to match your Sexy Fantasy: sub, Voyeur, Dominatrix, or Dominatrix sub Switch.

Follow me on social media including my CLBooks Coterie Fan Club below or on your favorite channels below and subscribe to my newsletter at **bit.ly/ CLBooksNewsletter** for a **Free Book**.

Fulfill Your Desires.

xoxo

Charmaine Louise

bookbub.com/authors/charmaine-louise-shelton

facebook.com/CharmaineLouiseBooks

instagram.com/charmainelouisebooks

tiktok.com/@charmainelouisebooks?

goodreads.com/charmainelouisebooks

STEELE International, Inc.
A Billionaires Romance Series Book 5

Justify My Desires Roger & Leonie Part III

Click on the link below or visit books2read.com/u/
47YwKA to get your copy.

Justify My Desires Roger & Leonie Part III

Books in the Series:

Discover My Desires Sebastian & Lola Prequel
(Available Exclusively to Subscribers)

COMING NEXT: JUSTIFY MY DESIRES ROGER & LEONIE PART III

"*Because of the testimony provided by both the plaintiff and the defendant, the evidence brought forth, and of my careful deliberation, I determine Roger Steele and STEELE International, Inc. should—*"

"*AAAH... MON DIEU!!*"

"*Qu'est-ce que—*"

"*Oh, Mon Trésor!!*"

"*Leonie!! What's wrong?!*"

"ROGEEERRR!!!"

My fiancée Leonie Beaulieu's ferocious roar of my name snaps me back to the Parisian hospital's bustling operating room and out of the hell of the pretrial courtroom.

What an emotionally charged day...

From making love to Leonie so intense it felt as though our souls blended to the rollercoaster ride of the court-room right before the pretrial judge's determination on the prosecution of the case and now she's in labor.

Damn.

WHOMEVER SAID money is the root to all evil wins the gold medal.

Delia Fucking Shaw wanted more than my billions. She had her sights set on the ultimate prize… Roger Steele of the media-dubbed STEELE Quaternity.

They consider my three brothers—Sebastian, Malcolm, Harris—and I the most sought-after of the world's eligible billionaires. Although not a part of the group, Haley, our youngest sibling and the fraternal twin to Harris, has a multibillionaire status that attracts men to her like bees to honey. Not that we allow just anyone access to our baby sis —no fucking way!

I should have known Delia was up to more than simple flirting with the professor when I guest lectured one of my then girlfriend Leonie's classes at the Paris American Academy.

As my family's multigenerational multibillion-dollar company STEELE International, Inc.'s President of Resi-dential Properties Division, Leonie thought I would impart some of my knowledge on her classmates. She was in her last year for her interior design bachelor's degree.

Wanting to help her make a good impression on her professor, I agreed.

Leonie has always had an eye for design. The combination of being the world-renowned megamodel *The Lion* for almost nineteen years and as the daughter of an old, wealthy Parisian merchant family that travels seeking antiques, antiquities, and fabrics instilled in her a love for the aesthetics. Transitioning into interior design has been her dream for years. And in any way I could help her, I promised I would.

Unfortunately, it came at a price.

During the class, Delia flirted with me, and Antonio Velasquez flirted with Leonie. I gave him the look of death, and he backed off. Or so I thought...

The dick didn't learn his lesson then. So I had to teach him at their end-of-the-semester reception when I caught him kissing my girlfriend—MINE!

My training with a former heavyweight boxing champion primed me to knock Velasquez on his ass and then some.

Which led to restitution as a vast sum of money for him and a STEELE internship program with the Paris American Academy for two of their students in perpetuity. Unluckily, the first two recipients turned out to be none other than Delia and Velasquez. Pain in my ass number one and pain in my ass number two—initially in either order.

Now, Delia takes the top spot.

Although I'm sure she would have preferred the bottom

position with her writhing beneath me... Billions and a ten-inch cock.

Despite my best efforts to elude her unwanted attention, she managed to get at me twice.

The first with an unannounced and unapproved visit to my offices on the executive floor of STEELE Paris. My take-no-shit personal assistant, Françoise Faucher, thwarted Delia's double entendre comments and advancement. Françoise made it her personal mission to escort the intern from my offices to security for the reprogramming of her ID card access and to human resources for a refresher in protocol with the president.

The proverbial nail in the coffin came in the form of Delia insisting I speak with her on my way to the Interior Design Team's weekly meeting, at which she was a participant.

Against my better judgement, I allowed her to ride up to the conference room on my private elevator with me. Said elevator oddly malfunctioned, and we were stuck together in the dark for twenty minutes—no cameras, no help, nothing but the two of us. No one knows how the hell my elevator went on the fritz.

Delia's interpretation of the events on the elevator differs so greatly from mine. She filed a legal petition. A petition against me for sexual assault and harassment and against STEELE International, Inc. as co-defendant with a civil claim for none other than... a vast sum of money.

Meanwhile, for the last eleven weeks, the love of my life

has had to cope with the stress of this bullshit while pregnant with our twin boys. Already struggling with the fear of her mother's experiences with multiple miscarriages before giving birth to Leonie and her parents' subsequent inability to ever have children again compounded by Delia Fucking Shaw.

So instead of having her water break under normal circumstances at her family's ancestral estate *Le Beaulieu Manoir*—where we're staying to avoid the rabid media and stalkers—it happened in the fucking pretrial courtroom. Surrounded by protestors, onlookers, Velasquez, and Delia, Leonie screamed in anguish from the contractions and the ensuing gush of amniotic fluid protecting The Twins.

Pandemonium broke out.

I gave zero fucks about Judge Favre's pronouncement. My baby was in pain, and I would be damned if I didn't go to her.

Without approval from the judge or STEELE General Counsel Albert Perry, who's representing me and the company, I rushed to Leonie's side.

The expression of fear and hurt on her beautiful face struck me in the gut like a sledgehammer. Her pitiful cries galvanized me.

My eldest brother Sebastian and I carried her between us while my other brothers, our male friends, and security detail cleared a path for us. With Lola Steele—Leonie's best friend and Sebastian's wife—leading the way, we exited out the back of the courthouse. Then we hurried into one of the Mercedes-Benz Sprinters I leased to transport everyone during the pretrial.

Starr Knight—Leonie's friend, yoga teacher, and doula—called her OB-GYN Dr. Pierre Berger. Starr confirmed he was on his way to the hospital as the five of us sped off. My trusted driver Eric Vogler maneuvered the crazy Parisian traffic to get us to the hospital in record time. Thankfully, Starr kept Leonie relatively calm during the ride.

Luc Montaigne—Leonie's mentor and friend and the multibillionaire CEO and Chairman of the Board of his family's multigenerational, global banking empire Banque Montaigne—once again used his considerable influence as the major benefactor of the hospital to garner approval for a custom suite. This after he procured Dr. Berger as her doctor.

When we found out Leonie was pregnant, Luc demanded the top OB-GYN attend to her. Not just of the hospital, but of all France. Since this is the most esteemed hospital in Paris, Dr. Berger has his affiliation with it and serves as their OB-GYN department director and a practicing physician.

No sooner had the nurses settled Leonie in her suite did Dr. Berger arrive with his team. An anesthesiologist, two pediatricians—one for each Twin—two labor and delivery nurses, an OB tech, and a nursery nurse followed him into Leonie's suite.

They went to work in prepping her for the first stage of pregnancy, pre-labor. Dr. Berger explained in twin pregnancies, it can take up to thirteen hours for her body to be ready for the actual delivery. He expected the first Twin within two hours after and the second Twin less than twenty minutes later.

Leonie was a lot less fearful now that she was in the hospital's safety and under the doctor's care. She may have been better prepared, but still in the throes of labor as she experienced acute contractions.

Her golden caramel complexion flushed rosy from the sensations overtaking her body. Her feline amber eyes glowered at my wolfish gray ones, while French curses spilled from her lush lips. Her ass-long mahogany waves once pulled in a sleek ponytail, now in one thick braid thanks to Starr.

She and Lola fussed over Leonie as Sebastian and I hovered around her bed. Soon the rest of our family and friends arrived from the courthouse. Leonie's mother Josy and my mother Shelley hurried to her side, hustling Sebastian and me right out of their way. Haley joined them at the foot of Leonie's bed as she massaged her feet and calves to comfort her.

Surrounded by the most important women in her life, Leonie braved the pre-labor stage for just over twelve hours. Now, the ferocious Lion is loose...

"ROGEEERRR!!!"

"Oh, mon Dieu!!! Aidez moi!!!"

She squeezes the fuck out of my hand.

I wince from the bite of pain, but persevere. If she has to go through contractions and all, I won't wuss out and will remain by her side.

At this stage, besides the medical team, Starr is the only person with us in the operating room. Dr. Berger moved Leonie from her suite to here since twins can have complications during delivery. He wants to ensure all equipment and support are available with no delay.

Thank fuck since I would lose my shit if something happens to Leonie or to our babies. My thoughts drift back to the conversation we had early in her pregnancy before we knew we were expecting twins.

"Leonie, understand me clearly. If for any reason I have to choose between you and this baby or any other, I choose you always. You mean everything to me. We can try for another baby, or we can adopt a baby in need of a wonderful home. But you... You are irreplaceable, my love. Call me selfish. But I will not live without you, Leonie."

She speaks. But I cut her off with a firm shake of my head. I don't give a damn how harsh it may sound. But it's the damn truth.

"No! This is nonnegotiable. And we will not speak of such things ever again. Do you understand?"

Leonie nods, still sad.

"Words, Leonie. I will have your words," I demand.

She takes some time to consider.

I feel her body stiffen, and she sits up tall. The surrounding energy vibrates anew. Then Leonie stares me straight in the eye with a fiercely determined expression.

"*Oui, Roger. You are right, Mon Cœur. We will move forward from this moment on with only positive thoughts and words of love. You are the most responsible person I know*"—she smiles brightly as she strokes my cheek—"*But we will share the responsibility of our blessing together. I don't want you to think you have to be strong for both of us. I will not neglect your needs either.*"

So, God forbid, anything goes wrong, I set my mind. But I push the negative thoughts out and return Leonie's bone-crushing squeeze of my hand with a much gentler version to hers as I stroke her reddened cheek.

"Yes, my love? You're so brave and strong. We are so lucky to have you—"

"BULLSHIIITTT!!!"

Leonie snarls and swats my thumb from her face. The golden flecks in her eyes flash dangerously as she glares at me.

An unceasing slew of French curse words follow a particularly painful contraction.

Starr turns her head. But not before I glimpse the smile on her face. Her dimples deepen as her sorrel-brown eyes dance with mirth.

Even Dr. Berger coughs to hide his laugh.

I glance around the room, and others avoid my gaze. Suddenly everyone has an important task...

"Oooh... How much more?" Leonie huffs huskily. "*Mon DIEU!!!*"

Dr. Berger peers between Leonie's legs—the caveman in

me wants to carve his eyeballs out with a flint knife—to check.

"One more push, Leonie. You can do it. He's almost here," the doctor states, back to business. "Now!"

With what must be a Herculean effort, Leonie delivers our first Twin. Their piercing cries mingle in the tense air of the operating room.

Rodolphe Beaulieu Steele enters our world.

My eldest son. Named for me. Leonie nicknamed me *Mon Loup*, my wolf. His name translates to famous wolf.

Tears fill my eyes at the sight of mother and son.

My protective instincts kick in. I follow his pediatrician —Dr. Constance Taylor recommended by Dr. Berger—as she carries my son off to the side in order to care for him. I split my gaze between her actions and Leonie, who's being comforted by Starr. I confirm she's fine, then turn my full attention to Rodolphe.

"How is he?" I ask as I watch possessively over the doctor's shoulder while she tends to him.

She smiles at me and responds, "He's in excellent health! All ten fingers and toes! He weighs 5.2 pounds. An acceptable size for a twin. Congratulations, Mr. Steele!"

Relief washes over me. Then anxiety sweeps in when she places a freshly cleaned Rodolphe in my arms. When I look at her in a panic, Dr. Taylor smiles encouragingly.

I glance down at his red face. He may be tiny, but the weight of responsibility hits me in that moment. This is one of my sons, the fruit of my loins. I am his father. His safekeeping ranks as my utmost priority along with his soon-to-be-born brother and their mother.

"Roger? What's taking so long? Is he okay?"

Leonie's soft voice filled with concern calls me back to the operating room.

"He's perfect, my love. See for yourself," I respond as I stride over to her and place Rodolphe on her chest.

Leonie's face lights up with such love and joy when she stares at our son. Tears stream down her cheeks. Her fingers tentatively touch his soft jet-black hair, and his eyes open slowly.

Gray eyes and black hair. The Steele family traits continue.

Leonie peers up at me and smiles.

"*Mon Loup*," she whispers.

I bury my face in her damp hair and cry.

"FUUUCK... YOU!!!"

Stage three begins...

Rodolphe sleeps in a warm hospital crib while his younger brother is being born. And his father is being cursed out by his mother.

I learned my lesson the last time. Instead of speaking sappy words, I go for the Alpha male route.

"Leonie. You will push when Dr. Berger says and not a moment before. Do you understand—"

I didn't even see it coming.

Leonie slaps the shit out of me.

"Don't you dare pull that dominant bullshit on me right now, ROGER STEELE!!!"

She bellows, eyes shooting golden fire.

Struck speechless, I can only stare at the wild Lion before me. The tame and loving new mother of ten minutes ago disappears in a puff of smoke.

Yeah, fuck me…

THIRTY MINUTES LATER, a fatigued, not ferocious, Leonie rests in her suite's bed with our sons in skin-to-skin contact against their mother's body as she breastfeeds them.

The sight is so poignant; I have to capture it with a few photos by my mobile. The clicking attracts her attention, and she lifts her weary gaze to mine.

"Hi, baby. I love you so much," I breathe. "Do you need anything?"

Leonie shakes her head and pats the bed beside her.

I sit and brush my fingertips across her cheek.

She closes her eyes and nuzzles against my palm; a soft purr slips past her lips.

"*Non, merci, Mon Cœur, je t'aime aussi,*" she whispers, followed by a yawn. "Only you and our sons."

Gaspard Beaulieu Steele, my second son. Named for Leonie. Her parents nicknamed her *Mon Trésor*, and we name our son treasure bearer. His gray eyes and jet-black hair mark him as a Steele. A perfect baby who weighs a healthy five pounds with all ten fingers and toes.

A beautiful fiancée and identical twin sons. My heart swells. My family.

MINE!

***

Click the Link Below or visit books2read.com/u/ 47YwKA for Your Copy

Justify My Desires Roger & Leonie Part III

I dedicate this novel to those who never give up on true love and each other.

Fulfill Your Desires.

xoxo
Charmaine Louise

WELCOME TO
CHARMAINELOUISE — THE
SENSUAL LIFESTYLE

GLITZY. GLAMOROUS. STEAMY.

CharmaineLouise New York, Inc. invites you to indulge in *The Sensual Lifestyle* through **CharmaineLouise Books** and **CharmaineLouise Intimates**. CLBrands immerse you in *Sexy Fantasies* with CLBooks contemporary romance novels and give you *Sexy Under Things & Loungewear* with CLIntimates.

Charmaine Louise Shelton the Founder, CEO & Author of CLNY loves all things classic, elegant, feminine, and of course with an erotic edge! Favorite outfit of choice is a cashmere cardigan, leather pencil skirt, and seamed silk stockings with stiletto heels. Sexy Fantasy Type: sub with a dash of Voyeur. When not writing and designing, Charmaine Louise travels and spends time with her Maltese buddies, ZIGGY and Jynger.

CharmaineLouise — *The Sensual Lifestyle*

~ Visit online at **CharmaineLouise.com**

~ Subscribe to **CharmaineLouise Newsletter**

~ Find us on Facebook **@CharmaineLouiseNewYork**

~ Instagram @**CharLouNY**

CharmaineLouise Books *Sexy Fantasies* launched summer 2020. Sizzling, contemporary romance with your soon-to-be favorite Alpha Doms, Powerful Billionaires, and the women they lust after and love for second chances, insta-love, enemies-to-lovers, and more.

Want to chat it up and share your thoughts with other CLBooks Lovers? Read our blog, join our Charmaine-Louise Books Coterie Fan Club and follow us on my author pages and social media to be in the know about the book release dates, exclusive content, giveaways, contests, and more!

~ **Purchase your eBook and paperback novels from my Author Page by clicking here!**

~ Read and subscribe to our blog ***The World of Sex***

~ Connect on **Amazon Author Page**

~ **Goodreads Author Profile**

~ <u>**BookBub Author Profile**</u>

CharmaineLouise Intimates *Sexy Under Things &*
Loungewear debuted in 2003. Inspired by the sensuous
sirens and sylph swans of the past and present, the hand
crochet cashmere and silk collections are for the sexy:
hence, the line names Ginger — Bombshell; Diana —
Showstopper; Jackie — Timeless; Lena — Classic. Also
known as The Movie-Star from Gilligan's Island; Ms. Ross
The Boss; Mrs. Kennedy Onassis; Ms. Horne.

Do you thrive on seduction and being sexy lounging at
home? Read our blog and follow us on social media to
receive the tips, the latest additions to the collections,
private sales, and more!

~ Read and subscribe to our blog *The Art of Seduction*

~ Find us on Facebook **@CharmaineLousieIntimates**

~ Instagram **@CharmaineLouiseIntimates**

Fulfill Your Desires.

www.ingramcontent.com/pod-product-compliance
Lightning Source LLC
Chambersburg PA
CBHW071530110726
47908CB00007B/1821